FIRST IN

CHEEKY WITH THE FIRE CHIEF

DANIKA BLOOM

FIRE LILY PRESS

Published by Fire Lily Press

Library and Archives Canada Cataloguing in Publication

Bloom, Danika, 1966- , author
First In / Danika Bloom

Issued in print and electronic formats.
ISBN 978-1-7780384-5-7 (paperback)
ISBN 978-0-9730619-5-6 (ebook)

1. Title

Cover design: L.J. Anderson, Mayhem Cover Creations (ebook); 100Covers.com (paperback)

To my own hot, firefighter husband who may not have been my literal 'first in' but is definitely the first in my heart.

And, to Crazy George, the Deputy Chief who encouraged me to become 'one of the guys' in our small-town, volunteer fire department. Godammit, you're missed.

ABOUT FIRST IN: CHEEKY WITH THE FIRE CHIEF

When a feisty volunteer firefighter gets cheeky with her fire chief, sparks fly, donuts melt, and emotions burn.

"If you like hot, action-packed, firefighter romance, look no further. Danika puts you right on the front line in all the best ways." ★★★★★
~Cora Seton, NYT & USA Today bestselling romance author

Sophie

I thought for sure I had the fire chief job locked down. Until in walked Nick West, AKA Mr. April from the hot fireman calendar. I can't decide if he looks better in his uniform or in that picture wearing barely more than raindrops. I hate that he's so attractive. I hate that he stole my job. But I hate even more that what I feel for him isn't hate at all. Once we're forced to work side-by-side hiding my growing feelings will be impossible.

Nick

I'm used to women literally dropping their panties for me. What I'm not used to is having a woman be completely unaffected by my looks or my charm. I'd like to say I at least have her respect, but she seems pretty irritated that I got the fire chief job. The surprising part, she sees the man beneath the looks and the swagger and that is addictive. Nearly as addictive as her sassy mouth and compassionate heart. Now we're working close together in tight quarters and I'm done pretending I don't want more with Sophie.

"Superb firefighter romance! This book started off with a heart-stopping action sequence that sucked me in right away, and it was quickly followed by a plethora of laugh-out-loud moments as the exquisitely executed enemies-to-lovers arrangement is set up." ~Viper Spaulding, Goodreads

"Action packed, sexy, fun, engaging and emotional adventure filled with danger, suspense and undeniable passion... an edge of your seat read from beginning to end and so hard to put down." ~Kathleen Bradbury, Goodreads

"One of my top 10 books of the year. … It was also so very easy to get sucked into this world that was a mix between the tv show *Rescue Me* and Janet Evanovich's don't-take-no-sh*t main lead Stephanie Plum." ~Colleen Young, Goodreads

1

____

NICK

"Cool your jets, bro!"

I stared into my rearview mirror at the jerk riding my tail, flashing his Lambo's high beams. As if there were somewhere I could go to get out of his entitled way.

The wanker flashed me again. I opened my window, gave him the finger, then geared down to fourth and reduced my speed to the actual limit.

"Not pulling over so you can gun it to the next car and harass their ass for the next three miles," I said to the face I saw in my rearview mirror, which was also talking to me. Well, screaming at me.

I tapped my brakes three times to slow down just enough to be annoying, not dangerous. At least, it shouldn't have been dangerous but this self-centered dick pulled around me, passed on the double line, then pulled back in less than two car lengths ahead of me. He hit his brakes. And not just to be annoying.

I slammed my foot down, fast and too hard. I skidded sideways, directing my car away from the oncoming traffic lane. My wheels touched the soft shoulder and pulled toward the ditch but I'd done this dance a dozen times before on icy roads. Muscle memory overrode brain and I lifted my foot off the brake. My trusty Subaru straightened out and I steered back onto the road. Aside from a very tight sphincter and an adrenalin sweat, everything was fine.

Sadly, it was just another day on the Sea to Sky Highway.

I'd been driving this highway at least once a week since I turned eighteen—in winter to ski, in summer to mountain bike. And in the shoulder seasons, I still made the seventy-five mile drive and spent double the time with fit young things from around the world who were happy for a short-term, holiday fling. I'd like to say I'd settled down in the last ten years, but that would be a lie.

It never ceased to amaze me how many Lamborghinis, McLarens and Porsche 911s I'd see in the two-hour drive from Vancouver to Whistler. Cars that cost more than I could earn in two years, risking my life as a Vancouver firefighter.

My heart was still thumping when I saw tail lights up the hill on the road ahead. An unusual number of them. I tapped my brakes a couple of times to let the driver behind me know I was planning to slow right down. I didn't want to be the guy who rear-ended another car around a bend.

It was a good call. Twenty vehicles sat idling. Fully stopped.

"Shit!" I pulled out my phone and looked for a text. I called the number.

"Decker," barked a man's voice.

"Mr. Decker, this is Nick West. I'm going to be late. I'm south of Lily Valley by about five miles. Looks like an accident at the Point."

"Huh." That's all he said.

"You're not interviewing anyone else today, are you?"

"Nope, you're it."

"Great. I'll be there as soon as I can."

The cars ahead of me were turning off their engines. A sign that this was more than a fender bender. I grabbed the

First Aid kit from under my seat and took off toward the accident.

Two vehicles were smashed beyond recognition. Unfortunately, neither was the apple green Lambo, but I'd put money on the fact that he caused this mess. A dozen people had gotten out of their vehicles and were standing looking helpless. Being useless.

"Has anyone called 9-1-1?" I yelled.

Several people called back, "Yes."

"Does anyone have any first aid training? Any at all?"

Silence.

The cars were about 100 yards from each other. I ran to the closest one. An older man, probably in his seventies, was in the driver's seat. He was alone. His windshield was smashed and his face was covered in blood.

"Hey! Can you hear me? Hello?"

No response. I checked the pulse in his neck. Alive and unresponsive. Looking around I saw a middle-aged man in outdoor gear standing with what were probably his teenage daughters. I motioned him to come over.

He stared at me.

"Over here! Now!" I barked.

The teens moved with him.

"No. You," I pointed at the girls. "stay. You do *not* come over here."

Outdoor man jogged over.

"I need you to keep this guy company until the paramedics arrive. Don't touch him. Just talk to him. Say any shit you think of. Tell him about your kids, where you were headed, anything. Just keep talking and keep it calm."

I scanned the crowd and pointed to a couple of young guys, "Come with me."

They obeyed. We ran to the farther vehicle. It was bigger, taller, an SUV. The upside? Lower likelihood of catastrophic injuries. The downside—higher chance there'd be more than one person in the vehicle needing medical attention.

The driver was trying to get out but his door had been crushed. He'd rolled the van but thankfully physics had been on his side so he was wheels down again. All the windows were shattered.

I pointed at the guys with me, "Wait." Then I approached the driver's side, "Sir."

He gave me 'the look.' He was in shock, had no idea what had happened.

"Sir, you've been in an accident. What's your name?" I used my elbow to push away glass so I could get a better look inside.

"Oliver," he said, looking at me with wide eyes, tiny pupils.

Beside him, his wife I assume, had taken the brunt of the impact. They don't call it the suicide seat for nothing. Clearly he anticipated the hit and steered to try to avoid it. What he hadn't anticipated was the soft shoulder.

I motioned for one of the two guys to join me and spoke quietly to him, "This is Oliver. Talk to him and keep him focused on you. Don't let him look at his wife."

Crossing behind the van to see if anyone else was inside, I approached the woman in the passenger seat who was clearly unconscious. Her pulse was strong but there was zero chance she didn't have a serious neck injury. Just as I was about to call 9-1-1 myself, to advise dispatch to send three ambulances, Oliver leaned across and shook his wife's shoulder.

"Amanda!" he yelled.

I grabbed his hand and held it away from her body.

"Sir. Don't touch her. She needs paramedics. You'll do more harm than good."

The driver dropped his arm and stared at his wife.

I looked for the second guy, to get him to find a door we

could open so when first responders arrived they'd have quick access to stabilize the passenger. The idiot was walking away from me.

"Yo! Bro! I need you over here. No time to take a piss," I yelled.

He ignored me and started to jog—in the wrong direction.

Turning back to the first guy, I said, "Try to get the driver's door open. If he cooperates, let him stay where he is. But if he starts to touch his wife again, encourage him to get out. But don't pull or push him. Let him move on his own. Clear?"

"Yup."

"Over here," the runner called to me. He was twenty yards up the road and standing in the ditch, waving wildly.

I ran, hoping against hope that he wanted to show me some wildflowers. Wishful thinking. What I saw was so not good. I put my hand on the guy's shoulder and turned him away from the child laying lifeless in the mud. Despite a decade of emergency medical calls I knew that even I'd be needing to debrief this with a professional.

"Look at me," I said, forcing him to make eye contact with me, "Call 9-1-1. Tell them we need air evac for a toddler. Say Captain West of Vancouver Fire and Rescue is on-scene. Got it?"

He nodded and was pulling out his phone before I finished my sentence.

I dropped into the muck and rolled a child of no more than five onto my extended arm so I could pick him up with as little movement to his spine as possible. I needed him on solid ground. As I lifted him I took one breath to redirect my rage at the parents who didn't think car seats were necessary, into something a little more productive.

I gently lay him down on the pavement and checked his pulse. Nothing. But he was so small and my heart was pounding so hard I knew I might not feel it even if he had one.

"Hey little man, can you hear me?"

No eye flutter. No chest movement. I pinched his arm. No response.

The first guy had gotten the dad out of the van and was walking him toward me.

"Keep him away from here," I yelled. I pushed a button on my watch and started CPR.

A few hundred compressions later, I noticed that two fire trucks were on-scene. All my focus was on making sure the blood was circulating in this small body so that if he could be resuscitated he'd actually stand a chance at having a functioning brain.

Minutes passed.

"*Merde,*" I heard as the boots and legs of a firefighter in full turn-out gear stopped in front of me.

"Get me your AED," I said without looking up.

"It's being used," a female voice replied.

"If it's not attached to a body I want it now."

No response. I looked up and made eye contact with her, "*Now!*"

She looked startled. Deer in headlights. But she followed my command.

"Joe from Sophie," she said.

"Go for Joe," a voice on the radio replied.

"Has your driver got a pulse?"

"Weak. AED is charged," the radio voice said.

"Sir, how long have you been doing CPR?" She asked.

I checked my watch, "8 minutes 27 seconds." I stopped compressions, checked the boy's pulse. Nothing. "I need that AED. Now!"

"Joe, bring the AED to the other car. Fast. There's a kid."

"Scissors. In my kit," I ordered.

"I'm the Incident Commander, I—"

"I don't care if you're the fucking Queen of England. Get the scissors and cut this kid's shirt off."

~

Two hours later, I'd met and worked with eight of the crew of the Lily Valley Volunteer Fire and Rescue, including the event's IC, Sophie Beaulieu. I'd never seen such a small firefighter in my life. No way she'd make it on a career crew. Hell, the jaws of life weighed more than she did.

But she was smart and fast and worked well under pressure. There weren't that many decisions I'd have made differently in her shoes. I had to give her credit, she was a good Incident Commander. For a volunteer.

And damn was she ever cute. She could be a stunt double for Arya Stark, with her short, dark hair and those eyes... grey when she was barking orders at me—which I did not appreciate—but when we were taking a breath after the paramedics took over, her eyes were a shade of green that made you want to stare deep into them to see what kind of magic was burning there.

She was nothing like the women I was used to dating. Dating... that's a stretch. The women I was used to having pre-fuck drinks with is more accurate. The women I met when I needed to get out of my head and forget a hard day at work. They met the cleaned-up, buttoned-down version of me which was about as authentic as they were with their Instagram-perfect make-up and push-up bras. Women who were as hungry for distraction as I was.

In just two hours, I felt like I knew more about this pint-sized firefighter than any of those flings. And, I really liked being near her. In a situation that normally left me needing a lot of booze and a naked body to remind me that I was still alive, I felt alive just working alongside Sophie. Alive and happy, despite the shit show of a car accident with a fatality.

2

SOPHIE

I took a minute to appreciate the sunny day and the successes of the worst emergency call I'd had to command so far. The little boy was conscious when the air ambulance lifted off. The paramedics said we'd saved his life, which allowed me to believe he'd be fine. I pictured him with all his five-year-old pals at his kindergarten graduation party. I also pictured the Good Samaritan firefighter who could take all the credit for having made that possible.

I did wonder, if we'd had two AEDs, if the old man would have survived, though. I took a deep breath to loosen the tightness in my chest, keep the tears at bay. I squeezed the skin between my thumb and first finger hard, to refocus the grief.

The guys were busy either packing up the auto extrication gear or directing traffic. The cops and coroner were taking pictures and doing their thing. Nobody needed me right now. I could relax. My job was almost done. This was the easy part. The calm between storms.

Back at the hall I'd have an hour of paperwork to do, making sure all the first responder reports were filled in properly—which they wouldn't be. One of the downsides of a volunteer fire department is the variable abilities of the members. Joe's paperwork would be perfect. Buster's would be a hot mess.

I walked around Engine One to make sure all the equipment bays were properly loaded and that nothing was missing. In responses like this, where the crew is working in two different locations, leaving something behind—a pair of gloves, a balaclava or a traffic cone is almost expected. Except when I'm IC. This was my fourteenth call as Incident Commander and my record was perfect.

"Hey! Do you have a minute?"

My heart did a little leap when I turned and saw the man who both challenged my authority and hung around to help when he could have left two hours ago. He'd royally pissed me off but made up for it a hundred times over by being right to override me and for keeping the little boy alive until paramedics could take over.

"You're still here? I thought you left."

"I tried," he said pointing to his car, "but my car didn't seem to want to go quite yet."

That was a weird thing to say. He was in dress pants, now covered in mud. His white dress shirt was unbuttoned and untucked, sleeves rolled up, over a white t-shirt. Both looked brand new—they had that whiter than white quality that you lose after the first wash.

It was obvious that he trained to be able to climb thirty flights of stairs wearing fifty pounds of turn-out gear and that he could easily carry an adult woman over his shoulder without breaking a sweat. I had half a mind to ask him if he was in a fireman's calendar, as a joke…but really, I'd pay top dollar to hang a picture of those abs in my turnout locker. No. That's a lie. The guys at the hall would razz me too much. Plus, what good is a picture of a smoking hot body hanging in a place where you can't properly fantasize about what you'd do if it was in your bed with you?

"It's Nick, right?" I tried to play it cool, as if I'd have forgotten his name.

"Yeah. And you're Captain…"

"It's just Lieutenant—" I was saying as he put his hands on my shoulders and gently turned me so my back, and my last name were facing him.

"Beaulieu," he said with a pretty decent accent as he spun me back around. "Are you French?"

"My mom and dad were. And I speak it, especially when I'm mad, 'cause cursing in French is way more fulfilling than swearing in English. But, I'm a Lily Valley girl, born and bred." I was an idiot. He wasn't taking my life story. "My first name is Sophie."

"Well, nice job, Sophie. Hard call with such a small crew."

"Thanks," I looked down, not really great with compliments. And as my eyes traveled to the ground they stopped part-way… *oh dear*… could he tell I wasn't looking at my boots? He could only see the top of my head, right? Not the angle of my eyes. I hoped. Deep breath.

"Yeah, well, it would have been an entirely different outcome for that little boy if it weren't for you. I can't thank you enough. These calls are hard," I looked up and into his eyes. My breath caught in my throat. He had the kindest eyes ever.

"So, I was wondering if maybe it would be helpful for me to come by the hall and you know, help with the paperwork for the response on the kid. Since I was there and you weren't."

He actually didn't need to come in since he'd already given all the info that was needed to the paramedics who took over. But since he was offering… and since I had no legit reason to ask for his contact info…

"That would be amazing. I should be back at the hall in about thirty minutes. You can kill time in—"

"Shit! Right." He looked at his watch. "I forgot. I was on my way to a meeting. And, I *really* need to get to it."

"Of course." I felt the silver lining to what was an otherwise awful day, a day that would require at least three therapy sessions, evaporate. "It's all good. I understand."

"I know where you are," he said, putting his hands on my shoulders again, mild panic in his eyes. "When do you train? Can we connect then?"

"Yeah. Of course. Thursday nights. Seven pm. I usually get there early to set up before the guys arrive."

"Six? Thursday. I can be there."

"That would be great. Thanks again for jumping in. Saving that little boy."

He nodded and smiled. He had perfectly kissable lips. Of course he did because he was a perfect model for Mr. April, wearing nothing but the raindrops of spring showers. Could he tell I was shamelessly objectifying him? I forced myself to look at his eyes and stop imagining getting to know his mouth better.

"All in a day's work," he said.

He looked like he meant it. Just a normal day for a career firefighter. I bet he didn't even need trauma counseling after this. Our crew would, though few of them would ever admit it. Spending twenty minutes performing CPR on a body that doesn't come back to life—it affects you even if you tell yourself it doesn't.

I watched him jog over to his car. He moved with ease despite his size. He was so far out of my league, but I allowed myself to dream a little.

Two sleeps until Thursday. Two sleeps to find out if Nick, the calendar-worthy fireman, was a life-saving hottie who also kept his promises.

3

NICK

I punched redial then pulled my way into the slow-moving line of traffic, waving thanks to the person who let me in.

"Mr. Decker. Sorry. The call was a fatality. I'm just rolling now. Do you still have time to meet?"

I heard a tapping, like a pen on a glass tabletop.

"Did you engage with the crew?" he asked.

"Yeah. Saved a kid," I said hoping that would add a check mark to my positive column. "Hung around a bit to help with clean-up."

More tapping. Then silence.

"Did you mention you were meeting with me?"

"No. I told the IC, Beaulieu, I had to get going for a meeting. Didn't say with who."

I heard him exhale. "Good, good. Yes, please come in. Lots to discuss."

Decker's office was a full hour north of the accident and the department where I'd applied to be Chief. The fully volunteer crew I'd just spent two hours working with would be, if I had my way, under my leadership in a couple of practices.

I put my cruise control on, five clicks over the limit, and settled in for a drive I could do with my eyes closed, my attention focused on what I'd seen on the call and how I could use that knowledge to my benefit in this last interview.

The crew was sharp with lots of good skills. But there were some incredibly dumb-ass decisions made on that call. One guy, Smith, was a hotshot who freelanced, didn't follow orders and did what he thought was right rather than what he'd been asked by Sophie to do. I wouldn't forget his name and he wouldn't pull shit like that under my command. Cutting him slack was one of the few decisions I think Sophie screwed up.

She did a good job under incredible pressure, but she wasn't a career caliber chief. It was obvious that the crew didn't take her leadership seriously enough to follow her orders without question. And when that happens, and you get even one guy deciding to do his own thing—freelancing—shit can go sideways fast.

I'd seen pretty well every bad outcome to weak leadership and strong personalities in my eight years with Vancouver Fire and Rescue. I might be young, but I had more experience and a better call record than most guys five years older than me. I knew Decker had one other serious contender for the position. This was my last interview, make or break for my career.

It was clear that the fastest way to earn the chief's helmet in a real fire department—by 'real' I mean a career department, not a small town hodgepodge of old guys who like to get together once a week, play with big equipment for an hour then drink beer for three more—was to prove I had the chops to do the administrative side of running a department. Saving property and lives was easy. Every recruit did that on the daily. But not many could even file an accident report let alone juggle the budgets, the training and maintenance schedules, funding from the different levels of government for new equipment, insurance…

Even though I'd never actually done any of this work, I was fully confident I could figure it out in no time. What would it need? Read some shit. Make some decisions. Fill out paperwork. No different than showing up at a fully engulfed house, reading the situation, deciding whether to do an interior attack and risk losing a crew member or an exterior attack and pretty well guarantee losing the house, and then writing the incident report.

Chief's job was no different. All about weighing risks, trusting your gut and being decisive.

How hard could it be?

I pulled into the muddy parking lot of the regional district office. It was smaller than my home firehall. A lot smaller. The first time I met with Mr. Decker, the Emergency Program Manager for the Lily Valley Regional District, I was shocked that this office, with just a dozen employees, managed eight towns and unregistered villages that ranged in population from 1,050 to 20,000 residents. The staff and a handful of elected politicians acted as mayor, council and administrators. Every town and village had its own fire department, but until now only four of the eight had paid staff.

Even though Lily Valley was the smallest of the unregistered communities, it had a reputation for having the best trained, fully volunteer fire and rescue service in the entire southern part of the province. But after what I saw today, it was clear that the competition for that award was B-class at best. That's why they needed their first professional and paid chief—the village had just reached the population threshold to have one paid position and was looking at doubling its population inside the decade. That meant the pressure on the fire department would more than double.

It was unusual for the district to be looking at external candidates for the chief position but if the region's goal was to create a Class-A department, they needed a Class-A leader. This was a perfect chance for me to make my mark and climb several rungs up the career ladder in super compressed time.

"Nick!" A voice called from behind me.

"Hello, Mr. Decker," I put my hand forward to shake his and caught his eye as he looked down at my pants which were covered in dried mud. "Yeah. Sorry about my appearance. I pulled a kid from a ditch and was doing CPR on the shoulder of the highway—"

Decker turned away from me and started walking toward his car, "Come with me," he commanded.

I got into his F-450 and buckled in. "Not meeting at the office, then?"

"Nope. Couldn't get the meeting room and this office-2.0-open-concept-bullshit is not conducive to employment discussions." He said it loud enough not just for me to hear over his shoulder but for anyone inside the building to hear through the open window.

We drove through the center of town and out onto the highway. He had the radio on a talk show and didn't initiate conversation so I sat quietly. After five minutes of driving at close to double the speed limit, he pulled off at a greasy spoon.

"Take the table at the back," he waved his hand toward the restaurant but pulled his phone from his pocket.

I'd been dismissed. I ordered a black coffee. The waitress was refilling my mug when Decker finally came in.

"Coffee for you, too, Dave?" she asked.

He nodded.

"So, here's the deal," Decker said, getting right to

business, "half the council want you, the other half want So — someone else to fill the role. And the deciding vote is mine since the chief reports directly to me."

I nodded.

"You're not from here. You don't know the community."

I could feel the job slipping away.

"The other candidate is a nurse. What you saw today makes up the bulk of our calls: MVAs, strokes and heart attacks, and injury by misadventure, usually involving drugs and alcohol."

"I've been working shifts on the Downtown Eastside for eight years," I told him. "Medical calls are the bulk of my experience, too."

"I know," he said, tapping his teaspoon on the table.

I waited. This was not the conversation I'd planned for. I expected to get a low-ball offer for the salary and to counter with something more in line with what a city chief would earn. Then Decker would tell me the budget was the budget so I'd negotiate a thirty-hour work week instead of forty. At least, that's what I'd prepared for.

"Convince me I should shit my bed and piss off the area rep for Lily Valley and that entire village to hire you."

We held eye contact. He blinked first.

"I think you already know the answer," I said, hoping confidence was what he was looking for. "You pointed out that I'm not from here and don't know the community. You said it as a fact, not positive, not negative. So, I interpret that as a positive. In fact, I can assure you it is, assuming you want to have the best damn volunteer department in BC."

He raised his eyebrows and an open palm to me.

"So, at the call today I was able to stand back and watch the crew work. The IC, Beaulieu—you know her?"

He nodded slowly.

"I'd say she was the strongest member on the call. But—"

"But?"

"But she doesn't have the respect of all the members. Nobody should challenge the Incident Commander. The fact that a couple of the guys did comes down to leadership from the top. The chief has to wear that insubordination. It's the chief's job to enforce the chain of command."

"And?"

"And, since I'm not from here I'm not going to be swayed by emotions and worries that I'll upset the wrong person or hurt someone's feelings. You want a crew that's ready to go big once the new housing development is finished? I can make sure that happens. I've got a career attitude and career experience. Warm and fuzzy is not going to cut it. And if you hire from within—the other candidate is an internal, I assume?"

He nodded.

"You hire from inside and you won't be able to level-up. You need to break the current system to be able to build it properly. Know what I mean?"

Decker stirred his coffee.

"It's a pay-cut from your current salary. I don't have any wiggle room this year. Budget is set. Next year we could maybe pull another ten grand, but no guarantees," he said.

Yes!

"I understand. And if you can work with me, let me work the hours I need to, not expect me to sit at a desk for forty hours just to put in the *right* number of hours, I can work with the salary."

He tapped out what sounded like a morse code signal on the table.

"Six-month probation. I don't expect change overnight. But I do expect that you'll maintain our turn-out stats. Our crew may be rough around the edges, but our response time is the fastest of all volunteer departments in the province, our relationship with the ambulance service is exceptional, and member turn-over is virtually non-existent once new recruits make the commitment to stay after their three-month training period. In six months, if those baseline measures aren't at par with where they are today, you pack up and go back to the city and I'll eat crow and hire the other candidate."

Decker put down his spoon and reached his hand across the table. We shook. He sighed.

"Welcome to the management team. Now the hard part: telling the local they didn't get the job."

I nodded. "The current chief?"

"No," he said, closing his eyes and shaking his head, "The IC you met today—Sophie Beaulieu."

Shit. I'd already decided that I'd make her my deputy chief. What were the odds she'd be happy to work with me now?

4

———

SOPHIE

I couldn't stop thinking about Nick. In the two years I'd been a volunteer firefighter I'd never actually met a calendar-worthy fireman. The training we got was from retired career guys and other volunteers. And volunteer firemen are a totally different species than whatever gene pool lottery Nick had won his abs and biceps from.

The firefighters I knew were like a half-inch garden hose that's still bendable even with water in it. But Nick... he was a fully charged 3-inch attack hose, the kind I needed to sit on with my full weight to be able to control. Now there was an inappropriate thought and impossible dream—that I'd ever be sitting on Nick's hose.

The one thing it seemed clear that Nick shared with the firefighters I knew was a giant heart and a desire to be of service. But damn, I'd never had the hots for one of our own guys. Ever. And since all the eligible men in town were on the Lily Valley crew my dating life had been non-existent since I came home to care for Papa.

I was so excited to see Nick again that I had that nervous energy that makes me jumpy. I needed to run some of it off before practice.

"Max!" I called to my Bernese Mountain Dog. "Time for a run!"

Max bolted from the bed and sat at my feet while I put on my trail runners. I checked the time. I had an hour before I had to be at the hall to meet Nick so he could 'help me' with paperwork. Such a nice guy, not that I needed any help. The papers were already filed with the appropriate authorities. The investigation into the accident already well underway.

I opened my back door. Max ran to the edge of the property where it met the road and sat. He waited for my 'okay' signal to run across and then straight up the steep mountain trail to get into the forest. Uphill for the first five minutes and then we'd hit an old logging road that, on a nice summer day, we could spend hours walking. But today would be a short sprint to the river, let Max have a quick splash, then home for a shower.

As I jogged, I planned my post-shower, pre-practice prep. Make-up or my normal *au naturel*? Ball cap or messy hair? Crew t-shirt, men's cut, of course, which did nothing to flatter my small cup size, or one of my own? Jesus. It felt like I was getting dressed for a date, not to pull hoses and get wet and dirty… though the similarities between a good date and a good practice suddenly seemed quite… similar. I cracked myself up. What the hell did I know about dates, good or otherwise? Nothing, that's what.

My watch buzzed. I tapped to see a message from Dave Decker. My heart did a flip. He'd promised to let me know this week about the chief position. That job was what I needed to be able to stay in Lily Valley and in the house I'd grown up in. Without it, I'd have to move—not just out of the house but out of Lily Valley since the vacancy rate was zero and rents, when a place ever did come up, were insanely high.

We had that perfect combination of country life and city access, with no more than two hundred houses on the side of a totally wild forest and just over an hour from downtown Vancouver. Rentals here were as hot and expensive as the city since so many people wanted the work-life balance they could get living here and working there.

Entitled city folk. God, I hated them.

All Decker's message said was,

DAVID DECKER, SLRD

Coming thru on way from city mtg. Be at hall at 6pm. Make it?

I dictated a response,

I have another meeting at 6. Can't cancel. Can be there in 15 minutes. Can you make it?

DAVID DECKER, SLRD

20

"Max! Gotta go, buddy," I called to the forest. I stopped to listen for him busting branches. I whistled. A sound that was so loud and sharp it sometimes hurt my own ears. No dog noise. "Max!"

I waited a minute, kicking leaves. My gaze hit the ground and there was Papa. Well, not my actual dad but the way he'd been communicating with me since he'd died—a dime lay in the dirt. It was the third one I'd randomly found in the last three weeks. I bent to pick it up, and pressed it into the palm of my left hand. Looking at the tree tops I said, "I miss you," out loud then listened for his message.

In my head I heard his voice and his encouragement, *Go get 'em, mon chouchou.*

Mon chouchou. My favorite.

Mom used to get so mad when he called me that, but he'd wink and tell Mom that he'd said, "*mon chou,* shoo!" meaning, my sweetie, now get out of here and go play!

"Will do, Papa. Max! Gotta go!"

I figured he'd run ahead to the river. We'd spent enough time in these woods that I knew he'd come home on his own once he noticed I'd left. I turned and started back toward my house.

'My house' as long as I got this job and could negotiate with my siblings a rent-to-own deal. My eldest brother, who'd assumed the role of Executor of my parent's will, had had the house appraised immediately after Papa died and offered to sell it to me at market value, via a letter from the estate's lawyer. Of course, he knew I wouldn't be able to.

Not only had Mom and Papa forgotten to update their will after I was born, all eight of my loving brothers and sisters agreed that if I wasn't named, I wasn't entitled to my share of the inheritance. The only thing of value in their estate was this house which we'd all grown up in.

The great irony was that I *would* have been able to buy it if I hadn't taken two years away from my almost-career as a nurse to be a full-time caregiver for Papa while the rest of his kids just lived their lives as normal, visiting when it suited them, helping out never.

"Well, you're the best suited for the job, Sophie," my closest-in-age sister, Sarah, said, "since you have a medical background."

Another sister argued, "You're single, so it's not like you're giving up family time like we'd have to."

For the record, I wasn't single. I was actually engaged but we weren't living together since he believed you get married first, then you live together and have sex. Our plan was to tie the knot as soon as we'd both graduated from university. I had one semester left.

Richard, or Dick as I referred to him, said, "Hey, you're getting free room and board. You should be grateful that you don't have to work and you get to live in this beautiful place." Dick, who didn't manage to make time to visit Papa even once in the two years I was on a supposed free-rent holiday as his full-time caregiver. Papa agreed with me that Dick been appropriately named.

"If Pops has to go to a home, it'll eat into our inheritance. We all need this money. Do your part, Sophie." This from my second-eldest brother, Christian, who was, in my opinion, not at all appropriately named.

Eight older siblings and eight different reasons they all decided I'd be the one to give up my life. Not that I ever needed to be convinced or coerced by any of them. When Papa asked me if I'd be able to stay to help him out after Mom died it was an easy 'Yes.' I was on summer break from courses. The hospital where I was doing my practicum agreed to give me a three-month leave.

Papa had been diagnosed as palliative when Mom died and everyone believed it would be a miracle if he outlived her by even two months. What became quickly clear was that Mom, although doing her best with Papa and his cancer diagnosis, wasn't doing very well at all, through no malice or fault of her own. She was too old and tired to cook the food they both needed or to get outside so they could move their muscles and engage their brains.

Mom's death was unexpected, triggered by a stroke but, according to Papa, the result of her having given up the will to live knowing she'd be a widow before summer. So Mom willed herself to die which ironically, gave Papa the opportunity to outlive his death sentence by almost two full years.

But it wasn't my medical training that kept him alive so long. It was just being here, spending hours a day with him, talking, pushing him along forest trails in a tricked-out wheelchair we borrowed from the Red Cross. It was love that kept him going. And a kick-ass diet of healthy, vitamin-rich meals.

Papa beat the odds because he was a fighter and I gave

him a reason to fight. And I'm just like Papa. I'm going to fight to live in this house and raise my *one-day* kids here.

I pushed open the gate and bound up the back steps. No need for keys in Lily Valley. Or to lock car doors. Best place on earth.

I took a fast shower, brushed my hair and teeth, no time for make-up. Put on a ball cap, a department t-shirt, and steel-toe boots. I looked at myself in the mirror. Dressed for success as the new fire chief, which meant not dressed for success with Sexy Calendar Man.

Ah well, Nick the firefighter looked like the kind of guy who would be attracted to women who spent more than three minutes getting ready to go out. I knew I wasn't dating quality for this guy but I had hoped to impress him enough to have one night out, just one, to mark that fireman fantasy off my bucket list.

Maybe he had a fantasy of spending a hot night with the chief of a fire department! The thought made me laugh. I hopped in my car and headed to the firehall. The run had worked off about two percent of my nerves. I was practically vibrating when I rolled in to the lot. Decker was already there, standing at the door.

"Mr. Decker!" I said, pushing my hand toward him, "Great to see you!"

"Mmm."

The guy was not known for his warmth or conversation. He was an astute bureaucrat who managed budgets and relationships with precision. I unlocked the door and held it open for him. He gave me a look, the look that says, "I'm not supposed to let you hold the door open for me and now you've put me in an uncomfortable position where I know I'll make the wrong decision." I smiled, gave the door a little push, walked in and let him catch it so it didn't hit him.

He smiled. There. Problem solved.

"Chief's Office," he said.

All officers had keys since we all shared the deputy chief position when the actual deputy was acting for the chief. It was nice and democratic. No pissing matches for who had the most seniority or authority. In fact, I had the full support of the department to get this first paid position. The volunteer chief was even happy to take a backward step and assume the deputy position while he trained me.

I sat in the chief's chair and spun it around to face the desk behind me in this too-small-for-two-people office.

Decker pursed his lips like he was trying to suffocate himself by blocking his nostrils with top lip. It was not an attractive look.

I smiled.

He closed the door.

My heart sank.

5

____

NICK

I stood just inside the front door. Sophie's voice carried through the office door, as clear as if she was standing right beside me. I regretted having put on cologne.

"An external? You hired an *ostie de calisse* external candidate? I thought it was just a formality, you know, show that there was the appearance of fair competition or something."

The door flew open and Sophie exploded into the room like a Mentos mint dropped in a bottle of Diet Coke. She didn't see me and turned back toward the office.

"If you think for one minute I'm going to cooperate with your *connard*, external *foutu* hire for *my* job, you're delusional. In fact, if you think anyone in this department is going to welcome an outsider with open arms, I'm going recommend you see a neurologist because it is my professional opinion that you, Sir, have brain damage."

She turned and Storm Troopered her way toward the door to leave and stopping dead in her tracks when she saw me.

"Shit," we said at the same time.

She turned back to yell at the office. "Decker, since you're the big boss, you can hang around until seven and let the guys know what's happening. I'm out of here. Let's go," she said, grabbing my hand. "My work here is so done."

Shit shit shit shit.

"So…" I was at a loss, not at all sure how to proceed. This was an emergency scenario I'd never practiced. A quick survey of the patient. She was agitated, heart rate high, likely not seeing very clearly. "How about I drive?" Seemed like the safest call on multiple levels.

"Good idea," she said, voice full of rage, dropping my hand.

I started the car and waited for her to put on her seat belt. "Anywhere in particular? You want me to take you home?" I stopped at the edge of the parking lot waiting for instructions. "Left or right?"

A right turn would take us into the village toward all the homes. Left would get us onto the highway. Fifteen minutes north would get us to the next town where there were places to go.

When she didn't answer I looked over at her. Her eyes were closed and her hands were cupped over her mouth, like she was breathing into a paper bag. It seemed to be working. Her breathing slowed and deepened.

I took the opportunity to check her out in a way I wouldn't have been able to if her eyes had been open. I seriously ogled her. She was… *wow.* No airs about her. The kind of woman who looks sexy in her boyfriend's t-shirt. I imagined her in one of my t-shirts. She'd be able to belt it and wear it as a dress.

She opened her eyes. I quickly moved my gaze from her breasts—which I could argue I was only watching so closely to make sure her breathing was stabilizing—to the windshield.

"Go left. I need a drink and I don't have anything at home."

We drove in silence. What could I say? *Hey, sorry you got screwed out of a job you thought was yours. I hope you'll change your mind and show me the ropes.*

We drove in silence along a stretch of highway between the village of Lily Valley which had nothing but houses and the fire department, and the closest town, which had a few restaurants, bars and a couple of grocery stores.

"Turn left at the lights," she said, "please."

I looked at her and she smiled. She was breaking my heart with her sad smile and those eyes. Goddamn gray-green gorgeous.

"Here," she pointed at a seedy-looking bar. "It's a dive so I know I won't meet anyone I know."

That smile again. Killing me. She led us to a table in the back corner by the pool tables and dart boards.

"Come here often?" I tried to joke.

"Only when I'm on a date with a guy I'm too embarrassed to be seen with." She actually laughed.

I grabbed my chest and feigned deep hurt. "What can I get you?"

"Rum and Coke. No ice. A double? Do you mind? I'll pay you back."

I waved her off and went to the bar, ordered her drink and a Kokanee for myself.

"So," I put the drinks down and held my breath. I wanted her to finish her drink fast. First, so she wouldn't have anything to throw at me. And second because I figured she was a lightweight drunk; I hoped a happy one.

"So," she said, "what you saw back there. It didn't happen. I don't want to talk about it or think about it. Deal?"

I nodded. If I followed her rules she couldn't then want to kill me when she found out I was the bastard she had a hate-on for. Could she?

"I'm sorry I can't help with the paperwork on the kid," I said, not sure if she'd want to talk about anything related to the department, but also not sure what else we could talk about.

"No big deal. It was actually all taken care of by EMS. You gave them your contact info, right?"

I nodded.

"They'll call you if they have questions. But… you know that… you do this way more often than me…" I could see the penny drop. She smiled. "Why did you offer to come up? Wait… is this a… a date now?"

She was adorable. I made a face.

"No! No way. When I take a woman on a date, she doesn't have to sanitize her hands after touching the entrance door. No. This is definitely *not* a date. Don't think that for a nanosecond. It would ruin my reputation as a suave and de boner, calendar-quality firefighter."

"Oh my god!" she was laughing. "Full of yourself much? De boner? Are you twelve?"

I shrugged. "It's a French word. I thought you'd know it. And aren't all men really twelve when you strip away the muscle and the five-o'clock shadow?" I flexed my pecs for effect.

"So, Nick, the full of himself calendar-quality firefighter… and I'm not arguing that calendar thing by the way… in fact… never mind…" She blushed and looked away. "So, tell me about yourself. You from Vancouver? Got brothers and sisters? What's your sign?"

"Straight to the heart, the important stuff. Okay, born and bred in East Van. I'm an only child. But I have three to five brothers, depending on how you count them."

She raised an eyebrow.

"Long, boring story. Needs a spreadsheet. And, I'm an Aquarian. How about you?"

"Well, born and raised right here in the Sea to Sky. Left for a few years—well ten years, actually—and came back two years ago to take care of Papa after Mom died. I've got eight brothers and sisters but... I'm more like an only child." She pointed at me like she knew her family story was as good as mine. "And I am on the cusp. Some years I'm an Aquarian and some years I'm a Pisces."

"So, you're complicated."

"I prefer multi-faceted or unpredictable."

"How long have you been a volunteer first responder?"

"Just two years. Joined the department as soon as I came home since there wasn't anything else to do around here, social-wise."

"Only two years? You're a damn good IC, given you've only had two years' experience."

"Thank you for noticing. And I would have been a damn good chief, too." She gave me a scowl and finished off her drink.

"Another one?" I offered.

"I don't know. I'm a two drink drunk and that was a double, right?"

I nodded and smiled. I could see her considering another. "I bet they water down their rum in this high-class establishment. It was probably more like a single..."

"You know, you're right. That did taste heavy on the cola and light on the rum. Okay," she said, "One more would be amazing."

I felt a bit bad knowing I'd just misled her since I'd watched as the bartender cracked open a brand new bottle of Bacardi White before he poured a full two ounces into Sophie's cup. She seemed like she'd be a happy drunk and I figured if she found out who I was tonight, I'd stand a better chance of survival if she was half-cut.

By the time I had her second drink in hand, she'd racked the pool table.

"Do you have a table in your hall?" she asked.

"No. You do?"

"Uh-huh. And I kick ass and take names."

"I heard that the guys let you win because you cry when you lose." I pushed my bottom lip out and faked a little cry.

"You heard that did you? Check your sources, buddy. I bet I can beat you."

"What's the bet?"

She thought for a second, her smile growing. "Winner gets to decide *after* they win."

"Unpredictable, indeed. Okay, I'll take that bet. But you break. Deal?"

"What? You're just going to hand me the game?" She laughed and shook her head.

"Um, no. Ladies first, I mean."

Sophie rolled her eyes.

"So tell me how you have eight—eight?—brothers and sisters. Are you Mormon or something?" I asked.

"Or something. Catholic but really my parents just loved kids and always wanted eight of them."

"And… number nine?"

"I was a seriously late-in-the-game, *Oops*. My next oldest sibling is ten years older than me. She's thirty-four. And, wrap your head around this one—my oldest brother is fifty-four!"

"That's older than my mom."

"Uh-huh. And you know what? Every last one of them is a *connard*."

"Translation?"

"Bastards."

"All eight of them?"

She broke the triangle of balls and pocketed a solid.

"Papa died a month ago," she lifted her plastic cocktail glass to the ceiling and said, "Cheers, Papa. I love you!" then continued, "And I just found out that I'm not named in the will."

"Jesus. That's brutal."

She stood back, eyed the table and walked around it as

she spoke, "Sure is. It was dated two years before I was born. Just a dumb oversight. But my good Christian brothers and sisters are claiming that since I'm not named, I have no right to share in the inheritance. And," she pointed her pool cue at my chest and poked me gently, "they're kicking me out of the family home unless I can pay market rent which is like two grand a month. Without the job as chief… I'm *fucké*. I was counting on that salary."

She pointed out her shot, took it and missed.

"But I'm not talking about that tonight. Your turn, Pec Man," she said bumping me with her hip.

God, I loved how playful she was. How could I take this job now? I'd have to wear the guilt of her being evicted from her family home, on top of stealing her job. I scoped the table and took a shot.

"Scratched! You scratched!" She danced around the other side of the table and called, "Seven in the corner."

It went straight in and the cue ball was lined up for her next shot.

"Four in the center pocket. My side," she smirked at me.

It looked like an impossible shot with three bounces. And… she nailed it.

"You are so going to suffer when I win!" she said standing on her toes and leaning as far over the table as she could to make her next shot. She missed it.

"You let me have that one," I said, pretty convinced that she had actually blown the shot to save my ego. There were so many striped balls, the table looked like a smashed up zebra. I sunk the thirteen, but in the wrong pocket. I gave the table back to her and sat down to watch as she checked out the set-up, then looked up and unapologetically checked me out. She walked around the table three full times, keeping her eyes on me.

"You're not thinking of winging one of those balls at my

head are you? You look like you're setting up the shot to take me out," I finally said, projecting my fear.

"I'm imagining your punishment when you lose, for being so arrogant. I'm just amusing myself."

"Arrogant? When was I arrogant? I've been nothing but your humble servant all night, driving you to your favorite club, buying you drinks, listening to you go on and on about your woes…"

"You, sir," she poked me hard with the pool cue, probably harder than she intended—I hoped harder than she intended, "accepted my bet which means you thought you could beat me. You probably looked at my size and my long eyelashes," she batted them for effect, "and figured I was a pushover. Didn't you? I bet you don't lose very often, do you?"

Her tone was playful but I could see the seriousness in her eyes.

"No, you're right. I don't lose often. And never to a girl—"

She whacked my shoulder with a solid punch. Maybe she wasn't a happy drunk…

"Let me finish! Geez. Never to a girl since I only have brothers."

"Are you close to them?"

"Super close to one brother in particular. But yeah, close to them all. I'll tell you the story one day when you're not kicking my ass. But the point is, I didn't take the bet expecting to win. I took it since you'd think I was chickenshit if I didn't. And for the record, I'm hoping to lose. But to lose fairly. So to be clear, I'm not letting you win."

"Letting me win? Oh my god! You *almost* had me there! I was like all 'oh, what a nice *not* arrogant guy and then you had to go and ruin it by assuring me you're not *letting* me win? The arrogant tag stands."

She took her shot. Pocketed the last two solids and stood over the table with five stripes and the eight ball.

"I suspect this is hard for you, losing to a girl who happens to have earned a rank in the fire department in just two years of service."

That little jab at my position stung. My chest tightened and I clenched my teeth and my fists. I bet my nostrils flared, too. I spoke slowly to make my point,

"The difference," I said, "between a volunteer and a career firefighter—"

As I spoke Sophie, who had been standing a few feet in front of me, turned her back to face the pool table and then fell backwards towards me. I caught her easily and lifted her into a cradle hold. She looked up at me laughing.

"The difference is that you're a trained professional who knows exactly what to do in an emergency—thank you for making my point for me—and I just play the part on TV. But, I'm a trained pool shark, so," she wiggled out of my arms and dropped back to her feet, "if you want to end the game now, I'm happy to walk away and call it a draw."

Whoah. I'm not sure if she realized it, but this firecracker of a woman was seriously skilled in anticipating an emergency situation and changing the direction before it happened. I stared at her, processing what I was feeling, which was that I wished I could wake up in a parallel universe where Sophie and I would have a chance at hanging out again, getting to know each other and maybe even—no *definitely*—making love. *Making love? What the hell? When did I make love?*

"Hello?" Sophie said, "Should I take my shot or do you want call this game?"

She pulled me back to the moment.

"What? And miss what I'm hoping is a spectacular victory dance? No way. Bring it. And then tell me what I lose in this bet. I'm on the edge of my seat."

"Eight ball far left," she said. She made the shot and this time jumped into my arms. Before I had a chance to react, she dropped her mouth onto mine and gave me a Jesus-I-could-hold-her-here-all-night kiss. And just as my thoughts turned dark and dirty, she pushed herself away and sat down at the table as if nothing had happened.

"Um," I walked over and sat across from her, "Not what I was expecting. So, what was it I supposedly lost in this bet? Because from where I'm sitting, it looks like I'm the big winner. I'm just a dumb guy, so can you maybe explain it to me, please."

"That, Calendar Man, was just a test to see if you were worthy of your punishment for thinking you could beat me."

"And, did I pass?" The way she'd jumped away from me I feared I'd failed.

She bit her bottom lip then murmured through her teeth, "Flying colors."

"Thank goodness, cause you know I don't do well with failure. So, what's the punishment?"

"You have to come back to my place, take off your…" She looked me up and down in a way that made me feel totally fine that she'd caught me checking her out.

Don't say shoes. Please say pants.

"…your shirt! And pose for me so I can have my own personal calendar fireman photo to hang in my…"

She stopped again and was smiling so hard I started to laugh.

"On your ceiling?" I offered.

"Yes! On my ceiling! That is what you've lost. Your soul to a photograph."

My good cheer was swallowed by the realization that I had lost my soul, but not to a photograph. To the job I hadn't started yet. To the fact that I'd spent the last sixty minutes letting Sophie believe I was a good guy when in fact, I was the devil. Her devil, at least. I debated whether I had to tell her tonight. The only thing I wanted to do was take her home, take off my shirt, and her shirt, my pants, and her pants, and lose my soul inside her.

"One more for the road?" I offered.

"I shouldn't. I'm going to feel this tomorrow. But… it would be rude to say no, wouldn't it?" She slurred just a little.

"Not rude at all. You could have soda and lime. Whatever you want. Or nothing. It's all good. You're the boss."

She looked directly into my eyes, "That's right. I'm the boss. Take me home and let's get me my photo."

6

———

SOPHIE

I was feeling just a bit drunk. I couldn't believe I'd told him my fantasy. Well, the first part of it. Actually, I couldn't believe I kissed him. And that he actually seemed kind of interested in kissing me back. Guess he must have had a thing for chicks in uniform or women who wore men's clothes… whatever! I'd take it. Not that he'd promised more than a photo or two of his chest.

But if he offered more, I wouldn't be the one to say, "No, no. You've been too generous already."

It was just after 7pm, Decker was probably delivering the news about the new chief as I sat here and got shit-faced with Mr. Arrogant Calendar Man. I really should be there, I realized. What kind of message would it send if I wasn't? That I was a sore loser? That I was a too upset to be there—which would, of course, be interpreted as crying, not angry.

"I should really go back to the hall. It was unprofessional of me to storm out like that. And if Decker is going to tell the crew about this new chief we're all supposed to follow, I want to be there to ask some questions so I'm prepared to take this guy on."

Nick nodded. He looked so empathetic, like he got it.

"Have you ever been passed over for a job you thought was yours for the taking?" I asked him.

He looked thoughtful for a minute. Dumb question, I realized. This was the kind of guy who failed at nothing, was given what he wanted before he knew he wanted it.

"Not a job. I've been a firefighter since I was twenty so, you know, just doing my thing there. But yeah, I know how it feels to be overlooked," he said looking lost in thought.

"Prom queen left the dance with another guy?" I gave his arm a nudge.

"You kidding? I left the dance with all the girls," he said rolling his eyes. "Nah, it was my dad. I'm his first-born son and the last one he ever had time for. Unless it was to compare me to my little brothers, tell me how much smarter, stronger, faster they were." He shrugged his shoulders. "Doesn't matter. Not like I need a dad now, right? Hell, most guys my age *are* dads." He made a face like the very thought of being a dad was terrifying.

"How old are you? Thirty?"

He pointed his thumb down and shook his head.

"Twenty-eight?" I tried.

He nodded.

"Right. And who says we're supposed to be settled down and have it all figured out by twenty-eight? Career. Family. Kids. Mortgage."

Nick shrugged his shoulders.

"*The Man*, that's who. You know what *The Man* can do? He can fuck himself, that's what," I said pointing straight at him.

Nick shifted in his chair. Oh no, I was making him uncomfortable.

"I don't mean you. I'm not mad at you. You're not *The Man*. I mean, you are kind of like the *perfect* man," I realized too late that my mouth was saying what my brain was thinking. "I mean, I don't think you're the kind of man who walks into a room like he owns it and screws the little people. I mean, you probably screw the beautiful women, but..." *Oh my god shut up, Sophie.*

Nick's head tilted and his mouth twisted, like he wanted to say something, but he stopped himself. He was fully focused on me. Not checking his phone or looking up at the TV screens. This was the best *not* date I'd ever been on. No doubt his mom raised him right.

"I'm sorry. I'm babbling. It's just, I should have been given that chief position," I said more to my drink than to anyone.

"I thought you didn't want to talk about that."

"I didn't. But now I do. Let's say you were in my shoes. What would you do? Would you quit—I mean it's just a volunteer position so it's not technically quitting—or would you stay and give this outsider a chance? Or, would you stay and make this guy's life a living hell?"

"If I were in your shoes—"

"I'm definitely leaning toward Option C. Give him a run for his money. See how much of a chief he really is. I bet he's some old, retired dude from the city. That's what they like to do in towns our size you know, bring in some old guy who's burned out and needs to supplement his shitty pension. He won't give a rat's ass about us, just sees the job as a chance to make more money. You know?"

"You might be surprised at—"

"You saw me at that accident. Do I not know how to manage an incident? I do, right? I've got the only perfect record for making sure we don't leave equipment or tools or gear behind after a call. I know that's not the chief's job, but I'm great with small details. Chief needs that quality. And the team respects me. You saw that, right? Sorry. I'm not letting you talk. Here," I handed him my empty tumbler. "You hold the talking cup now. What would you do?"

He took the glass and held it in both hands. Then he

looked up and held eye contact with me. He had such a calm energy. The kind of energy that people trust in an emergency. He didn't jump in with an answer, he took time to think. How many men did that? None in my experience.

Except Papa. He'd learned how to listen, knew the value of letting Mom say her piece, giving her space to think before tossing in his opinion. He did the same with me, let me talk myself into my own answers.

Nick pointed at me, "So, your first option, quitting. Who would you be hurting if you quit? Like really, who would suffer the most?"

Sweet baby Jesus, could this guy be any more perfect? I'd expected him to tell me what he'd do, direct the focus back to himself. That's what we all do… *If I was you, I'd…*

"Huh. That's a great question. I guess the community? I mean, if I quit I know that at least four other guys will leave, too, in solidarity. Without them we'd be slower on our calls and the people who would pay for that are the people who need us. Good point, Calendar Man. Quitting is off the table. So, we're left with me rolling over and taking it in the backside or coming at this new guy like a chainsaw gone wild. Chainsaws are fun, right?"

He didn't laugh at my dumb metaphor. He was taking this so seriously, like he really cared and wanted to help. I wondered where in the city he lived, if it was actually feasible to see him again, go on a proper date where I got dressed up and didn't get tipsy within the first half hour.

"So, same question, if you fly at this new chief like a chainsaw, who gets hurt? Could that approach kick back and hurt you more than him?"

"I don't want to talk about this any more. And I don't want to go to practice either. I want you to take me home and…" I couldn't say what I really wanted. I didn't want him to think I was that easy, because I wasn't. I was the opposite of easy, but it had been two full years since I'd been held by anyone and tonight I really wanted that. To lie in bed and know that everything would work out. The problem was that there wasn't one part of my body, heart, mind or soul that didn't want this man. And not in the innocent way. Even if just for one night.

"I'll take you home and take my shirt off for you. If you still want me to do that," he smiled and shook his head like it was a silly request.

"You save lives *and* fulfill fantasies. You're like a hot genie. Can you say, 'Your wish is my command, Sophie?'" I laughed at my challenge to him.

NICK

I needed another drink. I knew I'd still blow well below the level with two beers. And if I had another, so would Sophie. And given her size and state of inebriation, another double might save me from her going Jason on my ass without witnesses. Better, I decided, for her to find out who I am from one of her buddies in the department than me.

"One for the road, then?" I said standing. She didn't argue.

When I came back she was looking at her phone, a deep scowl made her look like a young, shrunken apple head woman.

"Hope the wind doesn't change," I said mirroring her scrunched face.

"What?" she said, thankfully relaxing.

"Here's your drink."

She pointed her phone toward me. "The new guy's name is West. West. What kind of dumb name is that?"

My gut twisted. I took the bottle from my lips, leaned back and placed it on the table behind me. Sophie didn't notice. She was replying to a text message, no doubt from one of the volunteers at the meeting.

"No phones at the table, young lady. That's rude when you have a real live person right here in front of you," I said, picking up her phone and pocketing it. I didn't want her finding out the bastard's first name while we were here. Sure, it would be nice to have a witness when she tried to murder me. But better for her not to make a scene in front of people who might gossip.

Adapt. Improvise. Prevail. That was my motto. What five minutes ago seemed like a good idea, now looked less than ideal.

"What kind of man comes to a town he has no connection to and thinks he can take over the tightest group in the community?" She shook her head I disbelief.

I nodded. Then I shook my head and raised my shoulders in a 'you got me' expression.

"That's not a rhetorical question," she said. "I'm serious. What kind of man does that?"

"I don't know. A guy who needs a job and has the qualifications?"

"Not his place," she said putting her drink down.

"Why is being chief so important to you?"

Oh man, I hoped she'd had enough to drink that she'd not remember this conversation when things went pear-shaped.

She looked at the table. Spoke to her rum and Coke. "I know you haven't had much of a chance to look around, but there aren't many jobs in this town for a woman. I mean, for anyone who doesn't want to be working in the logging industry or serving coffee or working a cash register. I'm a nurse. Or almost. I'd just gotten my final internship when I got called home. And I know it sounds awful, but I just can't see myself working at Walmart. You know?"

"So, why not get a job as a nurse?" I braced myself for what was probably a dumb question with an obvious answer.

She exhaled loudly and then sucked back the last of her drink.

"When I left Lily Valley, I swore I'd never come back. I was so ready to live in the city. And my parents seemed happy enough to send me away at twelve years old. I mean, I kind of get it. They were old, retired. And just plain tired. They sent me to a nice boarding school. I did well. Got a scholarship to university. Blah blah blah… didn't come home often since… what was here?"

I shook my head, "Family?" I asked since she seemed to be waiting for an answer.

"Yeah, well, my parents. My brothers and sisters were all long gone. I guess I thought that's what you do when you're from here: you leave. But when my mom died, Papa needed someone to take care of him," she looked up from her now empty mug, "Cancer. And on top of that he'd been paralyzed in a car accident about, I don't know, eight years ago. So Mom was a full-time nurse to him."

"And you took over your mom's job?"

"Well, yeah. At the funeral all my brothers and sisters voted that since I wasn't married and didn't have a job—which isn't true, I was working at a hospital in Halifax—and since Papa didn't have enough money for live-in home care and he refused to go into a government-run facility—which I don't blame him for—that I should stay and be his caregiver."

She stopped talking and seemed to be finished her story. But I was no more clear on why nursing wasn't an option for her.

"And your dad always wanted you to be the chief of a fire department, not a nurse?"

"I never finished my internship and now it's been over two years since I did my training, so to get a job is… I basically wasted four years of education. So, chief of a fire department sounds like as good a job as any. I'm good at it. I can use my medical training since most of our calls are medical in nature. And, I need a job, like yesterday because my *poutain de calais* siblings are saying that I'm welcome to stay in the house but making sure it's impossible since I know that what they really want is to sell the house ASAP to get their inheritances. The only asset my parents had was the house and they all want their share. So, I need to figure out how to earn enough money to pay market rent and save enough for a downpayment. I can't do that on less than a seventy-five grand salary."

"So, losing the chief job means—"

She interrupted me, "It means losing my house, losing the community that I actually love living in, losing my friends..."

"Basically, your life is in the shitter without this job?"

"Exactly. You understand. What would your life be without your job? Shit right? The fire department is family. Way better family than my own was." She looked up to the ceiling, "I don't mean you, Papa. You're the exception. Love you always." Sophie looked back at me and smiled. "I'm done. You owe me a photo shoot. Time to pay up."

It was just after 8pm when we drove by the firehall. Decker stood by his car, talking to a guy who was dead ringer for Hulk Hogan—he was as big as me, had a white biker mustache and a shaved head. The speed limit by the hall was just 15 miles an hour so I slowed right down, enough for Decker and this guy to see Sophie and me. They both waved for us to come in. I checked behind me. No cars. I slowed down and signaled. *Shit, shit, shit. Decker don't say my name. Please god, don't tell her I'm the guy who stole her job.*

"What are you doing?" Sophie yelled.

"They're calling us, or you, in. I thought you'd want to talk—"

"Drive! I'm done with them. And we have a date to finish. Or a not date. Whatever. I want pictures. You owe me."

"Your wish is my command, Sophie," I exhaled relief.

"Ha! I knew it! I get two more wishes, right? No wait! The photos don't count because they're part of the bet. You still owe me three wishes. Or is it two? Did that count as a wish?"

Saved by the drunk girl!

We drove about three minutes farther up the hill, past a few dozen small houses. She pointed to the biggest one.

"Pull in here," she said.

As I parked, a giant Bernese Mountain Dog ran to my car.

Sophie jumped out, "Max! I forgot I left you out. I am so sorry, buddy." She dropped to the ground and sat on the gravel, taking the dog's head in her lap. He probably weighed as much as she did. He melted into her.

"This is Max," she said. Both she and Max looked up at me. This is what unconditional love looked like. He wasn't mad she'd forgotten him, he was happy she was home. She covered his head in kisses and rubbed his exposed belly. "You must be starving. Dinner? Want dinner?"

Max jumped up and bound toward the door. She opened it without a key.

"You live here? On your own?" I asked looking up at the three-story mansion.

"With Max, right, buddy?"

"It's... big," I said stating the obvious.

"It is now. It wasn't when it was full of kids. Not that I was here for the best—or worst—of that. I was lucky enough to have my own room but most of my brothers and sisters had to share growing up."

She sat on a bench and untied her boots. I crouched down and followed suit, placing my own boots neatly against the wall and hanging my coat on a hook.

She walked down a hallway which led to the large kitchen. This was a kitchen designed for cooking and serving huge meals. She looked tiny in it, dwarfed by the fridge and the ten foot long table pushed up against the wall. Eight mismatched chairs sat around the three sides. She picked Max's bowl off the floor and pulled a container of meat from the fridge and vegetables from the freezer and mixed it all with hot water.

I pointed at the automatic hot water spout by the sink. "Tea drinker," I said as a fact, not a question.

"I can take it or leave it. Papa loved instant coffee. Emphasis on the instant." She smiled. "You hungry? I'm starving all of sudden." She grabbed two bananas from a fruit bowl on the counter and tossed one to me. Then she opened a cupboard and pulled out a granola bar. "Catch," she said. "Dinner. Want a tour?"

She grabbed my hand and led me through the rooms on the main floor, explaining some of the house's history.

"It was a rooming house back in the early part of the 1900s all the way through the sixties. That's when my dad bought it for a song. He and Mom had just gotten married. Back in 1966. They knew they wanted a huge family so they moved from the city where they'd been living with my mom's parents even after they got married. Once they got the house, they got to work right away on filling all the bedrooms. Come on! I'll show you mine."

She sure loved this house. I could feel it in the way she pointed out pieces of furniture, "this corner cabinet is responsible for this scar," she said pulling her hair off her forehead to show me a white gash just below her hairline. "And this radiator," she stopped in front of an ancient cast iron grill, "this is where I used to hide spiders since they'd come out from here and go right into that room," she pointed to the adjacent door. "That was my next oldest sister's room. She hated me but she hated spiders more." She wiggled her nose at me. "And before you judge me, she was too afraid to kill them so I was not responsible for sending innocent spiders to their deaths."

Her room was decorated as though she was still twelve. Posters of Justin Timberlake and Rihanna hung above a small white, IKEA desk. Her white bedside table matched the princess headboard on the twin-size bed.

"Oh my god!" I laughed out loud.

"Isn't it great? Like a time capsule to the mid-2000s. It seems a lifetime ago… but it's… just half a lifetime. But you can see why I need new posters, now, right?" She rubbed Justin's face and said, "Time for you to move along, Justin. There's a new kid on the block."

The way she looked at me. That same deep stare with those gray-green eyes that she gave Max. Damn. Did I give her those puppy dog eyes back? I had a bad feeling I had. I felt myself harden—and I don't mean my pecs. I turned before she could notice. I hoped.

"Um," I said catching my breath, "should we go back downstairs to do this silly photo thing? I'm not sure I'm Timberlake quality, but I am more age appropriate." I took two steps out of her small bedroom.

"Hey! Where do you think you're going?" Sophie grabbed the back of my t-shirt and tugged me hard backwards. I stumbled and hit my shin on the corner of her bed.

"Son of a bitch! Ow!" I spun and sat on her bed, exposing the fully erected tent in my chinos.

No doubt Sophie saw. She bit her bottom lip, her nostrils flared as her chest rose. I couldn't take my eyes off the Lily Valley logo over her left breast and her eyes were not moving from the demonstration of my appreciation of the way she filled in her department issue casual wear. I covered my crotch with my hands.

"Nothing to see here."

"You're blushing," she said, once she had no reason to be staring at my zipper.

"Yeah, well, when I was twelve Rihanna was one of my go to's, if you know what I mean," I tried to deflect, not sure why. If she wanted me, I'd love to bite her bottom lip. Kiss her bottom lips. But she was drunk. And she was going to hate me in the morning or as soon as she found out that I was her enemy number one. As much as I wanted to try to win her over before she found out she needed to find any reason to like me, this was not the way.

"You wanted a photo. That's what I'm here for." I pulled off my t-shirt and flexed my pecs, left then right. She made a little squeal and did a silly happy dance. She was sexy in a way that said, *I have no idea how sexy I am.*

"I have to get my phone," she said running downstairs to the front door where we'd dropped our coats.

I took the opportunity to think about prostate exams and nail fungus. Anything to move the blood away from my cock, back to my limbs. I flexed my biceps to warm them up.

Sophie yelled up the stairs, "Oh no! I forgot my phone at the bar!"

That's when I remembered I'd pocketed it to protect myself from her learning the first name of the new bastard chief.

"Dammit!" I yelled back. "Don't worry, I'll swing by and pick it up. But let's get these photos taken. We can use my phone."

She bounced up the stairs. "Okay. But let's be quick. I need my phone in case Papa..." She stopped mid-sentence. "Never mind." Her glow extinguished in a heartbeat. She dropped down beside me on her bed. She dangled her feet for a couple of seconds then pulled her knees up to her chest and rocked back and forth. "I'm feeling a little woozy."

"Yeah. You had a good six ounces of rum tonight. I'm guessing that's more than your normal Thursday night consumption," I said rubbing her back.

"Mmm… that feels nice." Sophie pulled off her t-shirt and rolled onto her stomach. "Please rub it more."

Her skin was warm to my touch and she moaned lightly as I let my hand run from her shoulders to her waist. Back and forth with a small jump over her bra.

"You can take it off so you don't have to lift your hand if you want," she said sounding like she was falling asleep.

"You're sure?"

"Mmm-hmm… feels good. Your hand feels so good."

I was glad her face was buried in her pillow so she couldn't see how good she felt to me. Too good. I undid the clasp of her bra and she wiggled her shoulders, leaned up on one arm and pulled it out. I caught a glimpse of her nipple. It was small and pale and looked to be as hard as my cock suddenly became.

I let my hand brush down the side of her breast and up her side ribs. She arched her ass just enough to let me know how good it felt. Up and down, my flattened hand covered fully a quarter of her back. I gently ran my fingertips along her spine and her hips tilted even higher. Her hands reached below her waist and she pulled her jeans off, giving me another look at her breast and nipple as she squirmed out of her pants down to just panties.

"Rub my legs," she said almost dreamlike. "Please, Nick. I'll use one of my wishes if I have to."

I wanted my own genie at that moment but I wasn't sure if I'd wish for Sophie to ask me to fuck her or to fall asleep, so I could leave without causing more damage. She reached behind her and felt for my hand, found it and placed my palm over her butt cheek. My fingers fell between her thighs.

She spread her legs just enough to be clear that she wanted my hand there. I allowed my finger to press gently against the moist fabric covering her pussy.

"Do you have condoms?" she asked.

I leaned down and kissed the side of her face. "No. No condoms."

"No fair," she whispered. "I wish you had condoms."

"You cannot know how much I wish the same." I pulled my hand away from her underwear and she moaned a sad, "Nooooo," but before she'd finished protesting I'd sucked two fingers and pushed them under her cotton panties, between her folds, and was teasing her opening. She flipped herself over onto her back, forcing my fingers out and stared up with so much longing I thought I'd come just looking at her.

Sophie pulled off her panties and lay there, totally uninhibited and so fucking sexy in her confidence I had no choice but to pull my cock out since it was going to break in half if I didn't free it.

"Can I make you come?" I asked.

She closed her eyes and arched her back. I took that as consent and dropped to my knees at the foot of her bed. I pulled her body down to the edge and put her legs over my shoulders so I could bury my face in her. She was sweet and salty and throbbing. She came faster and harder than I expected. I wasn't ready to stop. I sure wasn't ready to leave, but I knew I had to. I knew if I stayed I'd lose self-control and do something we'd both regret in the morning. Well, her more than me.

I picked her up, lay her down with her head on her pillow and covered her with her blanket. She kissed me hard, one hand on my cock, just holding it. She was fading. Falling into a drunken, post-climax sleep.

"Lay with me," she murmured.

"Much as I'd love to, really love to, I've got to go back to the bar and get your phone. And I've got work in the morning so I should really get going."

"Please? Just for a minute?"

She rolled over with her back to me, clearly trying to make room for me to spoon her. And as much as I hated myself for leading her on, I couldn't resist. I lay on top of the blanket to avoid accidentally ramming my raging hard-on inside her. I held her until her breathing told me she was asleep. I kissed her on the head and rolled away, forgetting how narrow the bed was. I caught myself before I fell to the floor but ruined my attempt to escape without waking her. Sophie sighed and rolled onto her back.

"Will I see you again?" She looked at me with those eyes that made me feel safe and unconditionally loved.

"You will."

"Promise?"

"Yeah, I promise."

"You're one of the good ones, Nick," she said as if to herself. Then, "Nick. Nick. What's your last name?"

I swallowed hard, and pushed myself back into my pants before I answered. I reached across her for my t-shirt and leaned down and whispered, "West. Nick West." Then I stood and made a b-line for the door.

Sophie whispered, "Glad to meet you Nick West. Drive safe and see you soon. I hope." She curled up into a ball and looked like she'd fallen into a peaceful sleep.

I took the stairs three at a time, pulled her phone from my coat pocket and added her number to my own phone before I put it on the bench she'd sat on to take off her boots. I went to the kitchen and looked around for paper to leave her a note. There was a whiteboard and markers. I wrote,

Forgive me.
xox Nick

I left Sophie's seriously considering calling Decker to let him know I'd changed my mind, to tell him to give the job to Sophie. She could do the job well enough. I mean, I knew I was the better fit on some levels, but she wouldn't have been a bad choice. Not by a long shot. Me taking the job now? Maybe a bad choice.

I needed to talk this out and as much as I hated feeling like I wanted Dad's thoughts, that's who I called on my drive home from Lily Valley.

"Hey, Dad. How are things?" I could hear the sounds of a loud bar behind him.

"Nick. Good, good enough. Did you hear that Dylan won his last case? My guess is he'll make partner within the year."

"Yeah, I heard. It was in the news. It's great," I said truly happy for my brother.

"I'm putting money on having three of the four of you boys hitting Vancouver's Top Thirty Under Thirty list."

I let that settle, knowing which son he didn't expect to give him that bragging opportunity.

"So, Dad, I was hoping for some advice—" I stopped talking since he started to talk to someone else. I waited for him to finish, "If you have time."

"You got it. What do you need? I've got two minutes before Dylan comes back from the bathroom. We're celebrating."

"I get it. I was offered a job, a promotion. Sort of."

"That's great, Nick. Remind me what comes after… what's the rank you've got?"

"It's actually in a different department, as chief."

"Chief? That's a hell of a promotion! I'm proud of you, Nick," Dad's voice sounded sincerely proud until he said, "Who'd have thought you'd become a chief? Wonders never cease, eh?"

Fuck you, Dad.

"Yeah. Who'd have thought? So, here's the thing. It's in Lily Valley with a volunteer department. The first paid chief position."

"That's wonderful, Nick. That'll make the news, won't it?"

"I guess. I don't know. But it's a pay cut of twenty-five grand a year. What do you think? Worth it or should I stick it out and work toward chief in the city? It'll take at least another ten years. If at all."

"Nick, Dylan is back. Here, say congratulations to him."

"Hey, big brother," Dylan said, sounding apologetic.

"Little asshole. Way to go, wiener. On the fast-track to partner, I hear."

"Yeah, well, we'll see. I'm just happy I won this one. Super nice family being royally screwed by a development company. So, what's new with you?"

"I have a chance to become chief of a volunteer department. Got the offer. Means taking a pay cut, but… might be good in the long-run… was asking Dad what he thought but, he's a little preoccupied right now."

"Yeah, sorry about that, bro. Does the job sound like something you'll enjoy?"

"Yeah, actually, it does. Aside from the fact that a local is probably going to try to murder me in my sleep since she thought the job was hers," I said.

"Lily Valley's a nice place. You could do worse. I think you should take it. Ah shit, Dad wants the phone back. Drinks on Friday? My place?"

"Sounds great. Congrats, eh. I'm super proud of you," I said to my high-achieving brother.

"Whatever," Dylan said in that way that people who get lots of praise can just shrug off the compliments since they know there'll be another one soon enough.

"Nick. It's Dad again. I'm really proud of you son. Chief. Wow. That's fantastic. What a day. Twenty-eight and chief of a fire department! We might just have four out of four of you boys making that list. Clearly I did my job well, didn't I?"

"Yeah, Dad. You did. Thanks for—"

"Gotta go, Nicky boy. Shoot me a message with all the details of your new job so I can share the good news."

And he hung up.

Love you, too, Dad, I thought, giving my phone the finger, but feeling no more sure about my decision.

The contract from Decker was in my inbox when I woke up the next morning. I read it over—didn't need no stinkin' lawyer to interpret it. It was exactly what Decker and I had discussed. I had six months to prove I could maintain status quo and from there, once I had a good handle on the assets and areas that needed improvement in the department and with the members, we'd put a growth plan in place. I'd choose the hours I'd spend in the office but I also had to attend eighty percent of calls, not as the Incident Commander, but just to observe.

Before I signed it I just wanted to gauge Sophie's reaction. Would it be a deal breaker?

I texted her and held my breath,

> I had a really great time last night. It's Nick btw. :)

After what seemed like a lot of typing and erasing since it took a full two minutes to send this message, I got,

SOPHIE

> See you soon, I hope. I owe you. :)

When she asked my last name I was sure I was a goner,

but hallelujiah, my genie powers seemed to be working overtime.

SOPHIE

> Nice to meet you, Nick West. Wear your cape next time we get together. I've always wanted to be a sexy superhero's sidekick. :O

I printed Decker's contract, signed it, scanned it, and emailed it back feeling like I'd just won the lottery. Then I went to my chief's office to negotiate a six month leave of absence. Could I make it a trifecta: the job, the girl, *and* the security—just in case the girl got tired of me?

8

SOPHIE

I woke up with a raging headache. What time was it? I leaned over to check my phone. *Not there... Where was it...* pieces of the night came back at supersonic speed. I touched my body. Naked. Stark raving naked. Yup. Not a fantasy. *Way to go, Sophie. I'll bet he'll be calling real soon, you salope.*

I picked my t-shirt and panties off the floor and put them on. I found my phone at the front door. He'd brought it back. What a sweetheart. I shuddered at the memory of his touch, soft and firm, gentle and assertive. *Oh my god, I let him eat me.* I slumped on the bench mortified. I was so needy. What had I given him in return? Blue balls, that's all I could imagine. He gave up his night to babysit me and I thanked him by letting him bring me to bliss, then I sent him on his way.

Or did I? I didn't remember telling him to leave. But I must have, otherwise, he'd be here. Wouldn't he? Max lay down beside me and I rubbed his belly with my foot as I scrolled down the list of texts I'd missed last night... seven, eight, nine of them. All friends in the fire department.

I sighed and let the disappointment of having not gotten the chief job overtake me. I'd held it together all night with

Nick. Now I could express how I really felt and that was one part sadness and one part fear which equalled one hundred parts pure rage at the committee that chose an outsider to lead our department. And the inconsiderate *connard* who thought nothing of coming to our village to take over the heart of the community.

I clicked on a couple of messages,

> **DAN**
>
> Sophie, sorry you got fucked over. You deserved that job.

> **LYNNE**
>
> This sucks. If you want to fight, I'm on Team Sophie.

> **MARTIN**
>
> Lots of us are willing to quit if you do.

My phone pinged. My heart and gut did a little flip. Maybe it was Nick.

"This might be important, Max," I said, standing up, suddenly filled with nervous energy again.

> **UNKNOWN**
>
> I had a really great time last night. It's Nick btw. :)

I pressed my thighs together tight to control the squirmy urge that suddenly filled my panties.

> I'm embarrassed. Sorry I got drunk.

I saw that he was typing a reply and I waited. Then the typing stopped. No message came. I waited. I worried. What had he typed that he erased? Should I mention that I'm not really such an easy lay? That it was just a hard day and it's been a long time since I'd had any kind of physical attention and… yeah, that's exactly what I should do, reinforce how needy I am. I typed,

> *Hope to see you under better*
> *Hope next time I'm*

I typed and erased my own message a dozen times before I finally settled on,

> See you soon, I hope. I owe you. :)

UNKNOWN

I'm glad you're still talking to me.

That seemed weird.

> Why wouldn't I?

Nothing from him. I typed again,

> What don't I remember?

A long pause and then his reply,

UNKNOWN

My name? I'm sorry.

I thought hard but couldn't remember his last name. And why would it matter anyway?

> Unless it's Beaulieu and you're a long-lost cousin I don't care what it is.

I waited. No reply.

> So what is it?

I watched my phone to see if he'd started typing. What the heck? Had he walked away mid-conversation?

> Hello?

UNKNOWN
West

Nick West. Sounded familiar, like a superhero's name.

> Nice to meet you, Nick West. Wear your cape next time we get together. I've always wanted to be a sexy superhero's sidekick. :O

Laughing at myself and how unusually comfortable I was with Mr. Arrogant Calendar Man, I went to the fridge to get some yogurt and saw the message on the whiteboard.

My stomach dropped. Wait a minute… West… I'd just heard that name… it was a dumb name…. a bad name… Oh no, no, no, he can't be…

I scrolled up my screen to find the message I'd read last night right before Nick bought me my third drink.

LYNNE
New chief. Some young guy called West.
He starts in two weeks.

"Crisse de câlice de tabarnak d'esti de sacrament."

I burst into the chief's office without knocking. Not my usual approach, but today was not a usual day. Max stayed in the meeting room, no doubt sniffing around looking for chips that had fallen on the floor during a post-practice debrief.

"What do you know about this new chief, Murray? Have

you met him yet? Did you interview him?" I was spitting nails.

"Good morning, Sunshine. Who pissed in your coffee?"

"That's exactly what I'm trying to figure out," I said, dropping into the chair beside his desk.

"Have a seat," he said, with a smile that made me even more angry.

"Murray, seriously, did you have anything to do with this Nick West guy coming in and taking over?"

He shook his head. "The only role I played was giving the suits my opinion about the strengths and weaknesses of the three guys from this department who applied."

"Who other than me?"

"You know I can't tell you that, Sophie."

"Come on, Murray—"

"And what does it matter anyway? You know I was behind you one hundred percent. I still hold that you could do the job. But—"

"But what?" I didn't even give him a chance to finish. I realized I was too mad to talk so I stood up, made fists and swung my arms like I was skipping rope. Murray pushed his chair back and away from me.

"You should go for a run, or go upstairs and kick your energy into that weight machine," he suggested.

"I met him, you know."

Murray nodded.

"How did you know?"

"I saw you two drive by last night during practice. Didn't see him leave right away so I assumed you were good. That you'd come to some kind of agreement."

"Yeah, well, you assumed wrong. He lied to me. Led me on. All night, buying me drinks and acting like he could relate to what I was going through. Arrogant *connard*." I stopped swinging my arms and sat back down. "I need the paperwork to quit, please."

"You're not quitting, Sophie."

"Yes I am. I can't work with him. He's…" I didn't know what to say. *He's too sexy? We would have had sex if one of us had been smart enough to have a condom? He made me come like I've never come before?* I don't think so. Murray and I were close but not like girlfriends kind of close. More like, 'I'd risk my life to save yours' kind of friends.

"I have to quit since I hate him too much to run into a burning building if he was to fall through the floor."

That was the level of trust and commitment to each other that we needed in the fire department. We had to know that every other member had our back and would be a hero to save our lives if it came to it. I could honestly say I felt that way about the twenty-nine members. I didn't always like them and there was no way I'd date a single one of them— you couldn't pay me enough and god knows a few thought they could buy my attention—but I *would* run through a live fire to help pull every last one of them out. But if West fell into a burning hole, I'd be the first on-scene with a shovelful of dirt to bury him.

Murray was smiling. "At five foot five to his what, six foot three, and with him having a good hundred pounds on you, I don't think we really need to worry about whether you'd run into a burning building for him. Also, since the last actual house fire we fought was when you were something like six years old… I don't think anyone needs to worry about that."

"You know what I mean, Murray," I said, wanting to cry in frustration.

"I do. You're hurt. And your ego's taken a good hard hit. But until this job was posted you had no interest in being Chief, Sophie. Let it go. This isn't the career you want. You're a nurse for god's sake, being the chief of a fire department is a glorified paper pusher and number cruncher and a fucking ring master to a bunch of apes who, half the time make you wonder if they even speak English."

That's when I lost it. I tried to hold in the tears, hold back the grief, but the dam broke and the flood hit the man most unprepared to know how to deal with a crying woman.

"Jesus Christ, Beaulieu."

"I'm sorry. I know. You're right. Sort of. I love being a member of this department and I love this town and I just thought that it would be perfect since I need a job to stay here and Lily Valley needs—needed—a new chief. I got my hopes up that everything could work out."

"What are you talking about? What's happening?" he handed me a Subway napkin, only used on one side. "Blow your damned nose."

I'd not told anyone in town about my financial or housing situation since I was being positive, believing I'd have it sorted out before it was an actual problem. Papa always called me a Pollyanna. I took it as a compliment that I saw the bright side, the upside, the silver lining… but now I just felt naïve and stupid that I hadn't prepared for this.

"The short story is that I'm not named in the will and my loving brothers and sisters don't see any reason to add me. And, they want me out of the house yesterday so they can put it on the market and each get their money. I thought that if I got the job I'd be able to negotiate a lease-to-own deal with them. It's not like any of them are hurting for cash."

Murray massaged the sides of his horseshoe mustache with his right thumb and forefinger and tapped his desk with his left hand. He looked bad-ass, like a Hell's Angel, but he had a heart of gold. He'd won a medal for his bravery and service as a volunteer firefighter, risking his life when the town flooded and a dozen houses literally washed out to the ocean. I was still wearing onesies when that happened. Our house sat in the upper village, far from the massive flow when the dam up in the mountain gave way. Murray didn't hesitate, jumping into the freezing glacier water to pull people to safety. Five people survived because of him. But if you didn't know him, you'd cross the street if you saw him coming toward you.

He was the only chief I'd known since joining the department. He used his gruff exterior to keep us in line, but his heart was always right there on his sleeve. He was the kind of chief who would give you holy hell and publicly humiliate you if you screwed up, not to be a *connard*, but to make sure you understood how important it was not to do whatever dumbass thing you'd done. He used a hammer to keep us safe and alive. Some members understood that but others hated him for it; typically, the ones who didn't learn too quick.

I was a quick learner. He and I had come to verbal blows once though, after a practice. It was in my first month and I don't even remember what exactly I'd said to make him say it, but in front of everyone, he yelled, "That's life. Grow some balls, Princess."

And I didn't pause for a second, yelling right back, "If you hadn't noticed, I have a vagina and it's very sensitive."

You should have seen his face. I've heard lots of guys talk back to him since, but nobody has ever stopped him in his tracks like that. He blushed. And a few days later, I apologized. He acted like he didn't know what I was talking about. And since then it was clear that I was one of his favorite recruits. His *chouchou*, as Papa would have said.

It was clear he had confidence in me, since he made sure I was trained and ready to take an officer position when it came available. I'd only been a member for fourteen months. There were guys who'd been here three years or more who wanted the position, but it was offered to me.

I heard the grumbling about it being affirmative action and a way to avoid any kind of sexual harassment problems since the department had some truly sexist undertones.

Having two of the six officers being women gave the appearance that we were a little more woke than the reality.

"You have a lawyer?" he asked.

"Was hoping I wouldn't need one," I said.

Murray shook his head and gave me the look he uses when someone messes up a pump operation or rolls a hose backwards.

"It's not like I have a lot of options here, Murray. I got a free thirty minutes from a lawyer in town but he's like $200 an hour."

"I know a guy—"

'Murray," I said, feeling pathetic, "I have no money. Like, bank account zero. I can't afford a lawyer. I can't even afford dog food, right now. Papa's pension checks have stopped so, I need a job. Like last week. I needed that chief's salary."

We sat in silence for a several seconds.

"Maybe you're not thinking about this from the right angle," Murray said. "You say you need a job, but really what you need is cash flow. Right?"

I raised my hands as if to say both, "No shit, Sherlock," and "That's how people get cash flow, with a job."

"Have those rat bastard siblings of yours agreed to let you stay if you pay rent?"

"No," I said. "Nothing's been offered, just threatened," I said making air quotes, "off the record." Two sisters had told me that I'd be sorry if I didn't move out and let things settle as Mom and Papa had intended, meaning, with me obliterated from the family history.

"Start thinking outside the box, kiddo. I'll do the same. We need you here. The town needs you. The department needs you. I'm not going to let you leave without a fight. I know your vagina is sensitive but I've never met a woman with balls as big as yours."

Murray pulled a used paper towel from the recycling bin and handed it to me, "Get out of here you cry baby. Take

Max for a run. Clear your head. I'll help you figure this out on one condition."

I wiped my eyes. "What's that?"

"You stay and make this hotshot new chief work for his salary."

9

NICK

Murray seemed like a good guy. I knew he was firmly in the Team Sophie camp but he didn't let that stand in the way of going above and beyond the call of duty to make sure I started my first day with enough info to keep me from crashing and burning on take-off. He did me a solid by bringing pertinent files down to the city so we'd not be interrupted by angry volunteers. We spent all day Saturday going over the financial situation.

The department had a seriously healthy bank balance. I'd never seen anything like it, the way this place was run. They got an annual budget for maintaining the hall and trucks and paying all the expenses of running a regular fire department—less the staffing costs, of course. But that didn't mean the volunteers weren't paid. Sort of. The regional district gave the department $10 for every hour a member was either at training or on a call. Weekly training was two hours every Thursday night, and typically twenty to twenty-three of the guys attended. That was a minimum of $400 a week into general funds. And then there were call-outs, billed at a minimum of an hour, even for the bogus false alarms or medicals when the ambulance beat them to the scene. They could count on two trucks rolling and at least a couple of members waiting stand-by at the hall.

All in, they were billing taxpayers a good $30,000 a year. That was money the members got to spend in whatever way they collectively decided. Most years that meant a nice Gore-Tex jacket or a water repellant hoodie and a stack of new t-shirts, all with the department logo on them. There was pride in this department and the guys liked people to know who was a part of it.

Even with the swag and the community events they paid for, they never spent out the money, so the day Murray showed me the books, there was over $50,000 sitting there collecting one percent interest. Such a waste. I mentioned that one of my brothers was some hot shit financial advisor-investor. I thought it might make sense to move at least half of that cash to a portfolio to help it grow.

"It's good idea," he said, "but you need to get better than sixty percent of the members to vote for it. Lots of these guys live for the day and see no reason to tie money up like that. The other half don't want to risk it. They know what's there and that even though it's not earning interest, they aren't losing money either. Talking budgets at the monthly business meeting is like being married to thirty wives."

"You married?" I asked Murray.

"Three times. Widowed this last one."

"I'm sorry."

"Too bad I didn't meet her in my twenties. It would have been a fun life. You know who reminds me of her?" he asked, with a wicked grin.

Since we only knew one person in common, of course I knew who he meant. "I can't imagine," I said. But really, all I'd been doing was imagining her. I raised my fingers to my nose, feigning an itch, but really I was wishing that I could find just a hint of her smell on them. I took a deep breath to move the blood into my lungs, direct it away from the place it kept traveling every time I thought about looking up at her with her head lying beside that damned Hannah Montana lamp.

And to be clear, she didn't get me hot in an innocent, young thing kind of way. Quite the opposite. I've never met a woman as confident as Sophie Beaulieu. I can't tell you how many women have refused to let me go down on them since they hadn't had a wax in a week, or needed to take an hour-long bath before letting me even finger them. Sophie was all natural. Had a 'take me as I am' quality about her and dammit, I wanted to take her again and again and again.

Murray pulled my thoughts back to his ugly mug and the job at-hand.

"Time for beer," he said. "Enough of this bullshit."

It was already after five and we still hadn't gone over the personnel files. That was going to be another full day.

"I have a guest room. Sheets… might be clean. They're clean-ish. You want go for food and deal with the rest tomorrow?" I offered.

Murray checked his phone, sent a text, then said, "You're buying."

"Can't afford it. I just took a twenty-five thousand dollar pay cut to do this job," I said with a laugh.

"And you're going to tell me all about why you'd do that over a few Buds."

I took him to the Firefighter's Club, a bar that was owned and operated by the Burnley Fire Department as a way to make their budget since taxpayer dollars didn't quite cut it. It was a dive, but it had cheap beer and the food was good enough. The best part was that hipsters and the young crowd avoided it. I was the youngest person there.

"So you have a hot shot brother?" Murray asked.

"I have three hot shot brothers."

Murray made a face, "Your poor mother, having to raise four of you."

"Actually, I have three mothers. But just one dad."

"Busy guy. Or careless," Murray said.

"A bit of both. I was the result of a short-term fling. By the time I was one, Dad had hooked up with my step-mom. She already had a son my age, my step-brother, Adam, the finance guy. She and Dad had two more boys, my half-brothers, Dylan and Josh. Then my mom got knocked up again by some guy I don't even remember. But that gave me Morgan as my third half-brother."

"Christ, that's a confusing soap opera," Murray.

I shrugged.

"I also have one brother who isn't related by blood but is as close as a brother since Mom, Morgan and I lived in this shared house situation with him and Becky, his mom, until I was eight."

"Sounds like hell," Murray said.

"Not at all. By the time I was a teen I had three houses, three families to choose to stay at, so if one of them was pissing me off I just went to one of the other ones. Kind of sweet actually. Nobody ever really knew where I was. And no one ever worried. Lots of freedom," I said hoping I sounded more convincing about the beauty in this arrangement than I felt.

"So, why a career as a firefighter?" Murray asked. "You got in young."

"Nepotism."

Murray laughed.

"Dead serious. Dad knew the chief. I'd dropped out of university after three semesters and this was like his version of army camp for me."

"How old were you?"

"Just turned twenty."

"He must be proud, your dad," Murray said without a hint of sarcasm.

I laughed. "Are you kidding? My brothers are all killing

it in their careers. Did you hear about that case where the development company was trying to force an elderly couple from their home in Kerrisdale so they could demolish the block?"

Murray nodded. "Yeah, the couple was just awarded twice the value since the developer was so sleazy in its dealings."

"My brother Dylan was their lawyer."

Murray didn't say anything. He took a pull on his beer. Played with his mustache. "You and your brother close?" he asked.

"Yeah, why?"

"Does he owe you any favors?"

I laughed. "Obviously. Don't you have younger siblings? Constantly covering for them and taking shit so they could shine like good little assholes."

Murray stared around the room and then said, "Good. Drinks and dinner are on me. And now you owe me one."

10

SOPHIE

Murray asked me to come to practice an hour early. He said he had a gift for me. A newspaper article naming me chief would have been nice. Or maybe adoption papers, naming me his heir and offering me my inheritance now. Or a bottle of spiced rum. I'd be happy with that.

In addition to his Harley Davidson branded pick-up truck, there was an Audi in the parking lot of the firehall. It wasn't a car I recognized. And the driver was, no doubt, a person I'd not want to know.

Audi drivers were assholes. The whole lot of them. They drove our stretch of highway like entitled dicks—yup, always men—never bothering with signaling and driving at stupid speeds to pass in the merge lanes, as if getting one car length ahead would make even twelve seconds difference.

Murray was in his office with his door open so I called a cheery, "Hello," when I walked into the meeting room.

"Right on time," he said, and I heard two chairs scrape across the floor.

He walked out ahead of a much smaller, albeit normal size man, same age bracket as me but definitely not the same income bracket. He was wearing a suit. Tailored, for sure.

This man was not an off-the-rack kind of guy, that was obvious. His hair was perfectly styled, his glasses were professional but funky with a little horn rim action. If I hadn't seen his car before seeing him, I might have swooned. But I knew better.

"Sophie Beaulieu, meet Dylan Rhodes. Dylan, this is the young woman in question."

I gave Murray a side glance and extended my hand to shake this over-dressed stranger's.

"Nice to meet you, Mr. Rhodes. And what's being questioned?"

"Chief Rollit was filling me in on your recent challenge with an inheritance," he stopped and said, "I'm sorry. I should have said, I'm sorry for your loss."

I shook my head but laughed. He was a well-dressed amateur.

"Thanks. Murray was telling you about my personal life? Seriously?" I mouthed 'what the hell?' to my not-so-trustworthy confidante.

"It's a fascinating case, from what he's shared—which was just the basics. It's one I'd love to hear more about, Ms. Beaulieu, if you're willing to give me the details."

"And why would I give Mr. Dylan-the-Audi-driver the details of my family situation?"

Murray put his hand on my shoulder and turned me to face him. He spoke to me like I was hard of hearing, "Because Mr. Dylan *Rhodes* is a lawyer who has space in his *pro bono* portfolio to take on something that is a bit unusual and could get him a splash of media attention when he *wins* the case."

The penny dropped. I smoothed my feathers and sat down, motioning for Mr. Rhodes to do the same. Murray now put his hand on the lawyer's shoulder, looking at the clock. "You can't meet here. Guys are going to start showing up in about twenty minutes and you won't have any privacy. Take him back to your place, Sophie. Let him see what's at stake."

"Murray, seriously. Not cool. Sorry—" I turned to face Mr. Dylan Rhodes.

Mr. Rhodes interrupted, "Not at all. I totally understand. But Chief Rollit is right. It would be better to meet where we can get into details without interruption. Is there a coffee shop in town?"

"There's nothing in this town and the closest coffee shop is a fifteen-minute drive."

"Happy to drive us," he said.

Yeah. Not getting into a car with an Audi driver.

"Fine. We can go to my place." I smiled at the lawyer and scowled at my chief. "I'll be right back," I said, jogging to the far side of the room to the door that led up the stairs to our recreation room.

We were, like all fire departments, a dry hall. But that didn't mean we didn't have beer on the premises. It just meant that we had to pay for it and could only drink it at specific times. At least, if we were drinking in the rec room. But I was going to take a couple home. I didn't have money so I wrote an IOU for $5 and pulled two Buds from the fridge. I stuffed the cans into my hoodie's kangaroo pocket and bounced down the stairs, two at a time.

"Ready when you are," I said. "You okay with dogs?"

"Love 'em."

"What about that fancy-ass suit of yours. Is it okay with dogs"

He laughed. "It's not been marked yet, so I think we'll be okay."

"Right, then. Follow me. It's a three-minute drive. Speed limit is 20. Can your Audi go that slow?" What was wrong with me? I had a chance at a free lawyer and my snark was on fire. "Sorry," I said. "Too many car accidents involving Audis. I've got a bit of a bad attitude about them."

Mr. Unmarked Suit smiled and graciously accepted my apology with some snark of his own, "I know what you're feeling. I've had my share of train wreck relationships with French Canadian chicks. I've got a stereotype to overcome here, too."

I liked this guy. I mouthed a 'thank you' to Murray.

Dylan drove a safe distance behind me and signaled at all the turns. I could see him singing along to music and tapping his steering wheel from my rearview mirror. He made me laugh when he caught me watching him and started to head bang.

We pulled into my driveway and before he turned off his car, rolled down the window so I could hear the song he was listening to: Nirvana's Teen Spirit. He was mouthing the words silently.

I sang along out loud, with the wrong words, "A mulatto, and a bow wow," but he turned off his car so I was caught singing, "I'm a Skittle, I'm a Beatle. Yeah!" acapella.

"Good pipes, Ms. Beaulieu," he said with a laugh.

"It's Sophie. And leave your jacket in the car. No need to get dog hair on it just for formality sake. I've seen the serious suit. First impression has been made. And," I tapped the hood of his car, "recovered from, Mr. Rhodes."

"Dylan."

After I'd gotten us each a glass for our beers, we sat on the couch in my living room. He pulled a yellow legal pad and a fountain pen from his briefcase.

"So," he said, "tell me your story. Why am I here and how can I help you?"

I took a deep breath. My first thought was, *You could figure out how to have that* connard *new chief fired,* but I held my tongue and focused on the bigger picture.

"This house is why you're here. And the fact that I have eight brothers and sisters who are all in agreement that since

Mom and Papa forgot to put me in their will, I have no right to an inheritance."

"And you think your mother and father would have wanted you to have your share?"

"Mom, I'm not so sure, but Papa? One hundred percent."

"I know it may feel rude of me to ask why you're so certain, but I'm trying to understand what you're up against and what kind of story your siblings may be telling each other, and their lawyer, that has them thinking you don't have a right to an inheritance."

"Because Papa and I talked about me raising my kids in this house. Even though I'm a few years from thinking about having kids, I know that when I do I want to have and raise them here. Not just in this town, but in this actual house. Papa and I even drew up elaborate plans for how we could renovate the five small bedrooms on the second floor into three that would give my kids room to build blanket forts and Lego towns and have sleep-overs. We figured out how to put a half-bathroom in each bedroom, so when the kids were teenagers they wouldn't have to wait in line while one obsessed over a zit or did things teens do that they'd die to have anyone know about."

Dylan chuckled. "Do you have those plans? Is your father's writing on them?"

"Yeah. You want me to get them?" I said standing up.

"No," he said motioning for me to sit back down. "Right now I just want to hear your side of the story."

"The one thing Papa and I never discussed was how I'd pull it all together financially," I said. "I let myself believe that Papa and I would make this happen together, ignoring the fact that when I arrived, right after Mom died, the doctors had given him three months, on the outside, to live. He had stage four lung cancer. I was there to make his last months comfortable and to drive him to doctor appointments.

"But Papa defied both the oncologists and the odds and lived without most people in town ever knowing he was sick. He'd made me promise not to tell anyone. And so we acted like he had a decade of life ahead of him. We did such a good job that I'd actually started to believe it."

Max sighed.

"You, too, eh, buddy? Anyway, reality came crashing in when the pain in his shoulder got so bad he needed morphine and the doctor did an ultrasound and found a new tumor. He went into the hospital on Friday for day surgery, but the oncologist took one look once he'd been cut open and closed him up again, saying there was nothing they could do at this stage. Papa was admitted into the palliative care ward and he allowed a morphine drip to be inserted. We both knew what that meant."

"I'm sorry," Dylan said. "That must have been hard."

"Papa asked to have a priest come to see him on Saturday and told me to call my brothers and sisters, most of whom hadn't come to visit him in months—even the ones who lived in the city." I took a deep breath to push back tears and exhaled rage.

"Even my *puttard* oldest brother, who drove right by the village every damn weekend never bothered to stop in to visit once during the whole ski season. Papa died on Sunday just before midnight but only three of my brothers and sisters managed to make getting to see him a priority. But after he'd gone, boy was everyone quick to have an all-family meeting to read his and Mom's will."

I handed a copy to Dylan who read it to himself until he reached a section I'd highlighted, which he read out loud,

"3.4 In the event that both André and Marie die before all the children have started their own families, the child/children living in the home may stay until such time as they are married. If said child/children are under the age of majority, either an older sibling shall live with them or a full-time nanny shall be hired with her pay being drawn from the equity in the home."

He looked at the last page of the will.

"This was dated in 1994. What year were you born?"

"1996. I had a lawyer confirm that even though I was well past the age that good Catholic parents might expect a daughter to be married and in her husband's capable care," I couldn't help but roll my eyes, "that I might still be entitled to stay in the house. But he said that didn't mean I wouldn't have to fight for the right. He said it might give me some breathing room but no oxygen.

"He also said that even if I won the right to stay in the house until I was married, which, he said was a long-shot especially since I'm not named, I'd at least have to pay all the expenses of maintaining it since the caveat didn't say anything about staying in the house for free."

"I agree with him," Dylan said. "And your siblings don't want to rent the house to you, I take it?"

I laughed. "No. They actually said that I'd already lived rent-free for two years. But the part they like to ignore is the fact that in caring for Papa I was working full-time for free. The only money I'd had to spend was Papa's pension and old age security money. It was just enough to pay all the house bills and buy healthy food for us both. But there was nothing left over for me to spend or save.

"And to be clear, even though I hadn't eagerly volunteered to be Papa's full-time nurse for two full years when I started, I had accepted the job willingly and once we had our routine established, I felt like I'd won the work/life balance lottery. I didn't resent one minute of my time caring for him, in fact, it was probably the best two years of my life."

Dylan and I held eye contact for several seconds.

"So to be clear," he said, "your siblings were happy to consider you a member of the family while you were here caring for your father and not being paid?"

"Basically."

It was only 7:30 when Dylan tapped his pad and said, "I've got what I need for now."

"And does it meet your *pro bono* standards?" I asked, fearful that answer was No.

"There are a few loose ends I need you to tackle before I can answer, which, actually," he breathed out loudly, looking a bit uncomfortable. "I realize this sounds… well, rude, but are you one hundred percent certain that you are the biological child of your mom and dad?"

"Wow! That's out of nowhere," I said, sitting up.

"Well, a thirty-year gap between you and your eldest brother… that's unusual. Honestly, unlikely."

I was angry at the suggestion but I'd had this conversation a hundred times, every time someone found out that my brother Dick was so much older than me.

"Mom and Papa were good Catholics. Mom was 48 when I was conceived. And yeah, I was a huge surprise but there was no way she'd have had an abortion, so," I shrugged my shoulders. "Here I am."

He stared at his paper and I stared at him.

"The reason I'm questioning this is because your siblings are doing their damnedest to exclude you from the will. It makes me wonder if they know something that you don't."

Dylan looked up, caught my stare then held his hands up as if I was pointing a gun at him. Which I might have been, metaphorically, with my eyes.

"Do I need to do a DNA test to prove it?" I asked, putting my hands on my hips.

"Are you willing?"

"Let's say, in the highly unlikely event that we find out my mom and dad are not really my biological parents, what happens then? Am I S.O.L. or could I still have a case to be included in the will?"

He took time to think. I watched him. I could almost see the thoughts spinning in his mind since his facial expressions kept changing and he was ever-so-slightly nodding and shaking his head.

"I bet you're a terrible poker player," I said when he looked up from his thoughts.

"You'd lose that bet. I'm the best bluffer you've ever met. And, to answer your question, it depends. I see four possible outcomes. First is that your mom and dad are your biological parents, second is that you were adopted and don't share any blood with the family, third is that your mom had an affair—"

"Impossible," I interrupted.

"—and fourth is that you are a blood relative, but actually the child of one of your older siblings." His face said, 'I'm sorry.'

It's not like I hadn't had those same thoughts at different times in my childhood, the terrible teens, and even when I was doing my medical training. But Papa insisted I was a product of his and Mom's love. I had to believe him.

"Fair," I said. "And if it's anything other than I'm a full blood sibling, I'm screwed?"

"Not exactly," he said. "From a legal point of view, if you are a full sibling who was not in the will, likely as an oversight, you can argue that directly to a judge and get a ruling which is 99 percent sure to be in your favor. If you were adopted and there are adoption records, same deal applies. It's just paperwork and an hour in court.

"But, if you're not a blood relative and there are no adoption records, you'll need a lawyer to argue that you are still a legitimate sibling based on the fact that they raised you as their daughter and everyone who knew you believed you to be their child."

"And, if one of my sisters is actually my biological mother?" I asked, trying to picture which sister would have been most likely to have gotten pregnant out of wedlock.

"That's where the case gets interesting. And that's the only version of this scenario that I'd take on *pro bono* since I could do something, if not precedent-setting, at least newsworthy."

"Murray wasn't joking? You're only interested in cases that get headlines? That's kind of sleazy, isn't it?" I looked over at Max and willed him to come over and pee on Dylan's leg.

Dylan took a deep breath and sighed. "I don't think it's sleazy, but you can choose to define it however you want. I'm ambitious. I want to make partner before I hit thirty. The way to do that is to bring clients to the firm. And I attract clients by winning cases that make the news. And it's not like you wouldn't benefit. You'd be getting at least $10,000 of legal services for free and walking away with about a hundred grand in your pocket that isn't there right now. It's a no-lose bet for you."

"Maybe," I said, imagining how a very public case could impact me and, if one of my siblings was actually my parent, their life. I didn't see rainbows in my mind's eye, I saw tsunami-sized storm clouds.

"How would the DNA test work, though, since my mom and dad are both gone? What will it show without their DNA to compare to?" I asked.

"There will be a bit of a gamble here. We'll be counting on the fact that one of your siblings has had the test done—"

"I know for a fact that two of them did, to see if they inherited the gene that was connected to Papa's lung cancer," I interrupted Dylan.

"That's good. And then one of them will have had to have made their family relationships result public. Do you think either of them is interested in finding long lost cousins?"

I shrugged. "And what if I have the DNA test done but neither of my siblings made their results public?"

"Big Catholic family like yours? I'm confident we'll find a thread that will be enough to connect you to the family tree if you are a blood relation. And, if it's not enough to prove whether you're a sibling or not, I'll petition the court to have one of your brothers or sisters have the test done."

My stomach churned at the thought of poking at the hornets. "I'll think about it."

"I'm not saying you have to do it. But I am saying that without a DNA test—or you coming up with a $2,500 retainer fee—there's no point in having another discussion. But, my secretary will still send you a summary of our conversation from my notes and, if you decide to pursue the DNA test, the next steps—getting all your legal details, birth date, social insurance number, approval to pull your credit report… basic stuff to start a new file." Dylan stood to leave.

I walked him to the door and Max pushed past us, out to the front yard. He gave me his 'Can I do this?' look standing next to the Audi's front tire. I shook my head and Max walked away.

"I really, really appreciate you coming up to hear my story. I hope you don't feel like you've wasted your time," I said, sincerely.

"Not at all. It's a fun drive. My favorite highway to open up and see what my beater car is capable of," he gave me a wink and he was right, I wasn't sure if he was bluffing or being serious.

"Well, please keep it to the speed limit until you pass under the bridge at Porteau Road. That's the edge of our response area. I don't want to have to scrape your ass off the pavement if you crash tonight."

I wasn't bluffing and I'm pretty sure he understood that.

I waved as he drove away and saw, out on the street, something shiny. A brand new dime right in the middle of the road.

"What are you trying to tell me, Papa?"

11

NICK

With zero chance of finding even a broom closet to rent in Lily Valley, I checked the bylaws and confirmed that there was nothing in them to say a member in good standing could not sleep in the firehall. It's not like it was going to be a sacrifice for me. The Lily Valley hall had a shower, a small but full kitchen, a giant screen TV and wifi. There was also an airy space above the truck bay that was home to exercise equipment (never used, Murray told me) and storage shelves. The heavy-duty hooks in the exterior wall suggested that the space was used to practice high-angle rescues, over the pony wall, into the truck bay. Smart.

The loft ran the entire width of the hall, a good forty feet wide and at least ten feet deep. It wasn't that much less space than my downtown condo and, with a little Marie Kondo-izing, had all I needed to make a home until something better opened up in the village.

And it wasn't like I wasn't used to sleeping on a cot or a couch. What I hadn't shared with Murray was that since I wasn't living full-time in any of those family homes growing up, once we all hit our teens, I bounced from couch to couch, not bedroom to bedroom, since nobody thought that it was worth having a bedroom for a part-time resident. Dylan was always good enough to let me crash in his room when he wasn't sneaking a girl in.

I moved the BowFlex from the wall farthest from the door to closest. The other guys might not be using it, but I would.

I unloaded my car, just a few duffle bags of clothes and books, a night table, lamp, and fold-out cot. At the far end of the space, away from the door, I created my camp.

I pulled all the turnout gear, helmets and boots off the shelving and looked each piece over. Most of it was so far past its useful life that even the Red Cross wouldn't send it to developing countries. I loaded it all into my Subaru and drove to the city so I could store it in my storage unit, in case Decker had an idea for it. All I could come up with was dropping it off at Value Village so they could be the go-to source for hobo fireman costumes next Halloween.

I was only gone four hours but in that time, missed a call. Good thing I wasn't officially starting until Monday morning. So many members had responded that I had to park up the road. I made a mental note that Sunday afternoon seemed to be a good time to find members at home and available to come in for extra training.

When the trucks rolled in after the call, I was in the loft, hanging a sheet to give my cot space some privacy. I stood to let them know I was there but before I yelled, 'Hello,' a member below yelled, "Is Sophie still here?"

I took a step backward, so I could see her without being seen myself.

"Yeah, I'm here," she called from the other side of the two trucks that separated the lockers on one side of the hall from the other.

"So, we have a plan to welcome this new chief," a male voice called. Lots of laughs.

"Oh, yeah?" Sophie said.

"Everyone gather around," the same man's voice said. Lots of shuffling and chatter. "I saw the West guy's contract. He's got six months on probation. All we have to do, to make sure he doesn't get the job permanently, is stop showing up. If our response times go down, he's out. Who's in?"

Lots of swearing and apparent enthusiasm. Great.

"You guys know I'm as pissed off as you all are—" Sophie started to say.

"Damn right to be pissed off. That was your job he stole," the same guy said, with Tony Robbins enthusiasm.

I so wanted to stand up and see who it was so I could give him a special welcome myself.

"But," Sophie yelled over the jeering, "not showing up for calls won't hurt West as much as it will hurt the community. Think about it. If someone needs medical attention and we don't show up, West won't suffer. The person who needs help will. As much as I want to make it clear we're not happy with the decision, we can't take it out on the town. That's not right."

Mumbles of agreement.

It took all my effort not to look over the side to see her. It was nice to hear her voice. I'd wanted to call her, to explain or *something*, a hundred times over the past two weeks. To try to smooth over what might have actually been the start of something nice… but what would I say? What could I say to fix the fact that I'd basically led her on for an entire evening. Oh, and stolen a job that everyone and their brother thought was rightfully hers.

"Okay, what if we stop coming to practice but still show up for calls? Will that make the point?" a new voice said.

Lots of verbal shrugging, "maybe?" "I guess so." "I don't know."

And then a voice I recognized boomed over the rest of them, Murray, the volunteer chief who was handing his stripes to me. He'd been clear with me that he thought Sophie should have been given first crack at the position but also knew that new blood would make the transition to a more focused department a lot faster.

"Until tomorrow morning you are a department under my command! In this firehall, there will be no talk of insurrection, backstabbing or otherwise undermining a senior officer. Or a fellow member, goddammit. Now or ever. Am I clear?"

A variety of voices answered weakly in the affirmative.

Then the trouble-maker leader again, "Beers at my place now. We can talk about whatever the hell we want there. Sophie, you in?"

I couldn't hear her answer over all the other voices saying they'd be there.

∼

I spent Monday in my office, pulling and sorting the training files on all of the members. It seemed haphazard, figuring out which members had achieved which qualifications. The mishmash of paperwork didn't give me a very clear picture of how well-trained each individual was or if, as a whole, the department was meeting the National Fire Protection Association's standards for fire fighter professionals.

What that told me was that Thursday night practices for the next three months would be focused on running through the basic tests and making sure every member knew and understood the codes and met the standards expected of all fire departments in North America.

I called Murray and told him my idea. He warned me it wouldn't be popular since there were several members who were great with the hands-on but had challenges taking written tests. He said that every volunteer chief who'd tried to get this department up to standard had given up, including him, since it was more hassle than the paycheck warranted. And everyone knew that even if the department wasn't meeting international guidelines, there was nothing the NFPA could or would do.

The hassle was that certain volunteers would need to be let go. But, since I *was* getting a reasonable paycheck and it *was* part of my job description to meet those standards, the guys could whine and whinge all they wanted and not sway me.

I compared what I'd figured out about the training level of the members against the records on the number of practices and calls each member had attended in the last four years, since the department had started tracking.

By dinnertime, I'd formed a solid picture of which members made the core of the department. Sophie, of course, was in this group of eight who attended every practice, virtually all calls, and took on extra leadership duties, some as officers. At the other end were six guys who were dead weight. Everyone else was somewhere in-between.

I checked my watch. I had under an hour until Murray, Sophie and four other members were expected for their once-a-month officer's meeting. Murray had agreed to lead this last one and share the plan he and I had developed. We needed, *I needed*, full buy-in from the officers to successfully implement the plan. All I knew so far was that I had Murray onside.

He arrived fifteen minutes early with news that Sophie had texted that she was stuck in traffic and would try to make it. Bob, the guy who'd been leading the insurrection after the call, didn't make up an excuse, just said that as long as I was sitting in the chief's office, he'd be on leave. Duly noted and thank Christ I wouldn't have to refrain myself from knocking him down from his high fucking horse.

No word from Lynne, Martin or Joe, but Murray felt

confident they'd all arrive on time and with attitude. I asked if he expected good or bad attitudes and he said that all attitudes were good as long as they led to the change the department needed.

I liked and respected Murray. I was pretty sure he'd not formed a solid opinion of me yet—aside from maybe, 'has potential'—but I wanted to prove to him that I was the right hire for this job.

At five to seven I slipped into my office to print out copies of my suggestion for how I'd move us from where we were to where we needed to be. Lynne, Martin and Joe all arrived together and came in quietly, saying reserved 'Hellos' to Murray who was sitting at the big meeting table drinking what looked like weak, black coffee.

Sophie arrived a couple of minutes later.

"Oh good. I thought I'd be late," she said sounding flustered.

"How'd it go with the lawyer?" Lynne asked.

"She was nice but I don't have as much confidence in her as the other guy. So, undecided? But one thing is clear now—I won't be able to fight this for as long as my sibs will. I mean, they are eight of them paying for one lawyer. And they all have these convenient things called jobs. So, unless I get *pro bono* representation, I'm screwed."

"Ah, honey. We'll do a GoFundMe for you, Lily Valley-style. You think it would help?" Lynne offered.

"Anything would help at this stage," Sophie said.

I didn't want her to know I'd overheard this, so I texted Murray,

> Take everyone to the bay and show them something that needs to be fixed on Engine One. Give me 3 minutes.

"Before West gets here, I want to show you what Dipshit

Number Three did on the call yesterday when he drove over the train tracks," Murray said.

Moans and chairs scraping as they all left the meeting room. I slipped out of my office and up the stairs to the kitchen and rec room. I cracked open the door to the loft area to listen to the conversation which was about how much it was going to cost to replace the heat shield that had been damaged when the truck was taken too quickly over the uneven railway tracks.

"It was a rookie mistake and it shouldn't have happened. You gotta make sure these hot shots understand the stakes of not paying attention," Murray sounded as mad at the officers as he was at the guy who'd done the damage to the truck.

When he suggested they go back to the meeting room, I silently closed the door and made my way back down the stairs with speed and a good amount of noise.

I flew in at the same time as they all did.

"Hello!" I said, "Sorry I'm late. Glad to see you all here. Is this everyone?"

Murray said, "All but Bob, but we won't wait for him."

Knowing glances between the others.

I refrained from saying hello to Sophie specifically, from asking her how she was, from telling her that I really was sorry and that I hoped she'd come to accept me as a friend and respect me as a chief.

"So, I assume you've all read my resumé. If you have specific questions about my experience or qualifications, I'm happy to answer those. And I know I'm not the most welcome choice to take this leadership role. I understand that Sophie was a strong candidate for the position and that she had the support of most members."

Everyone at the table looked at Sophie who stared at the table.

"Which means I also know that you're all in a difficult

position as officers, having to be the feet-on-the-ground, enacting and enforcing my vision which I'm guessing, no matter how brilliant, some members are not going to like."

I was looking at Sophie when I said the word 'brilliant.' She shook her head and mouthed the word. That threw me. Dammit.

"Um, so, I just want you to know that I will do everything in my power to support you."

Blank stares from all. Not even a head nod or a weak smile.

"All right. Well, Murray has given me a ten-thousand-foot view of the situation here—"

"Situation? I didn't realize we had a situation," Joe said.

"Maybe that was the wrong word. Let's start with each of you telling me who you are, how long you've been with the department, and where you see your own personal strengths and weaknesses as an officer. From there—"

"Seriously? Are we being group job interviewed?" Lynne interrupted.

"No. No, not at all. Murray and I have a draft plan and I'm just trying to ascertain who would be best to fill the different roles. For instance, I know that Joe is considered your most experienced and skilled mechanic... but I don't how you, Joe, feel about being singled out as the officer best suited to work with me on making sure we're maintaining our equipment to the best of our abilities. I'm also curious to know how interested you are in training other members to learn the ropes. So, fill me in," I said, making eye contact with each of them, although truthfully, when I got to Sophie, I looked at her mouth since I couldn't bring myself to see her hate. I saw enough in her clenched jaw to make me consider packing my duffle bag and ending my probation five months and twenty-nine days early.

Nobody spoke. And then Murray and I spoke at the same time, with a firm, "Alright then!"

I nodded at Murray.

He sighed. And then boomed.

"Look! You hate Nick because he stole something you all thought belonged to someone else. Get over it. Number one, Sophie was never a shoo-in, and you all knew the district was interviewing other people. Five in fact, and two others from this department, in case you hadn't heard, which, you probably didn't since it's confidential. So keep that quiet. But get the fuck over yourselves.

"Nick West is your chief now. He's got six months to prove he's got the balls and talent to get this department where it needs to be in five years. If you think we can keep operating this way once our population has virtually doubled, you're on crack.

"So, answer his question. Follow his orders. And remember what you are—brothers… and sisters," he said looking at Sophie, "who have to leave your shit at the door since your lives are in each other's hands when we're on a call.

"I'll start," Murray continued, still using his general's voice, "I've been with this department longer than you've been alive, West. Forty years with a short break in there for some prison time. I've lived in this town since I was small. I've worn that chief helmet so many times I can't keep count."

Murray took a deep and his voice softened, "I'm tired and too old for this shit. I can't keep up with you any more. This is my last meeting. Sunday was my last call-out. I'm counting on you to keep this department together since one day you'll be responding to my house with me on the floor having a fucking stroke or heart attack. I need you bastards in fine form to make sure I make it to the hospital alive so I can harass the nurses."

Joe, Martin, and Lynne all let me know their strengths and where they thought they could use extra training. And then it was all eyes on Sophie. I forced myself to look her in the eyes. I broke contact first. Gave her the win. And she took it.

Unlike the others who sat in their chairs to introduce themselves, Sophie walked to the front of the room and stood directly behind me, at the head of the table. My chair squeaked on the concrete as I turned so I could face her. She was standing so close I could have pulled her into my lap. The thought made my balls tighten.

12

SOPHIE

It had been two-and-half weeks since Mr. Decker, master of all the fire departments in this kingdom of tiny towns, had thumped me on the head with his scepter and kicked me into the moat. Two-and-a-half weeks minus six hours, since Nick West, the man who'd stolen my job had also stolen a small piece of my mind. And by mind, I mean he'd gotten into my head since I'd let him into my pants where he made a sneaky bastard left turn into my heart.

And he didn't even leave me with the photo he promised.

Worst. Genie. Ever.

It would have been so much easier to be mad at him if I had a picture I could obsess over, pick apart and find the flaws in. Sure, his eyes were a gorgeous blue in a dark and dirty bar, but what did they really look like in the light of day? Or, the light of the incandescent bulb in my Hannah Montana bedside lamp?

Maybe he had perfect abs and a chest that made my own chest heave to look at, but for all I knew he was a tentative hugger with a limp handshake and limper dick. Actually... I knew his dick wasn't limp. Damn him. So what if he had a powerful tongue? Who cared that he was a good listener, not just to my words but to the way my body responded under said tongue?

God, I hated him.

Hated that he didn't need Zac Ephron-perfect teeth to have a perfect mouth and smile.

But more than anything, I despised him for the fact that after spending just two hours with me he acted like he knew what made me tick. His arrogance at the fact that he knew I'd remain a committed volunteer because I cared about my community more than I cared about my ego or my self-esteem or keeping the house I actually loved so I could stay in this dead-end town and raise my non-existent, maybe never-to-be, kids here… I hated him so much.

By the time it came around to me sharing where I thought my strengths were and where I could use some support, I was so angry and so horny it was all I could do to not excuse myself to the bathroom for five minutes of self-love.

I wanted West to be as uncomfortable as I was. The best way, I figured, was to get right up in his face, see how he responded under pressure and figure out what his buttons were so I could push them the way he'd pushed mine.

I stood at the white board with my ass to his back until he turned his chair, presumably to see me. I twisted around quickly, knowing exactly where he was, took a step forward, toward him, and stood talking to the guys in the room with my crotch just six inches from his face.

I was wearing black leggings, a department issued, size small, men's t-shirt, and my steel toe boots. One hundred percent normal attire for a practice, since jeans were never comfortable under turn-out gear. No matter that this wasn't a practice. These clothes, I hoped, would be one hundred and twenty percent perfect for getting West riled up. If he looked straight ahead and stuck out his tongue he'd find the exact spot he'd explored two weeks earlier. If he looked up to see my face, he'd have to look past my breasts. They weren't huge, but they were there. I sucked in my belly and expanded my chest.

Game on!

I spoke slowly and deliberately. "My strengths, as I see them, are that once I make a commitment to something, I'm all in, whether that be to quit a damn good job to come home to care for my dad, or," I tilted my pelvis just enough that West would notice but the rest of the guys wouldn't, "keep a time-consuming volunteer job to be of service to *my* community," I said bending over to speak the last words inches from West's reddening face.

I turned to the white board and picked up the black marker. I drew a line down the centre and wrote 'Strengths' on one side of the line and 'Weaknesses' on the other.

"I work hard," I said, writing the word 'HARD' in all caps in the Strengths column. "As for my weaknesses," I turned around and stumbled so that I fell right into West's lap with my left hand on his not-at-all-limp cock. "Oops, sorry," I offered, pushing off heavily, making him grunt—in pain, I hoped, "I can be clumsy, sometimes."

I wrote 'CLUMSY' in the Weakness column to the muffled laughs from at least two of the guys. I caught Murray from the corner of my eye. He was biting his lower lip, trying to suppress a smile. That egged me on. I loved performing for Murray. He was like an adoptive grandpa. Just a couple years older than Papa, he was protective of me. But, unlike Papa who'd always pushed for me to be more serious, Murray encouraged me to have fun, as long as I was being safe about it.

"Hmmm... well, since I'm looking at my weaknesses

now, I guess I should add that sometimes I can be a little harsh in my delivery of information. Would you agree?" I looked at the Joe. He nodded then covered his eyes as if he didn't want to see what was coming. "So, I guess I could sum that up in a word as having a sharp tongue." I wrote 'TONGUE' on the board directly beside 'CLUMSY'.

"Huh, well that doesn't look very good, believing I have more flaws than strengths in front of our new leader, does it? What's something else I'm good at?" I looked into West's eyes and then at his bulge. I snapped my fingers, "I know! I have a perfect record on call-outs. I don't..." I squinted my eyes as if thinking of the perfect word, "cock-up." I turned my back to the room and beside 'HARD' I wrote 'COCK-UP.'

Murray couldn't contain himself and let loose a guffaw. West was now standing beside me. I took in his size. My forehead was at the same height as his throat. I had half a mind to head butt the smile off his face. He didn't look arrogant now. He looked mighty uncomfortable. Instead, I just looked up him, standing far too close for comfort, and said, "Not sure what kind of extra training I'm going to need. Boss."

As I stepped aside, West grabbed the eraser and wiped the board clean. But not before I noticed Lynne snap a photo. She shook her head at me, her eyes asking, 'What are you up to?' I winked at her. She was the only person who knew about my mini-fling and my mixed-up feelings for our new chief.

"Five-minute break," I said with authority, but I doubt I was heard over West who said the same thing at the exact same moment. We looked at each other. I'm not sure which one of us was more surprised.

"Game on," I said, as close to his ear as I could get. Nobody would have heard over the scraping of chairs. But as I turned to leave I saw that Murray was still watching. He put his left hand horizontally in front of his chest and moved his right hand, fingertips facing up, toward his chin, opening his fingers after he passed the still hand. He made the motion twice as he mouthed the word, "careful."

I got the message, loud and clear. American sign language for 'burn,' a hand signal we used to communicate during live fire training to indicate a door or surface was hot. He was telling me to be careful or I'd get burned.

I smiled and put my hands up in front of me like I was juggling invisible balls, silently letting Murray know that I knew I was playing with fire.

After the quick break, Nick said he needed fifteen minutes alone with each of us; the rest were supposed to read over some paperwork about different ideas for how to invest the money in our Member Retention bank account. I had lots of ideas but he called me in first. Great.

"Close the door," he said before I sat down.

"Yes, sir," I said, saluting him.

"Cut the crap. If you're going to stay on, Sophie, which I really hope you will, you need to work with me."

I couldn't help myself, "If you're going to stay on, Nick, which I really hope you *won't*, you need to work with *me*." I emphasized 'me' by placing both hands over my heart, dropping into the chair across from him. I had to sit sideways so our knees wouldn't touch.

He closed his eyes and rubbed his forehead with his massive hand. His fingers were long and strong, his nails were clean and cut short. I watched as he massaged his temple and remembered the strength of how his hands felt when he was gripping my ass, tilting my hips at just the right angle to—I inhaled quickly and shook away the memory before it had time to send any more blood away from my brain. I crossed my legs and pinched my thighs tight.

Damn you, Nick West. I don't do firemen. I don't do relationships, period. But I especially don't do local firemen.

"I'm sorry we got off on the wrong foot," he said, looking like he actually meant it.

"You could have told me as soon as you walked into the hall. You took advantage of me, let me pour my guts out to you and you pretended to care."

"I don't see it the same way. The very first thing you said was that you didn't want to talk about the chief position and I respected your wishes and fulfilled my promise to come and see you that day. I thought I was doing the right thing. The honorable thing by not making your night any worse."

"Honorable? Honorable? You… you…" I couldn't say it. *You went down on me and gave me the best orgasm I've ever had in my life. Pathetic sex life that it's been.* "you…" I pointed at my still very tightly squeezed together thighs.

And he smiled. The *connard* had the nerve to smile.

"I really enjoyed that. And from the feedback my tongue was getting, I'm pretty sure you did, too." He bit his lower lip and smirked.

Oh my god, he was so incredibly, annoyingly cute. And sexy. And I hated him for it.

"You're a pig. Who goes down on a girl the same day he meets her?"

His smirk had turned into a full on smile that I was tempted to smack right off his face.

"The kind of guy who doesn't carry condoms in his wallet since he never plans to get lucky on a first date."

"It was *not* a date," I sniped. "It was a bait and switch. And you lied to me."

"Never."

"Lies by omission. Same thing. I never in a million years would have invited you back to my place if you'd told me the truth about yourself."

"Which would have been a terrible loss for both of us.

Sometimes secrets are better kept, at least for a little while, don't you think?"

I shook my head. There was no way I could win this argument.

"So, what do we do now, Chief?"

"I was hoping you'd ask. There are a few ways we can take this and I'll leave the decision entirely up to you—"

"Then thank you very much for your day of service, Mr. West. We've really enjoyed having you but you can go back to the city and your regular programming now," I said patting his knee which was less than an inch from mine.

He didn't show any signs of frustration with me. He was unflappable.

"Murray really respects you," he said, "and he thinks that even though there are lots of members who have seniority, that you'd be my best choice as deputy chief. What do you think? Would you be willing to give it a try? Based on the little we've gotten to know each other I think we have pretty good chemistry."

He gave me that pain in my pussy smile again.

"You said there were a few ways we could take this. What are my other options?"

"You could stay as you are, a regular officer."

"I could step down and just be rank and file volunteer, too. That way there'd be a buffer between you and me."

He nodded, "You could do that but I think that's the least appealing idea. If Deputy Chief doesn't strike your fancy, you could simply resign from the fire department and—" he paused and stared right into my eyes.

As much as I wanted to see the arrogance that I knew lived behind those sparkling blue irises, all I could see was a man who clearly took life by the balls and enjoyed every second of it.

"And?" I asked, breaking the spell.

"—and be my girlfriend," he said standing up and

quickly moving away before my fist could make contact with his leg.

"This is sexual harassment," I said not sure if I was more angry or flattered.

"Joking aside, you've put me in a difficult position, Sophie. If I don't give you all the options, you'll give me hell for lying by omission. And apparently, if I spell them all out, you might charge me with flirting with you. Good thing my brother's a lawyer," he said giving me a wink.

"Sorry if I don't sound sympathetic, but you've put me in a hard place, Nick. Obviously, I'm not going to be your girlfriend. That's ridiculous," *because look at you and look at me.* "Off the table. I won't go back to rank-and-file since… well, since that's also ridiculous. Why would I give up authority? And who the hell would you replace me with? No one else is ready to become an officer."

Nick nodded. "True," he said.

"So that leaves me with either working as your right hand or status quo."

I took a step from his office and Nick put his hand on my shoulder, gently but firmly enough to turn me around to face him.

"Please consider the first option. I honestly think we could be a great team. And have fun working together to bring this department to where it needs to be in five years."

His hand was warm and sent a shiver right down into the crease of my Lululemons. He leaned over and whispered in my ear which made my Kegel muscles contract so hard my uterus slammed against my spine.

"I don't want to share this office with the runner-up, Sophie. I play to win and I need the best players at my side to pull this off. It won't be easy, but then, when was anything worthwhile ever easy?"

I tilted my head to face him and his mouth was close enough to kiss. Again. My tongue moved involuntarily in my mouth—which I realized too late, was open. I pushed my lips together and clenched my jaw as tightly as my vagina.

You will keep your calendar perfect body away from me, Nick West.

13

NICK

I had the good fortune of having Murray as an ally. He wanted Sophie as the deputy chief as much as I did so he gave me some pointers for how to win her over.

"She's as stubborn and independent a woman as you'll ever meet so whatever you do, West, don't be treating her the way you think you probably should. If it impresses those city women you pick up in fancy-ass bars, do the opposite to get Sophie's attention," Murray warned.

"I was thinking of inviting her out for dinner in Whistler."

Murray grunted. "She won't let you pay and she can't afford it. So, that's a no."

"Buy her flowers?"

"Have you seen her goddamned garden? Why would you waste money on cultivated crap when she can just walk into her yard and pick any flower she knows she loves having around? Nick, have you ever even had just a normal female friend?"

Sadly, that was a quick and easy answer. "Not a single one."

Murray sighed. "Do I have to spell it out for you? Jesus

Christ, I do, don't I? If you tell her that I told you any of this, I'll bust your balls with my own two hands. Understand, Chief?"

"Copy that. Busted balls for loose lips."

"First, I just want to clarify that you're trying to convince Sophie to accept the deputy position, not assume the missionary position. Is that right?"

I hesitated. I knew Murray liked me but I also knew he loved Sophie like a daughter. "Do I have to choose? Can't I have both?"

I was surprised when he said, "That's what I always say, 'Why choose just a piece of cake when there's pie on offer, too?' Okay, So Sophie only loves one thing in this world now that her dad's gone. It's Max. She'd do anything for that dog. Give up her own meal to make sure he gets enough calories to run wild in the forest."

I wrote, 'Max' on a Post-it note.

"Buy something for the dog and she won't refuse it. She'll be grateful. Tell her as deputy she can bring Max to work. I never let her bring the goddamned dog to practice since if I let Max in we'd have a fucking doggie day care here. But with you as chief, fly at it. You can make different rules for different members. They all hate you already so you won't lose anymore popularity points with the rest of the guys, but you'll earn a shit ton from Sophie."

I underlined 'Max' twice.

"Aside from the dog, what else?" I asked.

Murray grumbled and made sour faces. "She has a heart of gold and her natural inclination is to be the caregiver. You could hire her to deliver the first responder training instead of giving that work to an outsider."

"But, you could have given her the job. Why didn't you if she's so good?" I was starting to wonder if Murray might be setting me up for failure.

"Look Nick, I'm old. I've been in this department for

twice as long as you've been jerking off. It's an old boys club. We try to tell ourselves that it's not by letting women join, but the truth is, we've been operating on old rules. I can't change that. Honestly, I didn't have the balls for the fight so I did what I had to to make the girls feel as welcome as I could, but nothing to piss off the core. Which means not giving them too much authority.

"I was the one who told Decker and the Regional District that if we were going to mature as a department we needed to hire someone fresh and new. Sophie had two internal and two external competitors who didn't make it past the first interview. If it had been up to me, those two internals never would have gotten even one interview."

"Why's that?" I asked.

"Because all those bastards are just like me, only younger. Nothing would have changed. Sophie could have changed this place and brought us into the twenty-first century. I believe you can, too. I have faith in you. And with the two of you working together. Shit. This town will have the best goddamned fire department in the province. Guaranteed."

"To be clear," I said, "you think I should assign Sophie the job of doing the first responder training? She'll need the certification for that—"

"She's got it. Did it on her own time and dollar when she moved back. You know she's almost a fucking nurse right? This is shit easy for her. Second nature. She might need to do the refresher course or whatever the fuck it's called. Find out. Sign her up. Use department funds to pay for it."

"I can do that?"

"You're the chief, West. You can do anything you fucking want. Within reason. You pass things by the officers and make sure you go to the membership with the idea as a solid front. You'll get an earful from a few of the guys, but when it comes time to vote, anything that has all the officers onside will pass."

"Right, so to win Sophie's trust and support all I have to do is give her the room to use her skills and throw her dog a bone."

"You do that and I can guarantee you'll be throwing her a bone of her own."

I ignored the innuendo. Or at least, outwardly ignored it but inside I did a serious, *Hoo Haa!* "Thanks. I owe you."

"You just make sure you treat her respectfully inside and outside of the department or you know I'll hear about and I *will* hunt you down and cut you off at the knees. I've known a lot of women in my life and not one compares to our Sophie. The man who catches her heart is going to be one lucky son-of-a-bitch.

"Good thing I'm feeling like this is my lucky year, then."

I took Murray's advice to heart, starting with showing Sophie that I cared about Max by calling a friend who owned a natural pet food store that delivered food in the Sea to Sky corridor once a week.

He'd asked me months ago if I'd be willing to show up at his sister-in-law's stagette to surprise her and her friends with a strip tease. I'd flat out refused. But now I had a reason to degrade myself. He agreed that an hour of me playing sexy firefighter was worth three hundred bucks which would buy me six cases of frozen, dog food meat patties at wholesale. I had no idea how much Max ate, but, on his suggestion, arranged to have one case delivered every two weeks.

Then I sat down with the fire department budget to see what I could do to help Sophie upgrade her skills so she could take on more training responsibilities and get paid for her time. I knew it would never add up to the same salary as the chief's, but I figured it would help keep her in town and with the department at least a bit longer.

It had been three days since the officer's meeting. She hadn't submitted her resignation and I'd heard from Murray that she didn't intend to, that she was planning to stay and give me a hard time, within the bounds of allowable behavior towards a chief. I had that working in my favor: that she was respectful of the hierarchy in a fire department and understood how important it was to follow rules.

> Time to meet before practice tonight?

I texted her at 4pm, hoping I'd be able to announce my new deputy and my training plan at our pre-practice meeting.

SOPHIE

> Why?

At least she replied right away.

> I have an offer you can't refuse.

As soon as I hit 'Send' I realized my mistake. She confirmed that with her reply:

SOPHIE

> Sounds more like an order if I can't refuse it.

I waited two minutes and then sent,

> I'm making pizza. Come down in an hour?

SOPHIE

> Can't refuse pizza.

~

Sophie was five minutes early and had jogged down with Max, despite the rain. She peeled off her Gore-Tex jacket and wiped her bare legs dry with a few paper towels before pulling on yoga pants she kept in her cubby. She and Max both shook their hair to get the drips out. Either she didn't care that she had that just showered look or she knew it was a good look on her. My best guess? She had no idea how sexy the wet dog look was on her.

"Pizza's just about ready. Let's meet in the rec room," I said leading the way.

She breathed in deeply when we got upstairs. "Smells great. I'm starving. I assume the offer I can't refuse wasn't pizza?"

"It was one of the offers. I have a whole menu of them for you."

With food on our plates we each assumed a spot on our own couch to eat. She sat at the end closest to the couch I was on, which I took as a good sign since she could have taken the farthest side.

"I'm sorry we got off on the wrong foot. I had no idea that you were my competition for the job but since being offered it, I've had the chance to meet with your regional rep and Murray a couple times. Both think really highly of you and see leadership potential in you," I said.

She rolled her eyes.

"I saw it, too, that day at the car accident. But what I also saw were a few members who didn't take the chain of command seriously. They didn't follow your orders as the Incident Commander."

"Neither did you," she snapped, not holding back her irritation.

"It's true. I guess that was a prick move. As a career first responder with hundreds of these incidents under my belt, I had a better idea of who the priority patient was. But I did a shitty job communicating that I'd already sussed out the scene. I apologize," I said, meaning it.

"Have you heard whether the little boy made it?" she asked, softening. "We never hear about how people do unless they personally send us a letter or drop by to say thanks."

"He survived. He'll need a lot of physical therapy but the odds are high he'll make a full recovery."

"It was the right call. I'm glad you were there," she said, eyes cast down.

"Here's the thing. Bob's been clear that he's taking a leave until I'm fired and you heard Murray, he's retired for real. I need a deputy and I trust the little I've seen you working and what I hear from everyone is that you're the best person for the job."

She looked up from her plate and stared at me with glassy eyes.

"Okay, but here's the thing, even if I am interested in working with you, which, honestly, is going to be really hard since," she made a pained face then shook her head, "I need to find a full-time gig as soon as possible otherwise I'll be sleeping on a storage shelf," she tilted her head toward the door that led to the loft above the truck bay.

"Lucky for you I've already cleared off some shelves and you look small enough to actually fit on one."

She didn't look amused.

"Sorry. Listen, I crunched the numbers and I can offer you ten hours of paid work as the deputy at $25 an hour. I know it's not a full-time salary but, if you'd also accept the First Responder Trainer role, I can pay you a competitive contract fee each time you run guys through the program. Sending them to the city costs the department twelve hundred bucks per member. I'd like to keep that money here in the community. I'd like you to have it, if you're willing to take on that role."

That had her sitting up straight. "Really?"

"Murray thought you'd need to redo your trainer certification—"

"No, it's good for three years. I have fourteen or fifteen months left."

"Right. So you could get started immediately. I talked to a buddy in the city and he said that in his experience, he gets the best results running six guys through at a time—"

"That's seven thousand two hundred dollars. You're right; that is an offer I can't refuse."

"Hang on though. You haven't led a group on your own, have you?"

She shook her head. "I got certified but then Murray wouldn't give me the job. He said it wasn't personal, it was political."

"That's what he told me, too. I don't give a shit about small town politics. I just want this department trained up to NFSA standards as soon as possible. So, what I was thinking was to bring my buddy up to co-train with you the first time. Those first six guys you train, you'd share the fee, fifty-fifty. He's already in. You'd spend a couple days with him to get to know the agenda he's developed and figure out how you'll co-facilitate, and then three weekends, six full days, delivering the course." I let that sink in.

"Is it still an offer you can't refuse?" I finally asked when she'd gone a solid minute without saying a word. "I can pay you half your fee up front when you sign the contract. The other half the same day you finish the training."

"Okay, but what if all six guys don't pass? What then?"

"The restaurant gets paid whether you finish your meal or not. You'd get paid. But we'll select the six most likely to succeed for this first round. Five guys need to be re-certified within the next few months and you can help me ID one or two more who show promise. You have ideas of who those guys could be?"

I could tell by her body language that she was in. She was leaning so far over the arm on her couch toward me I thought she might fall over and into my lap.

"Do you have a print-out of the member list?" she asked.

I pulled a folded list from my back pocket. "I came prepared this time," I said with a wink. She got the joke and laughed out loud, which gave me an unexpected and uncomfortable rush.

We spent the next hour discussing the merits of offering first responder training to the different members. I learned her perspective on different guys' strengths and weaknesses, which aligned pretty damn closely to what Murray had already told me. The one area Sophie was less aware of were the members who worked to undermine her authority at any opportunity. Murray had been good enough to let me in on who those guys were, too. And, as far as I was concerned, none of them would get the opportunity of this perk.

"One more thing," I said, once we'd agreed on eight members we'd make the offer to, expecting a couple either wouldn't be interested or available, "what about the deputy position? I think we work well together, don't you?"

I have no idea what was going on in her head but the look on her face told me she was still hesitating.

"What?" I asked.

"Sharing that tiny office with you for ten hours a week?"

"Yup."

"I'm not sure that's a good idea."

"Because?"

"Because, honestly? I don't know how much work I'd get done with your pheromones floating around. Much as I hate to admit it, there's something about you that makes me want to get naked."

There was that rush again. Her directness surprised me, though it probably shouldn't have since she'd been really clear when we'd almost had sex about what was working for her. I decided to be just as honest with her.

"Then do what I do when I think about you."

"What's that?"

"Satisfy the urge."

Her smile lit up her face and her laugh filled the room.

"The contract is on my desk. Let's get it signed so I can announce your appointment at practice tonight."

14

SOPHIE

It had been six weeks—exactly forty-two days—since Papa died. Three weeks since we held his memorial service. Eighteen days since my loving siblings told me that I hadn't been added to the will and about twelve minutes since I read the registered letter signed by my eldest brother's lawyer telling me that I had thirty days to vacate our family home so they could put it on the market.

Three of the eight had come to visit me in the last couple of weeks. Or so they said, but honestly, they were clearly more interested in making sure the non-human contents of the home were doing okay. Everything was exactly as they all had remembered it the last times they visited. For my eldest sister, that was two years ago, for the sister closest in age to me, just a few days before Papa went into the hospital. They all took pictures. I wasn't sure if it was to argue with each other about who was taking what or try to figure out if I'd taken anything that now belonged to the estate.

I hadn't touched a thing that I didn't normally touch. Papa's clothes were still in his dresser and closet. His toiletries and medicine still in the bathroom. And his papers, books, and mementos still in and on his desk.

It was Sarah, my thirty-four year old sister who found the bank card with my name on it in the top desk drawer. She handed it to me with a shrug of her shoulders. "Probably from when we were kids," she said.

"What do you mean?" I took it with an amount of caution.

"Didn't you get an allowance that Mom made you put in your bank account, to save for college or hairdressing school or whatever?"

I shook my head, "I never got an allowance. Remember? I left before I was old enough to earn it." The memory stung.

"Oh yeah," she said without even trying to hide her irritation that I *got*, in her words, to go to boarding school. I saw it an entirely different way since I didn't want to be sent away. But at twelve, that's what happened. I was packed onto my very first plane trip and flown to Halifax. Mom couldn't stand to have me in a school where I might come home on weekends or for holidays, so she sent me as far from the Vancouver airport as possible without needing to get me a passport.

"Well, there might be enough for coffee at Timmy's. Assuming it's been building interest all these years," Sarah said, bumping the card that hung in my hand with her knee.

Sarah. My nicest sibling. In fairness to the others, none of them ever got to know me, so even though we're family, I'd always been this side note to them. I mean, I'm younger than three of my nieces and nephews. That's just weird to have an auntie who's younger than you. But since Sarah was ten when I was born, and the only girl living at home, she got to play dollies with me as her doll. Mom was too tired having to keep track of the three boys, all of whom, as I recall, were trouble-makers who never really acknowledged my existence. They were all teenagers so why would they?

Sarah blamed me for not wanting to have kids since she'd been ruined by the mothering experience so young.

She also said that the fact she still wasn't married was on my shoulders since all the nice men want kids and the guys who don't are all self-centered assholes.

Sorry for being born, Sis.

She took pictures of every damn thing in the house, from the junk drawer in the kitchen to the space in the attic that had once been Mom and Papa's bedroom, before the accident. She made me go with her to answer questions about where things were. Did she say please or thank you? I rolled my eyes at myself for even thinking that she might.

"I couldn't find Papa's bank statements," she said after she'd finished her audit.

I had no idea where they were or if he even got paper statements.

"I don't know. We went to the bank every other Saturday and he did whatever he needed to in person. I never stood with him. I never saw him take a statement either. So, I can't help you."

"Seriously? You want me to believe that you weren't managing his money? You were managing everything else for him."

"No," I said, feeling as wound up as a snake ready to strangle a mouse, "he managed all the bills and all his money. He was paralyzed, not incompetent, Sarah. Jesus. The only thing I could tell you anything about is what meds he was taking and when he needed to take them—which was often and why I never got to take a single day off for two years."

"Yeah, whatever. Free rent just an hour away from the most expensive city in the world. Cry me a river."

"I didn't see you jumping up to volunteer your life." I'd wanted to say that for so long.

"And that's the difference between you and me. I *had* a life to give up. As far as we could tell, you didn't—"

"I had a job. I had a nice apartment in Halifax. I even had

a fiancé who, if you look around, didn't manage to buy a flight to join me. So fuck you, Sarah. I *did* have a life. And now, my life is here. And you all seem to think that you can just toss me out and what?" I wasn't sure how to end that. That was my big problem. I had no answer to what would come next if I had to leave.

"Take a chill pill, little sister. You're still a kid. So young. Pretty enough that I'm sure once you move back to a city some man will see your charms. You'll be fine. Just think of the last two years as nice holiday from the real world. From having to be an adult. Yay, you!"

I sat in stunned silence for about six seconds before my pager went off. Saved by an emergency. The quick, loud beeping made Sarah jump and yelp.

"What the hell is that? Fire detector?"

"I'll be at least an hour. You may as well leave," I said, grabbing my pager and car keys as the dispatcher told us what kind of call we were all jumping to attention to attend.

"Lily Valley Fire and Rescue, respond emergency. Possible head-on collision three miles south of the forest service road. Police and ambulance have been called. Lily Valley Fire and Rescue, respond emergency. Possible head-on collision three miles south of the forest service road."

I was the fourth vehicle into the lot. The bay door for Utility One, our rescue truck with the jaws of life and AED, was already warming up. Engine One was also running. If we had enough people, that would follow since it had the traffic pylons and water and foam in case a vehicle was on fire, which happened more times than one might expect.

I pulled on my turn-out gear and jumped into the passenger seat of Utility One, the Incident Commander's seat. There was already a driver and two more guys were jumping into the back.

"Sophie, out!"

I turned to see Nick, all geared up, standing in front of the truck. "Take Engine One. I'm IC today."

I didn't pause more than a second since that was his call. I'd just been demoted to second crew. Captain of the second crew, but still. I wondered if he didn't put me in the driver's seat since he didn't trust I could drive Engine One. The idea made me mad.

Utility One pulled out with a crew of four, one empty seat, and I waited for more guys to arrive. Protocol was you roll with no fewer than four.

I checked my phone: 2:30. Turn-out weekday afternoons was always low since most people had lives and jobs. Most people weren't here 24 hours a day, seven days a week, 365 days a year. But I was. Murray usually was, too. But dammit, he'd retired.

I waited three minutes. Two more guys showed up and there we sat.

"Dispatch from Lily Valley Fire," I paged.

"Lily Valley Fire, Dispatch," came the reply.

"Can you repage the call, please?"

"Copy that. Repaging."

And the call came through on our pagers again. Within three minutes one more guy showed up. As he geared-up, I paged the Incident Commander.

"IC from base."

"Go base," Nick's voice came back.

"Engine One ready to roll with four."

"Copy that. Engine One rolling. We're just arriving and we've got fire. Traffic is fucked. You won't get through in the southbound lane so take the north lane at the lights. We'll make sure nothing's coming at you. Get the guys in air packs."

"Copy. Northbound lane. Air packs. Me, too?"

The guys in the back were already pulling on their

fireproof balaclavas and securing the straps of their Scott Air packs over their shoulders.

"You, too, Sophie."

"Copy." I put the radio back in the holder. "Matt, when we get there, pull up and position yourself so you can see the vehicle we'll be working on. You'll be on your own. You good?"

Matt was a great driver—one of our best since he drove a ten ton logging truck as his real job. He was always the first guy to put in the driver seat on a non-fire call. But he was new and hadn't attended an actual fire yet. Being driver also meant that he was the pump operator. Matt looked nervous, like he wanted to say something.

"You can do this, Matt. Take your time. Read the instructions. They're all there. We'll pull hoses and attach to output 1. You know how to add foam to the mix?"

He nodded.

"Good. Unless Chief says otherwise, run with about twenty percent foam. Got it?"

"Twenty percent foam," he repeated.

I pointed to the dash. "Put the truck in Park, keep it running, wait until you hear the engine disengage, push that button to engage the pump," his eye followed my finger and he nodded. "The rest is all at the back. You'll do great. I know you can do this."

"Thanks, Soph," he said over the screaming sirens.

"IC from Engine One," I said into the radio.

"Go Engine One."

"We can see you. Matt's on pump. First time. I need one guy to pull hose with us."

"Copy, on new guy. No one to pull hose with you. You're on your own."

I turned to look at the two in the back. "You have this? I'll be there as back-up."

They nodded and gave me the thumbs-up.

"Which one has a radio?"

Garry patted his chest.

"I'll be watching but if you run low on air before water, call me. I'm not putting my breather on until the first one of you needs me. Call me on the first beep. Got it? *First beep.* Don't wait."

They both nodded. And I knew they were both bullshitting. These two hot shots would go until they were out of air and then pull off their masks and attack without protection unless someone was watching them.

Matt pulled into position and the guys in the back jumped from the truck and pulled hose. They could have used a third set of hands but my pump skills were better than my strength so I stayed with Matt to make sure he felt solid with his role.

As the IC, it was Nick's job to watch everything going on at the call, not to actually be part of any of the hands-on work. Although I was focused on my team and truck, I couldn't help feel him watching and judging my performance. To his credit, he didn't interfere with any of my decisions. When it became clear that Matt was going to cave under the pressure of being the pump man, I pulled off my air tank and traded roles with him.

My team did a great job and got the fire beat down with water to spare. They got to take credit for putting the wet stuff in the right spots. I got to take credit for giving them the right amount of water flow and foam mix. I was feeling good and confident.

Nick called me over to stand with him as the rest of the crew cleaned up the mess on the highway, sweeping debris to the shoulder so we could get traffic rolling again.

"How you doing?" He asked.

"I'm good. So, how'd we do?"

"Proud to be part of this team," he said, giving me a panty-melting smile.

"I should go help," I said taking a step away from him, needing to get out of his energy field.

"Nope," he said, taking my arm and pulling me back into position beside him, "you should stand here with me. You belong at my side, Deputy."

And then we stood in silence until Matt came and told us that Engine One was ready to roll.

"Gotta go, Chief," I said. "See you back in quarters."

The drive back to the hall was quiet. It usually was when there were injuries. We all knew that one day we'd be attending a call when one of our own neighbors, or worse, a family member was being put in the ambulance. So far, in the forty-two MVA calls I'd been on, I hadn't known a single person involved.

Lots of the old-timers had known victims, though. Murray seemed to know every person who wasn't a tourist, but that's because he also knew half the people in the adjacent town. I knew virtually nobody outside our village. Something, I'd decided, I had to work on.

Nick had awakened my dormant sexuality and now that I had no reason not to date, I'd been considering the idea. Not acting on it yet, but actively thinking about it.

Back at the hall, while I cleaned hoses and helped refill air tanks, I pondered the qualities in a guy I'd be looking for. The post-call work took another thirty minutes and by the time hoses were washed and the truck re-outfitted, people were animated. Their energy fed mine and despite the argument with my sister, I was feeling happy. At home. Purposeful. And maybe even a bit datable.

I'd been a bit—okay, a lot—lost since Papa died, not knowing what I should or could be doing with my time. It's not like I had somewhere to go in the day, other than the forest with Max. As much as I know Max missed Papa I could tell he loved his new freedom in the forest since as a service dog he had even less freedom to be himself than I'd had. Now he was providing a new kind of service and companionship. One I knew I couldn't live without. He was my family now. Even if we lost the house, I'd still have Max.

I was the last one to go since I made it my job to check all of the equipment on both attending vehicles to make sure we'd be all set for the next call. The bay doors had been closed and everyone had yelled goodbye. Nick, I assumed, had either left without saying goodbye or was in his office.

I moved around the trucks, dancing like a fool, opening and closing all of the equipment doors, singing to myself, not too loud but not quietly either.

My phone chirped in my pocket.

Text from Nick.

"Ugh," I said out loud, stopping my happy dance.

I clicked the message and saw a video frame. Of me. In the hall. I clicked it and watched myself doing my best K-Pop dance moves right behind Engine One. It was taken from the storage loft. I looked up and Nick was leaning on the pony wall, smiling at me.

"Oh my god! Why are you spying on me?" I was mortified.

"Don't be mad," he said and my phone pinged again. Another image, this time a video selfie of Nick's naked chest, his pecs flexing and bouncing in time to my singing.

I watched the video and laughed out loud. When I looked back up at him he was leaning over to show me his still dancing pecs.

"Are you hungry?" he asked.

Sweet Jesus, what was he offering me?

"You mean hungry for a burger, I assume?" I said, but in my mind, I was wishing he was asking if I was hungry for something a little more raw.

"If that's what would make you happy."

His dancing pecs were playing on repeat on my phone. I

stared at them for a few seconds as I figured out what to say. What to do.

"I need a shower. And Max needs a run. So," it killed me to say it but I knew it was for the best, "rain check?"

He stood up and his goofy smile turned serious. "Sure."

I turned and walked toward the door, "You were great out there," I yelled back to him, "Not that you need to be told. But it was nice working with you. I'm glad I decided on Option A."

As the door closed behind me, I heard Nick say, "For the win!"

15

NICK

I don't know what it was that made me so hot for the smallest firefighter I'd ever seen in my life, but something about Sophie made me want to both fuck her brains out and protect her from guys like me. She had something that I'd never come across in another woman.

Maybe the fact that she wasn't trying, at all, to impress me or be someone other than pure Sophie. Maybe it was because she had no interest in taking a selfie with me and sharing it on her social media. I made a note to check out her Instagram and Facebook feeds. Or maybe it was the way she felt and tasted. The way she moaned that told me I was a god and she was my humble and very willing sex servant.

Every time I thought about that night, I got so hard I had to deal with it, so I tried not to think about her except when I showered. I didn't succeed. And now I had that sexy, goofy little dance to watch while I remembered how she tasted and sounded and felt. Jesus, I was going to become a four shower a day guy. Good thing I wasn't paying for the hot water.

Because I'm an optimist, I'd bought my first pack of condoms in over two years. I know it's probably weird, but even though I never had unprotected sex, if a woman wanted to have sex with me, she had to be the one who came prepared. Did that make me a prick? I don't think so. I think it actually made me a nice guy since it meant I could never pressure a woman to do more than she'd already been prepared to do before we had a few drinks.

On the other hand, I struggled to respect women who met guys at bars, let them buy them a few drinks and then offered their bodies as some kind of payment. And maybe that's not how they all thought, but that's always how it felt, like I was some kind of cock and wallet for hire. And I knew it was double standard since there were days I really wanted to find those women. But if a woman fucked me on our first date, there was never a second. Did that make me a prick? Probably. Did I care? Not in the least.

Sophie wasn't one of those women I'd meet at the Roxy or hell, even when the guys and I would go for wings at the Grill Girls Club. I can't even count the number of women who put my hand on their shaved, naked pussies under the table while we sat having drinks, usually watching a hockey game or some other sport on the big screen TVs. Sometimes I'd finger fuck them, only half paying attention since really, I was there for wings and the game. I imagine they thought I was trying to look casual, like nothing was happening. And on one hand, they were right. Nothing was happening. They'd get off. Or not. I didn't much care. They got to say they got finger fucked by a Vancouver fire fighter. Yes, one of the guys in the calendar. Mr. July, to be specific.

And me?

It stroked my ego for about five seconds. But didn't do a thing for my dick.

Sophie was an entirely different story. She was the first woman I'd buy condoms for.

And now I was on my way to town to buy burgers for her.

I figured I had a good thirty minutes before she'd start making herself dinner. I had no idea what kind of burgers she liked so I got her a Mama Burger, Papa Burger, and Baby Burger with cheese. Fries and root beer, of course. Then I got her a burger at a family restaurant. And since it wasn't too far out the way, I also stopped at Wendy's which conveniently shared space with Tim Hortons. I got her a burger and a salad and one of each kind of donut they had. Three boxes worth.

I pulled into her driveway and knocked on her door. Either not home from her run or in the shower. Damn. The burgers were in a thermal bag but… I debated going in and turning on the oven to keep them warm. Would that be too stalkerish? Did I care? Would she forgive me once she saw all the food?

I decided to go for it. I opened the front door and called her name. No answer. No sound of water from the shower. I took all the burgers out of their bags and arranged them on a cookie sheet that was stored exactly where one would expect, in the drawer under the oven. Put the oven on at 220, threw the burgers and fries in and then went to sit in my car, since finding me snooping around her house would be a step over the line, I thought.

I sat in my car playing Risk on my phone, listening to some weird mix of K-Pop bands on Spotify and doing my damndest to keep my hand out of my pants.

After close to thirty minutes I was starting to think that she wasn't coming home. Maybe she'd gone to a neighbor's for dinner. I went back to her front door to turn off the oven. It was locked. How the hell did I lock it? I didn't remember locking it.

I rang the doorbell and knocked at the same time.

Sophie answered, burger in her hand and mouth full, chewing what looked like the burger from the family restaurant. She waved for me to come in.

"How long have you been home? How'd you get in?" I asked.

She pointed to the back door, motioned for me to sit down and pulled the tray of burgers from the oven, putting them on the table in front of me. She'd already finished the Mama Burger and most of the fries.

"Eat," she said, "I met this genie a couple of weeks ago. He said that my wish was his command. He offered me three wishes, as I recall. I have to admit, I was a bit tipsy when he made the offer. Anyway, I wished for a photo of this arrogant calendar-worthy firefighter. Still haven't gotten it. But when I was out running with Max, I wished someone would make my dinner for me and look! I came home to all these burgers! My genie's not a total dud."

Goddammit she was sexy. She was still in her running shorts and a tank top. Her hair was a mess. Sweaty and dirty from the fire call. She smelled like smoke, the forest and healthy sweat. Fresh and rich.

"You haven't showered yet," I managed to state the obvious.

"Don't know about where you were raised but, in these parts, we tend to exercise and then shower. And, when someone puts dinner on the table, we sit down. So, no. Haven't showered yet. You either, it seems," she leaned over and sniffed toward my chest.

"Rude! This is a clean t-shirt," I said, sniffing my own pit to make sure.

"Seriously, please eat at least two of these burgers. I'm already stuffed past full. And I assume you got some for yourself. You weren't expecting me to eat them all, were you?"

"I have no idea what you're talking about. But I'll gladly eat whatever you don't."

"Me and Max. Which one is your least favorite? I'm giving it to Max."

As soon as Max heard his name he sat at attention by Sophie's leg. I pointed to a burger and she took it apart, leaving the bread on the baking tray.

"Dogs don't need the carbs," she said, placing the burger, lettuce and pickles in a bowl on the floor.

She sat in the end seat at the large kitchen table so I sat down in the chair closest to her. When I stretched my legs out, they bumped hers. Her immediate reaction was to move and make room for me, but then she allowed her knee to settle against my thigh. Oh, boy.

"This was really sweet. Thank you," she said without a hint of snark or sarcasm.

In the space of a nanosecond I thought of a half dozen things to say,

"It was nothing. I found it on the side of the road."

"I didn't get it for you, I got it for me, but you started eating it."

"I'm hoping I can earn my way back into your pants and that you'll want to explore what's in mine."

But I just smiled. Well, I didn't just smile. I readjusted myself in my chair, moving my leg away from hers since my cock was getting uncomfortable.

"Where'd you find a place to live? I'm actually surprised you did since the vacancy rate here is like zero percent. I've been looking for myself."

Then she scowled at me, "Wait a minute... did you also steal the only rental in town?" She pushed her chair back.

"No, I haven't found anywhere to rent. I'm living in the hall. You were actually singing and dancing in my bedroom this afternoon. Well, the ensuite to my bedroom."

"You're sleeping above the truck bay? Seriously?"

She looked appalled.

"But the truck bay is really freaking cold," she said after a few seconds of thought.

"And," I added, "it smells like diesel, sweat and stale

laundry no matter how much essential oil I put in my diffuser. But it's home. At least for now."

That got a smile but then her smile dropped and she looked at me with a scowl. Not an angry scowl, more of a concerned look, like an attentive mom would give a child who came home with a black eye and a poor excuse for how it happened. She looked at me. Looked away. Sighed. Looked out to the hallway by her front door. Looked at me again. Sighed again, louder.

"What?" I said, "You look like you're at a spelling bee and have just been asked to spell—" I couldn't think of a good word. A funny word that she wouldn't be able to spell. Dammit. Blowing the punchline. I'm such a moron.

"*Mon ostie de saint-sacrament de câlice de crisse,*" she offered.

"I have no idea what you just said. And even less idea how to spell it so, that."

"It's French. Obviously. And translated literally it means, *My host of holy sacrament of the chalice of Christ,* but really it's French for, *fuck me, what am I about to do?*"

"Wipe the mayo off your face," I said, leaning forward and running two fingers across her chin. She watched me take those fingers and suck them clean. "Delicious," I said as my cock threatened to escape my boxers. I shifted in my seat again.

"Come upstairs," she said, taking my hand and pulling me to standing. I tried to put my other hand in front of my groin to hide what was happening but there was no use. It looked idiotic, cupping the tent in my sweatpants, as if that would hide what was going on. And anyway, I prayed to the holy sacrament of the chalice of Christ that soon it would be free and I'd be able to breathe again.

16

SOPHIE

I got to the top of the stairs with Nick a couple of steps behind me. I turned around and came face-to-face—well face-to-giant-erection—with Nick's giant erection. I dropped his hand and pointed. "What is *that* about?" My voice sounded higher-pitched than I expected it to.

"You took my hand and said come upstairs. It's a Pavlovian reaction."

"No, no, no. Bad idea. Turn around. Back downstairs. Never mind."

"Wait! What? Why? I don't understand." He was breathy and the look on his face made me picture him as a little kid who'd just been told Santa didn't exist.

He didn't budge. He blocked the stairs so I couldn't get past him, back to the safety of the kitchen and living room. The public spaces where hard-ons did not make public appearances.

"Why in god's name did you pull me upstairs if not to have sex? Finally. Finally, have sex?"

"*Mon ostie de saint-sacrament de câlice de crisse de TABERNAK!*"

"You said 'Fuck me' again but you're sending me back

downstairs and you're mad that I have a *fucking* hard-on for you? What the fuck, Sophie? Fuck!"

"'Fuck me' as in, 'I'm an idiot.' Not 'fuck me' as in 'fuck me.' Jesus," I looked at him and realized how ridiculous this was. I smiled. "Fucking, hell."

"I have been so fucking horny for you ever since that night, Sophie. Please. It's killing me. Please. Whatever you want, your wish is my command," I hated how pathetic I sounded but she was still smiling. "I'm serious. Just let me rub your back again. Maybe a kiss. You enjoyed it when I ate your pussy. Didn't you?"

With me on the landing and Nick now standing just one step below, he was in perfect kissing position. I looked at his mouth. I felt the throb beneath my running shorts. The sudden wetness. But I was a stinky mess from the two hours in my turnout gear and then the run and the onions on my burger. I could not have felt less sexy. What was he seeing?

My tongue played against my teeth. I imagined it running along his perfectly not straight teeth. Pausing for a second on his slightly crooked eye tooth. My breathing got shallow and when I looked down from his mouth to his chest, I noticed his was, too.

"Bathroom," I said, not sure where my confidence was coming from other than horny desperation.

Nick, the arrogant idiot, just stood there. I was ten steps down the hall and he hadn't moved.

"What are you waiting for?" I said, my whole body was vibrating.

"I thought you had to pee," he said, looking desperately confused.

"No. I need to fuck. But before that I need to shower. So —" I didn't have a chance to finish since he was down the hall with his shirt coming over his head. I turned on the water and we both stripped out of our clothes and stood waiting for the water to heat up. I kissed his chest, which was where my mouth naturally landed given how tall he was. He put his hands on my shoulders and wrapped his thigh around mine, pushing his hard-on into my hip.

"Wait, this isn't going to work," I said tilting my head back to look at him.

He just stared at me.

"We still don't have condoms. We need a condom!" I felt like I was going to cry. As mind-blowing as the oral had been, I wanted more. I wanted him inside me. I needed his body wrapped around mine. I needed to feel the security of being held.

Nick moved his hands from my shoulders to around my waist and gently lifted me into his arms. I wrapped my legs around him and he kissed me. "I have condoms."

I reached into the tub and turned on the shower. While the water heated up, so did we. But I needed to slow down. I wanted to savor this moment since there would never be another quite like it. And, I was just a little scared.

Inside the shower, I focused my attention on soaping up a facecloth then asked him to turn his back to me, in part so I couldn't see his massive hard-on. It was so much bigger than my vibrator. It looked too big. I needed to catch my breath and calm my thoughts and I did that while soaping up his back.

He stood with his legs spread as wide as the shower base would allow, reducing his height by several inches so I could get the tops of his shoulders. When I got to his buttocks—I'd never seen such a beautiful ass in my life, not that I'd seen many and never standing in a shower with me—I accidentally dropped the facecloth.

Nick squatted to pick it up and turned toward me when he stood, showing me his fully engorged full frontal view again.

"My turn," he growled. He literally growled at me which made me laugh.

He squirted the soap directly on my body, across my collar bone, down the centre of my chest between my breasts and into my now trimmed but still not shaved pubic hair. He held the facecloth in his left hand but rubbed the soap around my body with his right, taking extra time to make sure my breasts and nipples were clean. When he got past my stomach, he cupped my right ass cheek in his right hand to steady me and used the facecloth to suds up the soap on my mound. He let a finger find its way from my ass to my folds and he gently touched my opening, teasing me mercilessly, sliding his finger between my folds then down to my vagina. His finger pushed in a just a touch, enough to let him know I was wet and ready for more.

I was breathless. Aching. And annoyingly unsure about how the next steps should go. I knew I had to be in control. I had to let him know without freaking him out and scaring him away. I squirted soap into the palm of my hand and wrapped it around his cock.

I stroked him from base to tip, squeezing tight on the up pull, and looser on the downward motion. I was faking it, hoping I was making it.

"Tell me what to do," I said, finally looking from his cock to his face. His head was back and his eyes were closed.

"You're doing it. Just keep doing that."

I worked his cock until the soap was gone and I started to feel friction.

"Can I suck you?" I asked.

He moaned which I assumed was consent. I squatted and brought the tip of his cock to my tongue, swirling around the head until I tasted his pre-cum. It was salty and made my pussy throb. I tilted my head to take as much of him into my mouth as I could. My hand held him firm at the base while I worked my mouth back and forth. Until this moment I'd never understood the attraction of giving a blow job but rolling my tongue around and up and down his cock, making him groan, felt amazing.

Nick gave a thrust that surprised me and I gagged. He pulled out, grabbed his cock in his hand and masturbated for three or four strokes before coming down my neck.

I stood up and smiled at him.

"I'm so sorry," he said.

"What? This old thing? Don't worry about it. I'll have the maids give it a wash and it'll be clean in no time." I don't know what made me say that but his look was so serious.

"Give me twenty minutes and I'll be good to go again," he said.

I didn't want to tell him that I was relieved. Twenty extra minutes to figure out how to give him the news that if he did get his boner back and decided to use it, he'd be the first in.

I'd done lots of things with my one and only boyfriend, but intercourse—a penis in a vagina—was where we drew the line. Good Catholic boy and trying to be a good Catholic girl… we defined 'sex' as the thing that might lead to conception. That was the one and only act that was off the table. All else was fair game. Not that we played often. And never, ever, even close to the way Nick played me the night he stole my job.

He gently, without hunger this time, washed the front of my body with soapy hands. I was still throbbing between my legs and hoped that he was still willing to help me sort that out without the use of his cock.

We got out of the shower and dried off. Nick wrapped a towel around his waist and said he'd be right back. I heard the front door open. When he came back in I heard him click the deadbolt into place. I did a little dance and jumped into my bed, pulling the covers up to my chin.

I was not expecting what he arrived with. Not a box of condoms, but three boxes of Tim Horton's donuts.

"What in the world?" I said, forgetting I was trying to be

a little more modest. I sat up and let the blanket fall away, showing my breasts.

"Open it," he said handing the top box to me.

Yup. It was an assortment of twelve different donuts but scattered between them were condoms.

"If your favorite isn't here, it'll be in another box," he said, flipping the lid open on box number two.

"What's *your* favorite?" I asked him.

"Close your eyes and let's see if you can figure it out."

I closed my eyes and listened as he put the box down then moved around to the end of my bed. I opened one eye. He had what looked like a Boston Cream in his hand. He pushed away the blankets at the foot of the bed, exposing my feet and then, with his left hand, grabbed both my ankles and yanked me toward him.

I fell backward and dropped the box I'd been holding.

"Eyes closed," he ordered when he looked up and saw me smiling at him.

Three seconds later, he pushed open my folds and slowly wiped the cool insides of the donut along my labia. I squirmed and tried to pull away.

"Hey. Stay still. I'm trying to eat my favorite donut."

He finished applying the filling and then his tongue slowly licked the coolness away. He licked with his tongue firm, up and down one side of my labia and then the other. Then his tongue went flat and he licked my whole sex in long, slow, warm and wet laps. I couldn't hold my ass on the bed. My hips tilted up and up as far as I could push them, seeking more contact with his mouth.

He pulled away.

"What are you doing?" I felt desperation when he stopped.

"Cool your jets," he whispered, "Just refilling my favorite donut."

His fingers massaged more custard onto my own cream puff. Then his expert tongue cleaned it all off again.

He had me so close to climax but I knew it wouldn't happen if he left my clit out of the play.

"Clit. Please," I begged and I didn't care, "please lick my clit."

He didn't stop to think, he just did. I melted into the mattress, and within six seconds flat the orgasm moved from threat to full attack. As soon as the vibrations started he thrust his fingers inside me. I could feel my muscles contract around them as he pushed deeper and deeper inside me.

It was intense. Too intense. I couldn't take any more and I tilted my hips down into the bed to force him out. I rolled away from him, panting. Gasping for air.

"Need water," I croaked.

Nick took one stride from the end of my bed to right beside me, placed the donut box on the floor and took its place, planting a wet kiss on my mouth, pushing his tongue between my lips to meet mine. I started to salivate and dry throat was no longer a problem.

He took my hand and placed it on top of his hard-on.

"That was not twenty minutes," I said inside his mouth.

"You inspire fast action," he said into mine.

I pulled my face away from his.

"Nick, we need to talk."

17

———

NICK

J esus Christ, is there anything worse than hearing, "We need to talk" when a woman has your throbbing dick in her hand? If there is, it's nothing I've experienced.

"Fuck now. Talk later," I said, I know it wasn't very romantic but I was worked up and I wanted to take this pocket rocket over the edge not have it fizzle out, leaving me trigger happy until god knows when I'd fuck again. I hadn't had sex, hadn't felt that full body connection, in months. I couldn't even remember the last woman I'd been in bed with. It was that forgettable. But I knew with Sophie that wouldn't be the case. She made me feel alive, not just horny. Big difference.

"It's about that," she said, sounding apologetic which made me want to scream.

"Did you not ask about condoms?"

She nodded.

"I was under the impression that condoms were consent for fuck—for intercourse, making love, whatever you want to call it." I was trying to sound calmer than I felt.

She nodded again.

"Then please, for the love of all things holy, what do we

need to talk about at this very moment when my hard-on is raging to be inside you?"

"Are you Catholic?" she asked.

"Am I *what* now?"

"Catholic?"

I could feel the blood leaving my erection. My woody was now just a semi. She looked up at me with apologetic eyes as it disappeared in her hand.

"I'm an atheist. Why? Why are you asking me this now?"

"Because… because, I'm still a virgin. And I know that taking someone's virginity can be a big deal. And, I thought it was only fair to tell you in case you decided that you didn't want to be the one to, you know, engage in the 'ultimate sin' with me."

She took her hand off my cock and I let her words settle. This was a mind fuck. Sophie was so hot and comfortable in her skin, and skilled… my cock jumped. A virgin? I don't think I'd ever slept with a virgin. I didn't even lose my virginity to a virgin. That girl was three years older than me. So on the one hand, yeah, the idea was hot, but on the other, what the fuck did she mean, ultimate sin? If I had sex with her would she get all weird and possessive with me? All biblical, you took my virginity now you have to marry me, shit?

"How old are you?" I thought she said she'd done four years of university but maybe I'd misheard. Maybe she was only sixteen.

"Twenty-four."

"Why are you still a virgin? How is that even possible? And if we were to have sex, what does that mean? To you, I mean."

"It's kind of a long story," she basically whispered.

I settled onto her pillow and pulled a mixed box of donuts and condoms from the floor.

"You have until this box is empty to finish your story

because once the donuts are gone, we'll have no choice but to move on to condoms," I smiled and tried to ease the sudden tension in the air.

"Only if *you* want to, once you have all the facts," she said, taking a double chocolate.

Thirty minutes and four donuts later, she was done her story. In a nutshell, she'd been engaged in a promise keepers style relationship and then she got called home to care for her dad. Her fiancé decided to stay in Halifax since Sophie only expected to be here for a couple of months. At about the five month mark, he told her he was with someone else. And she hasn't had any kind of physical relationship since the last time she saw him. Until me.

"So, if we have sex, are you going to expect me to marry you?" I asked with a goofy smile, trying to keep it light but also not sure if that was the moral to her story.

She had such an earnest look when she said, "Only if God finds out."

And then she bust a gut laughing.

I was confused. "So are you or are you not saving yourself for marriage? Because you seemed pretty keen on going all the way with me an hour ago and last time I checked, I hadn't offered you a ring."

Ouch. That came out a little harsher than I'd planned.

She stared at me, her eyes one second feeling like she was thinking dirty thoughts, the next that she was about to confess a sin. Or maybe I was projecting. Whatever. I was confused.

"Here's the thing," she said, propping herself up on an elbow and letting the sheet that had been covering her, fall away. Where to look? Her eyes or her tits? I had half a mind to cover her up but that was the last thing I wanted to do. I rubbed my forehead as she spoke, holding my hand so she couldn't tell where my eyes were focused. And it was on her left nipple which, as my own thoughts got hot, started to harden.

"So, what do you think?" Sophie bumped me gently with her free arm.

"Sorry. I was only half listening. What did you say?"

"No really," she said with a smile, "what do you think?"

"No really," I said with what I hoped looked like an apologetic face, not a creepy one, "I was too busy imagining sucking your nipple to hear what you just said.

"Oh. My. God," she rolled away and put her feet on the floor. "Never mind. I take it all back. That's my answer right there. It was a bad idea."

"Wait! What was a bad idea? Tell me. I might think it's a very good idea."

She was pulling fresh panties from her dresser drawer. I had to stop her. I jumped out of bed and didn't see the open box of donuts. I stepped right on top of it and slid, losing my balance. I fell on my ass with a thud.

That hadn't been my plan but it achieved the desired result. She dropped her underwear back in the drawer and came over to me.

"You okay? You hit the floor hard. Did you hit your back on the bed frame?"

I moaned, "Owww," sucking in air through my mouth, playing up what might end up being a small bruise into a sound that was worthy of a proper first responder check-up.

"Can you get up?"

I winced. "My back. I think I did something to my back," I said, making a face like I was in pain when I tried to stand.

"Stop moving, you idiot. You know the drill. Let me check you over."

She was still buck naked, kneeling beside me. My cock had been soft through her whole story, but it started to come to attention, as if poking up to get a better view of the show.

Her eyes were focused on mine so I'm pretty sure she didn't notice.

"I'm just going to do a quick scan, to make sure you haven't really hurt your spine. Can I touch you?"

It was amazing. She was in full-on First Responder mode, totally focused on me as a possibly injured patient.

"Tell me what you were doing before you fell. Do you remember?" She smirked.

"I think I was getting up to stop a woman I am really hoping to have sex with from getting dressed," I said.

"You think or you know? Is it possible you blacked out? I just want to rule out a mini-stroke," she said, biting her bottom lip but keeping her eyes very serious.

"I think I know," I held her gaze. "Yes, that's what I was doing."

"Your pupils are quite dilated. Have you taken any drugs recently, prescribed or recreational?"

"No, but I have eaten a lot more junk food and sugar than I normally do. I do kind of feel amped up, like I've just had a Monster drink."

She nodded, "Mm, hmm. I'm just going to check for broken bones or sprains. Let me know if anything I touch is uncomfortable using a scale of one to five where one is mild discomfort and five is excruciating pain."

I kept my look as serious as I could and nodded. She put both hands on my left shoulder and squeezed, then squeezed at intervals along my triceps, bicep, forearm. I lifted my arm before she reached my hand.

"Relax your arm, strong guy. Let me lift it for you."

I let my hand fall into hers and she palpated each finger and the palm. My cock was slowly engorging as I imagined her palpating it.

She repeated the check on my other arm and by the time she'd finished, I was standing at full attention, seated on her bedroom floor. If she noticed, she did a perfect job hiding the fact.

"I'm going to check your legs to make sure you don't have a broken bone or a twisted ankle since that could explain why you fell down."

This was the sexiest foreplay I'd ever experienced. I'd have never thought of myself as a doctor role play kind of guy but then I'd never had a doctor who turned me on or a woman who could pull off that fantasy with any credibility. She started on my clean foot and touched every inch of my calf and thigh, stopping less than an inch from my tight testicle. Then she moved from my left thigh over to the right and back down toward the foot that was covered in donut icing and fillings.

As she went, she asked every few seconds, "Does this hurt? No pain?"

I was silent but for my rough-and-getting-rougher breathing.

When she reached the second ankle she stopped and looked up at me. She was utterly serious.

"I believe I've found the source of the trauma. I'm going to get a cloth to clean the wound. Do not try to stand until I can assess the damage to your foot. Clear?"

I nodded, trying not to shake since I was holding in both laughter and a desperate desire to throw her on the bed to give my boner the full internal assessment it was screaming for.

Sophie came back with two warm facecloths. She wiped all the goo off my foot, making a show to be careful not to get any on her, explaining that in a perfect situation she'd be wearing personal protective equipment, consisting of gloves, goggles and mask. Once my foot was clean, she folded one cloth in on itself to have a fresh wiping surface which she used to clean the stickiness off of three condom wrappers.

If she didn't speed up the exam, I was going to lose my

shit. Well, my wad. It took all my inner strength not to take my cock in my hand and bring myself to climax since I was throbbing so hard for her.

She pretended to not see my aching cock when her eyes moved from my foot back to my face, but I could tell she had since a smile escaped and she bit down on her bottom lip to control it.

"Well," she said, her voice pinched, "I don't see any injuries that would prevent you from resuming," she paused and took a steadying breath, "your regular activities."

I couldn't do anything more than moan.

"There is one more thing I'd like to check, with your permission. It's a little unorthodox, but when I do a physical, I like to do a thorough job." Her breathing was as shallow as mine.

I nodded and she tore open a condom. She took it out and looked at it like she'd never seen one before. She held it between her fingers and stared at it, looked directly at my cock, made a funny face and then put the condom to her lips and blew inside it.

"No!" I barked, grabbing one of the unopened condoms from the floor. I stood, then sat on the edge of the bed. "Get up here," I commanded, smacking my hand on the mattress. She couldn't have moved faster, sitting down beside me. "Like this." I opened the package and placed the condom on my tip, grabbed her hand and held it under mine as we rolled it up my shaft. Once it was on I took her face in my hands. "Please let me use this, Sophie. Please. You're killing me."

Wordlessly, she lifted her legs into the air and around me so her whole body was splayed on top of her blanket.

"Is that a 'Yes?' That fucking better be a 'Yes.'"

"Yes," she whispered. "Will it hurt? It's so… big."

I just about blew it right then and there.

18

SOPHIE

It's not like I hadn't had things in my vagina before—fingers, a vibrator—but nothing the size of Nick's cock. I mean, how does that even work? If he pushed the whole thing inside me it would come up past my belly button. So obviously a whole lot was not going to be up and in my business. Still, how would he know when to stop pushing?

The more I thought about it the more I lost my nerve. He was lying with his belly and cock pressed against me, kissing my neck and collar bones. One hand was gently twisting my nipple and his other hand was holding himself up so he didn't crush me. I could feel the wet between my legs. My body was so ready to make love. But my brain wouldn't shut up.

"Nick?"

"Mmmm," he said nuzzling the side of my breast.

"I think I changed my mind."

"About what," he said moving his tongue to my nipple.

"About having sex?"

He stopped moving, as if we were playing freeze tag, and inhaled so hard his pecs expanded to twice their normal size. He exhaled and pushed himself up and off of me, then spun so his feet hit the floor. He was half-way to the bathroom before I said, "Do you wanna blow job?"

He stopped walking but didn't turn around. He went into the bathroom and closed the door. A door which didn't have a lock since locked doors weren't allowed in my parent's house. I pushed it open enough to see he had one hand on the sink and the other on his cock, moving up and down near the tip, really fast.

"Stop!" I pushed the door all the way open, bumping into him hard enough that he dropped his jerking-off hand. I met his eyes in the mirror's reflection. "Don't waste it. Come back to the bed. Please. I am *so* horny. And scared. And confused. *Please* don't be mad."

He inhaled deeply through his nose and barely moved his mouth when he answered, "I'm not mad. I'm frustrated."

"So am I," I offered. "Please let me help with your frustration. Please?"

"Your wish is my command," he said with no humor, adding a really snarky, "Princess."

I took his hand and led him back to the bed. "I'm sorry I'm a virgin. If it's any consolation, I don't want to be. And I really do want to lose it with you."

"Mmm-hmm," he said rolling his eyes.

"Lie down on your back."

He did.

"Cover your face with a pillow."

"With pleasure," he snarled.

I didn't want him to see me, to watch me as I debated with myself about what I really wanted right now. I knew what I wanted in theory, but in practice, giving up what I'd been told was sacrosanct to a god I no longer really believed in was still hard. Nick's cock, however, was starting to soften. I pulled off the condom and ran my tongue over his tip. It responded. I wrapped my hand around his shaft and slowly moved up and down while I swirled my tongue around his head. I could tell I was doing something right. I opened my eyes to make sure he wasn't watching me, then turned my head to change the angle so his cock wouldn't hit my gag reflex. I saw the unopened box of donuts on the floor.

He'd rubbed cream on my cookie, I wanted to do the same with his cock but I'd have to jump off the bed.

Nick moaned and tightened his ass cheeks which pushed hips and cock toward me.

"I'm going to come," he growled into the pillow as he grabbed my hand to stop me from stroking.

I took my mouth off and didn't move, but I did blow lightly on his engorged head.

"Stop," he said.

I did and he relaxed, letting go of my hand which released his cock.

I took the moment of no contact to jump off the bed, grab the first donut I touched then jumped back over his thighs. I landed higher up and harder than I'd expected since I was off-balance trying to keep from getting chocolate icing on my bedding. I was straddling his cock with my pussy.

I didn't move. I just felt the heat of his member melt into the length of my sex, like a hotdog in a bun. Getting my balance, I started to rub myself back and forth along his cock. There was no way he could penetrate me at this angle since his tip was far from my opening. I dropped the donut on the sheet so I could have more control grinding him.

He moaned. He groaned. He grabbed my shoulders and dug his nails into me. I lifted one arm and threw the pillow onto the floor so I could kiss him. He was too tall and had to tilt his head toward me while I reached my neck as far forward as I could. Our tongues swirled at the same pace and in the same pattern as my hips.

"Fuck me," he said, letting his head fall back onto the pillow.

I took his nipple in my mouth and when I turned my head saw that a condom was stuck to the icing on the donut. My toes curled as I felt an orgasm start to peak. I slowed my grind so that all my weight was focused on having my clit run along his cock. I came hard and loud. But I didn't feel done. My vagina was contracting on itself, squeezing nothing. I needed something for it to close around.

I put the condom in Nick's hand. "Open this. Put it on," I said.

He pulled the package to his mouth and tore it open.

I pulled my leg up and over to the side so he could see what he was doing. Once it was on, I straddled him again.

"Don't move. Don't thrust. I'm in charge," I said making direct eye contact. He stared at me with wide eyes.

"Copy that," he said. "You're in charge."

I positioned my hole over his tip and slowly pushed, allowing just a little in. Probably not even in, just pushing me open enough to know he was there. I pulled back and his cock dropped away, so I grabbed the shaft near his balls to hold him steady.

I was watching our sexes touch and retreat, touch and retreat. In a half-inch, then out. In just a little deeper. Then out again. I relaxed into knowing that he wasn't going to tear me open. I let him in deep enough that when I pulled back, he was still inside me. I placed my hands on his shoulders and continued the slow and gentle, up and down movement of allowing his cock inside me.

I was too much in my mind to enjoy it as much as I expected given how horny I was when I was playing at the edges. I looked at Nick. His eyes were closed and his mouth was open so I could see his lips forming an 'O' each time he exhaled. He looked like he was trying to meditate.

He opened his eyes wide, "I can't hold it."

"You can co—"

Before I finished the word, he grabbed my hips and

pressed me hard down on him. I screamed when his head smashed against my cervix.

His eyes went wide, "Sorry, sorry, sorry," he said, releasing my hips. I bolted off and away him so fast I didn't see the donut. My hand squished it and in my haste to pull it away I lost my balance and rolled off the bed and fell on the floor.

"Sophie, I am so sorry," Nick was up and squatting on the floor beside me. "Can you get up? Did you hit your head?" he asked.

The shock of the pile driver impact had subsided. There was no pain, just embarrassment.

"I appear to have injured myself," I said holding up my my icing covered palm and fingers.

Nick took my wrist and helped me sit then stand. He sat on the edge of the bed and directed my body onto his lap. He took one finger in his mouth and slowly worked his tongue from the tip to the base, licking then sucking until it was clean. With each finger, I lost more and more control. My pussy was throbbing again.

"I can't believe I'm still horny," I whispered

"We can't have you unsatisfied," Nick said, lifting me off him and laying me on my back with my legs hanging over the edge of the bed.

I came harder, faster and more times than I ever had before. It was exhilarating and exhausting. When I'd had more than enough I sat up and pulled Nick's mouth to mine. I kissed him lightly and drew him back into bed with me.

I rolled onto my side with my back to him and he pressed up tight, holding me in his arms, spooning me from head to toe inside his hug.

"Nick?"

"Yeah?" He pushed my hair away from my neck and covered it in slow kisses.

"Do you want to live with me?"

19

NICK

I froze. Did she just ask me to move in? After one night of admittedly the best sex I'd ever had. But she'd gone two years without getting any action. Anything with a pulse would have been an improvement on her dildo, even if it did have fresh batteries and rabbit ears. And shit, she was a virgin. She had nothing to compare the experience to.

But I did. Plenty to compare it to. And god help me, there was no comparison. I knew she thought I had a good body, which isn't new, what woman hasn't wanted to spread her legs for me? But there was something different in the way Sophie looked at me. Something different in the way she touched me. It was as if she was actually interested in all of me, not in telling her friends about having fucked me. I know it sounds arrogant, but women bragged about bedding me. And it bugged me to be treated like a piece of meat to be shown off.

With Sophie I just felt like she wanted to be with me, for me. And damn it felt good to not feel like I had to perform since I knew I'd be semi-publicly graded which, in all honesty, just made me want to do the minimum expected and see how far that would take me.

All the way, was the answer. It was pathetic. I had little respect for the women who were so obviously interested in the conquest and even less respect for myself.

But move in? That was just crazy talk.

"You know," I finally said, "your body has just overdosed on oxytocin, so I suspect that proposal was just euphoria talking. I'm going to pretend I didn't hear it so you can pretend the same and not feel embarrassed in an hour once you're back to normal. Deal?"

"Oh my god, Nick. I wasn't asking you to marry me. Yes, the sex was mind-blowing but jeez, Louise, you really truly are the most arrogant man I've ever met if you think that virgins will throw themselves at your feet after you've deflowered them."

Fortunately, she was laughing, but I felt like a tool.

"Busted? I guess I am a little bit overconfident."

"You think, Calendar Man? Look, I have this huge house with four empty and fully furnished bedrooms. And you're sleeping on a cot in a truck bay. I thought you could move in here. Pay me rent. You'd get a proper room and I'd have money for food."

I was glad her back was to me since I'm sure my face looked like I'd just been caught talking to myself in the mirror.

"Would you believe me if I said I was only joking?"

"Umm... not for one hot second. But that actually brings up a good point."

She pulled my index finger to her face and ran her tongue along the palm side before taking it in her mouth and sucking.

I felt the blood move south. If she didn't stop, this conversation would be prematurely ended. I rolled away from her mouth and pulled the sheet up to show her my semi-stiffy. She giggled.

"You're the one bringing things up around here," I said.

"If you move in, we have to have really clear boundaries about… whatever this is," she put her hand on my cock, "so that things don't get weird. I mean, if you're my roommate, and have your own room, and I have my own room, then we have to be clear on when—or even *if*—this is going to happen again."

She was swirling her thumb on the head of my cock as her hand pulled the shaft. I could barely understand what she was saying. All I could think about was how many times we could do this in a day. How many days we could stay in bed before Search and Rescue would be called to find us.

"I mean, I'd love it if it did but I have no expectation that it will," she said, pulling her hand off me and pushing her pelvis tight against me.

"You're an evil negotiator," I said, "using techniques that are *not* approved of by the United Nations. In fact, this is torture. I'm sure of it. And nothing I say in this state can be held against me in the light of day."

"I'm well aware. A very smart albeit arrogant man schooled me on the influence of oxytocin on decision-making and I know that when you're near my body that your own is debilitated by my sexual prowess and that you can't be trusted to make rational decisions. So, I suggest we finish what we started here, with your cock and my vagina, and continue this conversation in the morning when we're both so wrung-out that we never want to have sex again."

"Stop talking," I said pushing her onto her back so I could straddle her and see her face straight on, kiss her mouth and neck and breasts. She ran her fingers over her mouth in a "my lips are zipped" motion and relaxed into my touch. I gently took her nipple in my teeth and played with it with my tongue. She moaned and arched her back which brought me to full attention.

There was no way I'd be able to sleep in a room down the hall from her, knowing she was within reach, naked and warm and wet and welcoming. It would never work. Even if we had a rule about keeping to our own spaces, I'd break it. I know I would. I had to say no, but not until morning. Tonight, I'd pretend that this was my life and Sophie was— oh my god, I can't believe the word that popped into my head.

Just because it rhymed, I told myself. You've only just met this chick. Give it a week, maybe two, and she'll get sick of you. Just enjoy the moment, I coached myself.

And that's what I did. The moment and the next two hours. I enjoyed the hell out of them. It was pretty clear she did, too.

20

SOPHIE

I don't even know how many times in the last eighteen hours Nick and I had sex. I mean, how do you define sex? Is it sex if there's no need for a condom? A lot of what we did didn't need protection but holy mother of all things holy, it sure felt like sex to me. I'd even say making love, the beautiful connection of two bodies that just seem to get each other.

And it was so much more than just the way he made my body feel. He made me laugh more times than he made me come and I was a non-stop orgasm machine under his touch. I don't think my core muscles have ever gotten such a complete workout. That was one of the things Nick suggested that had me busting a gut: the idea that we record exercise videos for the As Seen On TV channel. He figured we could do two versions, one for prime time where the focus would be on the laughter exercises and one for after midnight which would focus on a lower set of core muscles.

I finally got the photos he promised me that day we went out. Most of them I'd be able to blow up and hang on my wall or ceiling without worrying about who might see them.

But a couple, if I ever had the courage to get them printed, would be just for me.

As perfect and gorgeous as Nick's body was, it was his heart and ability to make me feel totally at ease that made me extra hot for him. I mean, who'd have thought that an actual, real-life fireman's calendar model would find me attractive? I am so far from the supermodel body that I'd expect to see men like him with. Everything about me is pint-sized. My legs are not giraffe-like, my hair is short, my boobs are a double-B cup only for the elusive twelve hours a month when I'm ovulating. The other six-hundred-and-sixty hours of the month I don't even need to wear a bra if I'm not jogging.

Anyway, he made me feel beautiful and I could tell he wasn't faking it just to get some action by the way his cock reacted when he looked at me. He couldn't fake that with his eyes open, could he? No way.

I felt so comfortable with him, trusted him so much, I was thinking that I'd tell him about my dirty family secret. I'd never told a soul what I thought I'd overheard as a kid. Not Dylan when he suggested I might not be my parents' kid. Not even my ex-fiancé. I hadn't trusted that he'd not judge me or my family if he found out.

But Nick? I could just imagine the way he'd react if told him. He'd hold me in his giant bear hug and then kiss my neck and tell me he didn't care what my family did years ago, that he only cared about me, right now and going forward.

It felt so strange that I'd only known him for three weeks and that I thought I hated him at first. He was impossible to hate. I couldn't imagine anything he could do to make me hate him.

"Morning, gorgeous," he said, pulling me out of sleepy reverie and into his arms.

"Morning, handsome." I raised my head to kiss him. "How'd you sleep?"

"Sleep? I didn't sleep. I couldn't. My mind was going a million miles an hour, thinking of all the different episodes of our new YouTube channel's 'Get Fit Like a Firefighter' series and all the ancillary products. Books, of course. Greeting cards. Oh—and my best idea, the Sophie and Nick coconut oil sex lube."

Since neither of us were expecting such a sex marathon, we were not prepared for the hours of foreplay—which was really just recovery time—or the need for lube. Nick had the brilliant idea of using coconut oil. It's slippery as heck *and* delicious.

I licked my lower lip and tried to look serious. "Good start but I think it needs a better name than that."

"Okay then… how about, 'SophNic Lube?' And as our tagline, we could say… 'The lube you can heat to 400 degrees without getting burned'?"

"I like it, but it's not exactly clear that our lube is meant for sex, not motorcycle engines. How about…" I moved the blanket off of Nick's body and traced a line from his Adam's Apple down to his pubic hair. His cock twitched. "How about, 'Even if you can't have sex *with* a hot firefighter, you can have sex *like* a hot firefighter'."

"I like that, " he said, placing my hand on his thickening member. "But I think there needs to be a warning note, too, since sex between *two* hot firefighters is something only trained professionals should attempt."

I think he just called me hot. I melted into his body and breathed him in.

"So, what's on your schedule for today?" Nick asked.

"Well, that kind of depends…"

"On?"

"On whether you're going to move in or not. 'Cause if

you are, then I'll be emptying out one of my brother's rooms for you."

Nick gently lifted my hand off his cock and rolled onto his side. He wrapped his arm over me and rubbed my back.

"That's a really kind and generous offer, Soph. But I'm not sure it would be a smart move. If I move in here, when would you ever get a break from me? Between sharing an office ten hours a week and attending calls at all hours of the day and night, seeing me in your kitchen three times a day, I think you'd get sick of having me around pretty damn fast."

By the tone of his voice and the gentle look in his eyes, it felt like he really meant what he was saying. He wasn't giving me an 'It's not you, it's me' line when what he really meant was, 'If I lived with you you'd make me want to run unprotected into a burning building.'

"What if we give it a test run?" I suggested. "Do you think you could be honest with me if you decided living with me was too much? Because I can promise you that if you get on my nerves, you'll know. I'm not very good at faking that. And I don't let things fester, either. If it gets to be too much, I'll let you know as soon as I start to feel it so we can talk about it and come up with a plan to fix things."

I gave him a nudge so he'd roll onto his side away from me. I wanted to spoon him, hug him from behind. Most people tended to be more comfortable saying uncomfortable things when they weren't facing the person they were talking to. I hoped this would help him open up.

"I don't know. My track record's not very impressive when it comes to living with people," he said.

A tinge of jealousy burned in me. How many women had he already lived with? I mean, he was twenty-eight, so probably at least two or three.

"Well," I said, holding my breath, "I'm nothing like the other women you've lived with."

"Can't argue with you there since I've never lived with another woman."

I exhaled and hugged him tighter.

"Well then, I think it's only fair that I take your female roommate virginity since you took my, you know, actual virginity." I gave him a gentle bite on his neck.

"Let me think about it, okay? And," Nick spun around and grabbed me tight in his arms, "don't take this personally. This isn't about you. It's about me. I promise. I think you're awesome and I can't imagine what you could do to make me want to run away."

"Yeah, well, I think you're awesomer. I really hope you'll say yes. It's not like I'm asking you to live with me forever." The thought of 'forever' reminded me that I might be evicted. "We can try for a month, see how it goes."

21

NICK

Despite my reticence, Sophie convinced me to take a chance on her 'roommates with benefits' offer since living in the storage space above the truck bay wasn't ideal. I liked her more and more every day. As a roommate, she was smart, funny, warm, and kind. And the benefits? They were mind-blowing.

Although neither of us said that we were boyfriend and girlfriend, or that this was a relationship, exclusive or not, it was pretty clear to me that we were both living as if this was an exclusive relationship. It wasn't her first, but it was mine.

I was on the cusp of turning thirty and Sophie was the first woman I'd let get to know more of me than surface-level shit. She was the first woman who actually asked me questions that were deeper than what my favorite restaurant and position were. I had fun with her, laughed more in the last three weeks than the previous three years. She called me on my bullshit, told me when I was acting arrogant, expected me to contribute to household chores as an equal partner and made both going to bed and waking up moments I looked forward to.

I wouldn't go so far as to say I was falling in love, but I

was happy and for the first time in my life, felt like love without conditions might be possible. The only thing I was missing from my old life was time with my brothers.

Dylan and Josh had the day off and agreed to come up if I'd buy lunch and beer. The assholes both made double what I did with my pay cut. Oh, and then there was the extra thousand a month I was giving Sophie. When she figured out that I was paying her out of my pocket to be my deputy, she had a fit, told me I'd tricked her into thinking the paid position was legit. She was a proud woman and not one to accept the smallest amount of help. In the end, she accepted the two-fifty a week, but called it rent. Made no difference to me although I'd have willingly paid for both her deputy services and the roof over my head, which we might both be losing pretty darn soon if her siblings got their way.

The reason I'd agreed to pay for Dylan and Josh's lunch and beer was because I was going to be getting free advice from them. They didn't specify where we'd eat, so I took them to the shit-hole dive bar where Sophie had taken me on that fateful night. As the oldest brother not only was I allowed to be a dick, it was basically expected of me. And I hated letting my little brothers down.

We'd eaten our 2-star pub food and were on our second beers when I said, "Isabelle called and wants to come and visit for a couple of days, have a little vacation out of the city. My first thought was to see if Sophie would be willing to rent out one of the other empty bedrooms, kind of like a B&B. But—"

Josh interrupted, "But you're not insane, so you didn't make the offer. Tell me you didn't say yes to her visiting, dude."

"Well, I didn't say no. I told her I'd check with my landlady. She got kind of peevish with me."

"You want my advice?" Dylan added, "Take a hard pass on a visit. The very last thing you want or need is to have

Mom or Dad know you've met someone you might have even the mildest of feelings for. Mom will see that there's something going on in a heartbeat."

"Seriously, if you like this chick, keep her as far from Mom and Dad as possible," Josh said.

"I ran into them by accident at a brunch place in Yaletown last weekend. I was with a woman I've been out with a few times. It was a morning-after brunch. Dad called me an hour after they saw us—I was still *with* her!—and he starts in on me."

Dylan deepened his voice into a pretty damn good imitation of Dad, speaking far louder than he needed to, because that's what Dad does, he projects to make sure he is heard, "She's no good for you. If you pursue her, you can kiss your career goals goodbye."

I felt for Dylan. As much as I felt bad about being virtually ignored by Dad, this was attention I was glad I didn't get.

"And then, as usual, Mom chimed in, right Dylan? She said, 'You know he's right. You've worked hard for this. Don't blow it all for a nice piece of ass.'"

"Seriously? Isabelle said 'a nice piece of ass'?"

Dylan shook his head and rolled his eyes, "Not in those words, but it was the meaning."

"Her ass isn't even that nice," Josh added. "I mean, it's okay, but, no, not marriage worthy."

Dylan punched Josh on the arm. Josh hit back. I pushed my chair away from the two monkeys in designer clothes and laughed my ass off. I so needed this reminder that there were definite upsides to being the black sheep, underachiever in the family.

"So your live-work arrangement with Sophie is going well, huh?" Josh asked.

I hesitated since I didn't want to jinx anything, not that I'm superstitious or anything, but one thing Dad did a good job teaching me was to not get my hopes up too high before something was a sure thing. And what I had with Sophie? That was still too new to be anything but a nice reminder that there were women in the world who cared about more than just having social media posts designed to make everyone in their circle jealous of their lives. Sophie was as down-to-earth and as real as a person could be.

I'd never seen her in make-up. She didn't fuss about clothes and didn't own a single pair of shoes that she couldn't wear in the forest. She baked and made homemade pasta and she was a kick-ass first responder. If I had to define a perfect woman, Sophie would be it. Crazy thing is that I'd never have added all those things up if I'd not met her.

"I think so. I hope so," I said.

"What's that mean, dork? It's pretty simple, are you fucking or are you fighting?"

"We're not fighting," was all I'd give him.

"Then chill, dude. Dylan, you've met her. What do you think?"

"I liked her. She's got a spark about her."

"You see a spark in any woman with a pulse," Josh said.

"Hey! I resemble that remark," Dylan said, punching Josh's arm.

"Obviously she's into you, otherwise she wouldn't have invited you to live with her. Just don't go weird on her and fuck it up."

"But 'Weird' is his middle name."

"Josh, if you're the definition of normal, I'll take weird any day," I said.

"Seriously, Nick," Dylan said, picking up my beer to make sure he had my full attention, "you and Sophie are in the honeymoon stage right now. You know you'll have conflict eventually but I beg you, give her a chance. Don't run when things get hard—"

"That's what she said last night," Josh interrupted.

I felt a too-familiar pressure in my chest. That sensation of knowing that even though my dad or Isabelle or my mom or Becky rarely said it out loud, there were times that I knew they were hoping I'd take off to one of my other homes.

I pointed at my beer, still in Dylan's hand. He put it down and I took a long swig.

"Sophie doesn't seem to be judgmental like Dad," Dylan said. "She's not passive aggressive like your mom. And it's obvious that she's not a narcissist like Isabelle."

"Your point?"

"Trust her words, dude. Don't project your insecurities on the way she rolls her eyes at you or whatever the fuck it is that makes you run every time you meet a woman who's spent more than an hour with you and still thinks you're tolerable company."

"Which is how many... two women? Lifetime total?" Josh said with a laugh.

Josh's smile changed to a grimace as Dylan and I both landed punches, me on his left bicep, Dylan on his right.

"You bastards always gang up on me. I swear, you're the worst brothers ever," Josh said.

Dylan shook his head. "Mama's boy." He pointed at me. "Promise that you'll keep your shit together. You've been happy. Sophie seems like a good person. Don't fuck it up."

I held out my glass. Dylan and Josh held out theirs. We clunked them together.

"You guys are the best. As long as Sophie doesn't actually tell me to leave, I'm not going to be the one to flinch."

22

SOPHIE

I t had been three fantastic weeks since Nick and I became roommates. He chose the room with the biggest bed, which was just a double, but much better for sharing than mine. And, we'd shared it every single night since he moved in.

We'd developed a lovely rhythm both inside and outside the bedroom, sharing the cooking and cleaning up. We were trying to keep cool at the firehall since neither of us wanted the other members to know how embedded in the community Nick had become. It made for some uncomfortable practices and emergency calls with innuendo over the radio—*Sophie, come pull hose with me!* And *Sophie, set up a forward lay for me!*—that sometimes made me laugh and always made me horny for him.

I knew Nick was good people because he arranged a deal with a buddy of his to provide Max with high-quality raw dog food. He told me not to worry about how much it cost since his friend owed him a favor and this was how he was paying him back. I saw the invoices and it was true—there was no charge for the box of meat that was being delivered on Thursdays.

Just when I'd started to feel like my life was settling into something I could see as my future, I got a registered letter from my miserly siblings' lawyer. In a nutshell, it was a ruling that said since I wasn't named in the will, Clause 3.4 did not apply to me. Basically, I was now trespassing or illegally squatting since my employer no longer needed me to do my job.

The letter went on to say that the new owners of the home had all agreed that it would be in the best interest of the estate to a) put the house on the market as soon as possible, and b) have it vacant when it was being shown. They'd been generous enough to give me thirty days to find a new home.

I called Linda, the postmistress who knew about all the comings and goings of people in town including which houses had rooms to rent. She confirmed what I expected: Max, Nick and I were screwed.

I dropped the letter on the kitchen counter and pulled Dylan's contact up on my phone. I texted him,

> I'll do the DNA test. What's the worst that can happen?

I went online and ordered the test, paying for expedited shipping. I had no idea how this would help me not have to move, but I did have a strong suspicion that Dylan would be able to provide me with his *pro bono* services based on a memory that I'd fought to ignore or forget for two full decades.

When I thought my day couldn't get any worse, my phone rang. A ringing phone was never good news in my world since friends would text, not call. I'd have ignored it but the caller ID was the bank where Papa had his account. I took a steadying breath and smiled when I answered.

"Sophie speaking."

"Sophie Beaulieu? This is Denise Ramble of the TD Bank."

"Hi Denise. How are you?"

"I'm well. Thanks for asking. I was just closing up your dad's account for the lawyer and noticed that you've not been in to take care of the account he opened in your name."

"Yeah, my sister told me about it," I said giving Max a good ear scratch. "I guess it's been dormant for… well, forever. Do you need me to come in and close it?"

"No, neither. It was your dad's most active account."

"His most active?" I interrupted.

"Let me clarify. Your dad opened it and made deposits to it, but the actual account is yours. I'm not calling to say you need to close it. I was calling to see if you wanted to set up a time to meet to figure out how to invest the money in it. Right now it's in a non-interest-bearing account. It was the only account type that didn't have a service fee and your dad sure hated paying bank fees," she laughed.

"He sure did," I agreed. "I'm not clear, though, that account was set-up…" I did some quick math in my head, "twelve years ago for my allowance—"

Denise interrupted, "No, no, your dad created that account just over two years ago. He's made a monthly deposit ever since. Until—apologies. His last deposit was a week before he passed."

"In an account in my name?"

"That's right."

"And how much money is in this account?" I asked hoping against hope it was a thousand dollars. I said a little prayer to the Universe.

"Two hundred and forty—"

"Oh," I said, deflated. "Well, every little bit counts and this is a nice surprise. He left me a bank card but I don't know what the password is."

"Sophie, I don't think you heard what I said."

"Two hundred and forty dollars," I repeated back.

"Thousand. Two hundred and forty *thousand* dollars."

I laughed out loud. "That's not possible. He didn't have any income. You knew him. All he had was his government pension. We were living on the bare minimum."

"No, that's how much there is. He was taking equity out of the house every month and putting the cash into an account for you, to pay you for your time as his caregiver."

"But," tears pooled in my eyes, "but, he never told me that."

"No, and he made me promise not to mention anything to you until, well, until now, when his accounts were being settled. Assuming you hadn't found the bank card yourself and come in to see how much was in the account."

"Two hundred and forty thousand dollars? That's ten thousand dollars a month. That's ridiculous," I said still not believing her. Waiting for her to start laughing at the cruel joke.

"The going rate for a full-time, live-in nurse is actually almost double that, Sophie. But he wanted to make sure he didn't pay you more than would be defensible if one of your brothers or sisters wanted to challenge it."

"And they will," I mumbled. "Do they know yet?"

"They know that there's a $240,000 debt against the equity in the home, but they don't know where he was moving that money to every month. And it's none of their business if you don't want to tell them."

"But they'll figure it out pretty fast."

"They probably will," she agreed. "I'd recommend you come in, move the money to another account in your name that has no ties to your dad, and take a couple thousand dollars out to hire yourself a lawyer."

"Wow. Yeah. Today? Can I come in today?"

"I'm here until five."

I hung up and felt so many emotions. Relief. Gratitude.

Confusion. And some fear about the shit storm I was sitting in the eye of now.

I looked skyward. "Papa. Oh, Papa, why the big secret? Why *all* the secrets?"

I texted Dylan again,

> Change of plans. I can pay! Call ASAP pls. Thx.

I thought about calling Nick to let him know but decided instead to surprise him with a steak and lobster dinner with twice-baked potatoes. Every time I was getting groceries and asked if we needed anything, that's what he asked me to buy, which I never did, of course.

I got in my car and drove straight to town to see Denise and move that money to a new account. As I was going along Main Street, I saw a familiar-looking Audi parked outside the dive bar. What would the odds be that Dylan was in town and drinking in the bar you go to when you don't want to be seen?

I parked and pulled the bar door open. Sure enough, it was Dylan. He was sitting at the same table in the far corner where Nick and I had had our not date, the day he accepted my job. Dylan was facing me and sitting with him were familiar-looking shoulders and triceps and another man almost equal in size to Nick.

Why would Dylan be meeting Nick? I started to walk toward them and heard Dylan say in an overly dramatic voice, "She's no good for you. If you pursue her, you can kiss your career goals goodbye."

Dylan squinted his eyes at Nick who dropped his head into his hands. I couldn't hear what he said, if anything. But then the other man spoke, looking directly at Nick, "You know he's right. You've worked hard for this. Don't blow it all for a nice piece of ass."

What Nick said, clear as day, cut me to my core. It was stated as a question, 'a nice piece of ass'?"

I stopped dead in my tracks and quickly turned to leave before they saw me.

From shit day to best day to shit day again. I pulled my car around the corner in case they were getting ready to leave so they wouldn't see me, and let myself have a long overdue cry.

Once my eyes were good and swollen, I drove the two blocks to the bank to meet with Denise, half expecting that she'd made a terrible mistake and really, it was only two hundred and forty dollars she had for me. She was with someone when I arrived so I waited in the same chair I sat in every second Saturday when Papa came to do his banking. I hadn't been back since he'd died since my own account was at the credit union. One by one, the tellers came over to give me their condolences with sad eyes and then their big smiles of congratulations on my windfall.

When I was finally called in to see Denise I was equal parts pissed off and grateful.

"So, it seems everyone and their dog—except me and Max—knew about this not-so-secret account my dad had."

"Well, I'm not sure about that, but certainly all the tellers knew. He was so proud of you. He told every one of us that you were taking better care of him than anyone else in the world could. And how much joy you brought to his life after your mom died. He knew you'd never accept being paid to care for him, so he was doing this to surprise you when you wouldn't be able to refuse the money."

"I honestly don't know what to say."

"What do you think you'll do with the money? Take a well-deserved holiday somewhere nice?"

I shook my head, "No, I already live in the vacation paradise capital of the world. I just want to be able *stay* here." At that I had an idea, "What can you tell me about getting a mortgage? What would I need to buy my Mom and Papa's house?"

"Bare bones? A down payment of at least ten percent of the purchase price—which you easily have—and then proof of an income that would support the monthly mortgage payments. Not much more than that. I mean, a reasonable credit rating, which I assume you have."

"Okay, so what steps do I need to take to make this happen?"

Denise gave me a checklist of things I needed to pull together, starting with a house appraisal so I'd have a clear idea of how much money I'd need to be able to buy it. She gave me the name of the appraiser who was the bank's go to, someone the bank trusted.

"You can do this, Sophie! Your dad would be so pleased. I'll do everything in my power to help you get that house."

When I got home, Nick was standing at the stove, stirring a pot. Max was lying on the floor a few steps away.

"Homemade chicken soup," he said, "My second mom, Isabelle's recipe. You'll love it."

"Whatever. I'm going upstairs. Don't call me for dinner. I'm not hungry."

"Are you sick?" he asked, sounding concerned.

"Yeah, sick and tired of all the lies," I muttered under my breath. "Nope," I called as I walked upstairs, "just don't feel like company tonight." I gave a quick whistle. "Come on Max!"

I waited at the top of the stairs for Max who was taking his sweet time.

"Max. Come! Now!"

I could hear shuffling and then finally his nails on the hardwood. As he started to climb the steps I could see something tied to his collar. A Ziplock baggie. I waited for him to reach me, then pointed to my bedroom. He went in and jumped on the bed. I followed and closed the door. Maybe a little harder than I needed to.

"What have you got there? Cookies? What in the world?" I had to undo his collar to get the bag of what were three homemade chocolate chip cookies. They were still warm.

There was a knock on my door.

"Go away," I said, angry that I couldn't resist the treat from the traitor.

"I know you had a bad day," he said through the door, "You want to talk about it?"

23

———

NICK

"Not with you," she said. Her mouth was obviously full.

"What have I done? Did I leave the toilet seat up? Is that why you're mad at me?"

"No. Go away."

"Did I put the cutlery in the wrong spot again when I emptied the dishwasher?"

I heard her exasperated sigh, but she didn't answer.

"I saw the letter from your brother's lawyer. Don't be mad at me, Soph. I'm on your side here."

"It's not that!" she yelled. "Just go away."

I thought for a minute. I *could* open her door but I worried she might throw a shoe or a lamp at me, she sounded that mad.

"I know," I said triumphantly, "You're on your period. That's why you're mad at me for no reason!"

I heard her feet hit the ground. Hard. I stood right in the middle of her doorframe and when she opened it with her fists up at her chest, I spun her around. With her back to me, I hugged her tight, lifted her off the ground and carried her back into her room. I sat down on the edge of

Sophie's bed with her in my lap, ignoring her screaming to let go.

When she finally stopped struggling and yelling, I opened my arms and she retreated to the top of her bed, pulling her knees up to her chest. She rocked back and forth without looking at me.

"Talk to me, Sophie. Please. I can't fix what I don't know is broken."

"It's not your job to fix anything. You're my housemate. Nothing more. Your only job is to pay your rent on time. Do you think you can handle that without it ruining your life?"

That hurt. I had no idea where this was coming from. Stress, I assumed, from learning that she was going to have to go to war with her siblings and was most likely going to lose her home. I hated seeing her so upset. I put my hand on her knee. She jerked away from my touch.

"Sophie, what the fuck? I'm on your side, here. Maybe I can help you."

"I. Don't. Need. Your. Help. I have a lawyer." She looked up at me for the first time. "But you know that already."

"Yeah, my brother told me."

"Your brother? Dylan Rhodes is your *brother*? Oh, god," she looked at her legs again, then exploded up onto her knees into an attack position. "Why didn't you tell me Dylan was your brother? Don't you think that's kind of an important detail to let me know?"

"I didn't know he was working with you until—"

"Wait! How is it that Murray put me in touch with your *ostie de callis* brother? And why is he *really* willing to work with me for free? What did you do?"

She had fire coming out of her eyes.

I had a terrible feeling there was nothing I could say that would give her the answer she wanted.

"When Murray and I met that very first time, when he was giving me the run-down on everything I needed to know, he asked about my family. I mentioned I had a brother who was a lawyer. He knew you needed one and asked for his name which I gave him and then didn't think of it again. I didn't even know that Murray passed it on to you.

"As for why Dylan isn't charging you? If he's willing to work with you *pro bono* it's nothing to do with me or charity. All it means is that there's a chance the case will get print if he wins."

"So you knew I'd met with him and—"

"No, Sophie, I didn't. Not until this afternoon when you texted him. I was with him and his phone was face up on the table. I saw your name on the text. I asked him about it and all he said was that you'd had one discussion about a case. Nothing more. We didn't talk about you at all. So I know nothing. Nothing except you got a shitty letter today because it was on the kitchen table. And, since I'm not just a dumb guy who sprays wet stuff on hot stuff, I put two and two together and assumed that you must have met with Dylan about the fight with your siblings to be able to stay in the house."

"Uh-huh. Right," she said rolling her eyes. "You expect me to believe you didn't talk about me *at all*. I call bullshit."

I thought for a second back to my conversation with Dylan.

"No, you're right. We did talk about you a little bit—"

She crossed her arms in front of her chest. "So, why don't you tell me what you talked about when you were talking about me, then?"

I couldn't tell her I was worried that I was going to fuck everything up since it was all going so well. I didn't want her to know how every day I woke up and wondered if today would be the day she decided she'd had enough of having me around and would ask me to move out. How sexy would that be? Josh was right, I was a weirdo.

"I told him that I wanted to make you his Mom's chicken

soup for dinner and I asked him if he'd text me the recipe since she taught him how to make it. Which is what you smelled when you walked in."

Sophie looked at me disbelieving then put her head down.

"Anything else?" she asked avoiding my eyes.

"No. After that we talked about... I don't know, shit my brothers are doing."

Tears were falling off her face and she wasn't bothering to wipe them or hide the fact, other than by not looking at me. My heart was breaking for her. I couldn't imagine the level of betrayal she must have been feeling. My brothers, even though we were only half- or step-brothers, were a team, always watching each other's backs, and even fighting each other's fights.

"Sophie, what's really going on? You can talk to me. I want to help you."

"Do you trust Dylan? Do you trust his advice?"

"With my life," I said.

Sophie got off the bed and lay down on the floor beside Max and whispered to him while she pet his head. She looked up at me, "Why do you have different last names? That makes no sense."

My hands squeezed into fists and I could tell by the way I tried to steady my breath that my nostrils were flaring. I did not want to talk about this but she'd given me no choice.

"My father made me change it to my mom's last name when I was fifteen, okay?" I realized my anger was being directed toward Sophie. I turned to look out the window. "Dad didn't like the group of friends I was hanging out with with, said I'd amount to nothing and that there was no way my punk ass was going to sully his good name and reputation."

I watched Sophie petting Max from the corner of my eye and focussed on slowing my heart rate. I was triggered and knew that it wasn't her fault but that didn't reduce the emotions.

"You could have told me Dylan was your brother. I mean, why keep that a secret unless you're trying to hide something from me?"

"Sophie, I didn't even fucking know you were talking to him. If you want to be pissed at someone, go yell at Murray. Or fuck, why not take this out on Dylan? He could have mentioned that I was his brother. But no, of course he wouldn't.

"Fuck it, you know? I thought it would be nice to share a family recipe with you, but you know what? This whole family thing is bullshit. Your family are assholes. My family are assholes. Fuck the whole family thing."

"Well, we can agree on that." Sophie stood and faced me. "I'm sorry I thought letting you live here would be a good idea. I can't do this."

"Somehow that doesn't surprise me."

That familiar and unwelcome emotion—part confusion, part disappointment and part 'well, fuck you, too'—filled every cell of my body. I knew from experience that there was no point arguing, no point continuing the conversation. I'd been dismissed. It was time for me to go, back to one of my other homes, which, lucky for me, I still had.

I left without a word. Didn't bother to stop at the firehall to pick up my things, and drove the highway back to the city like I had lights and sirens on my Subaru. Made it in record time. I parked my car at my condo and grabbed a cab to the Grill Girls Club, intending to lose myself in overpriced beer and the attention of an oversexed woman. I ordered and looked around, making eye contact with two or three women. They smiled and I felt like punching the wall. I dropped a twenty on the table before my beer even arrived, stepped out into the cool spring air and walked the four miles back to my place. Alone.

24

SOPHIE

Despite the fact that I was pissed with Nick for lying, I was still heart-broken. And, although I was pissed with Dylan for thinking that I was bad for Nick, I still let him be my lawyer because he was confident he could help me. It's not like I was in love with stupid Nick West. Sure, the sex was mind-blowing and that soup he made the day he moved out was orgasmically delicious. But that's not love. That's just pleasure. And as every kid who's ever eaten a Family-size bag of M+M's knows, too much of a good thing becomes sickening.

It had been two weeks since I found out I was almost a quarter-millionaire. The appraiser told me that the fair market value for my parent's house was $900,000. Dylan helped me get a one-week extension on my eviction by letting my sibs know I was working on a plan to buy the house from them. Denise arranged a pre-approved mortgage based on a business plan Dylan helped me create to turn five of the six bedrooms into rentals. I'd have to do some renovations to create one more bathroom so there'd be three full baths. They'd be small, with just a shower, sink and toilet, but functional. In the rental market, we figured I could get $1000 a month per room. If I added five dinners a week, $1500.

The plan was to rent the rooms to international students who attended the fancy private university nearby. Lots of parents didn't want their kids living in residence, wanted an adult presence. I could be a bit like a foster mom, making sure they behaved themselves.

Denise loved the idea and the income projections were just enough to approve the mortgage. Dylan prepared a sales agreement for me to buy the house at market value and sent it to my brother's lawyer, giving them two working days to decide since I was up against my eviction notice if this didn't pan out. I thought he was being too cautious since why would they turn down the offer? I mean, it gave them exactly what they wanted and none of the hassle of putting it on the market or the cost of paying a real estate agent's fees.

Things were looking up and I was happy. Mostly. Except on Thursday evenings when I had to go to fire practice. And on the emergency calls we got that were on Monday to Friday, 9am to 8pm, since that's when Nick was in town. I assumed he'd just move back to his storage room space in the hall but he didn't, he was commuting to and from the city.

I had to stop in at the hall to fax some papers to Dylan on that first Monday after he left and he looked like hell rung out, like he'd spent the weekend partying hard.

"And *I'm* bad for your career," I muttered when I saw him.

"The worst," he replied, not looking up from whatever paperwork he was clearly pretending to be focused on.

Now we were down to the wire. My siblings had had 47 hours to do whatever they needed to do to finalize this house sale and send back a signed document to Dylan. I'd spent the morning talking to contractors since I'd have to get the renos done pretty fast to get income rolling in. Every day I waited was a day I was tossing away $200 in potential rent. I was willing to pay top dollar to get a good plumber here within the week.

My phone rang. It was Dylan.

"So, was I right? Nothing to worry about?" I said, prepping my best, "I told you so!"

"Hey, Sophie. Not exactly."

"Not exactly?" I said feeling immediately deflated.

"Your brother is a… well, an interesting man, I guess."

"He's a *connard*. Why do you say that?"

"He's made a counter-offer on behalf of the estate."

"Yeah? How much?"

"One point five million."

"What the actual fuck?" I was on my feet, adrenalin pounded in veins and thunder in my ears. "That's $600,000 more than market value. He can't do that, can he?"

"Sadly, he can. He could have just rejected the offer, which would have been less aggressive, actually. He clearly wants to show you that he's in control."

"The whole family had to agree to this?"

"I assume, but I don't know. Maybe he just asserted the power of his position as executor. Maybe he bullied the others. I have no idea. His lawyer just emailed the documents. Not even a cover note. I'm so sorry."

I sat back down, grief and sudden exhaustion overwhelmed me.

"What now?"

"Well, unless you can reason with him, which I have zero confidence in at this point, you have to move by the eviction date. Sophie, I am truly sorry. I expected some pushback but not this level."

I felt like throwing up. I was in too much shock to cry, almost too much to even breathe.

"Maybe they'd rent the house to me? Can you ask?"

"I can. I will. But, honestly, Sophie, I think you'd better start looking for a new place to live."

"Three weeks…"

"I'm so sorry."

The next morning my doorbell rang at 8am. I was sound asleep after spending much of the night awake fretting. I ignored it, pulling my pillow over my head. The bell rang again, accompanied by hard knocking and a voice, "Sophie. I know you're home."

It was my sister, Sarah.

I plodded to the door, unlocked it without opening it, then went back to my room and closed the door. I didn't want to see or talk to her. And apparently neither she nor my two brothers who were with her cared to see me either. I listened as they walked through the rooms talking. I couldn't hear what they were saying when they were downstairs, but up here on our bedroom floor and on the floor above, their words were as clear as if the walls were made of nothing more than wallpaper.

"So we all agree to take care of our own bedrooms, right? Clear them out, emptied."

"Yup."

"What about Mom and Papa's bedroom?"

"I think everything else in the house should be moved to a storage space. We can go through it all later, figure out who gets what."

"I was hoping to snag a couple of Mom's rings now. I'm

the only one who isn't married, so I thought I could have her engagement and wedding rings," Sarah said to John and Patrick.

"No, that's not fair. We need to have everything appraised first. You can't just start taking things before we know the value of everything."

"Seriously, John, you're not going to wear them."

"Maybe I'd like to give them to Becca when she's old enough to get married."

"She's six for god's sake."

"Why don't we have the jewelry appraised first and then we can create a spreadsheet of who's taken what and the values. If you want the rings, Sarah, I'm fine with that. And John, seriously? But let's get them appraised first," Patrick said.

"Did you see Mom's jewelry box upstairs?" John asked.

"Yeah. It was on the top shelf in the closet. I'll get it."

Sarah went upstairs and the other two went down. I hated them. I had decided to not bother fighting the will since Papa had taken care of my share and then some. It didn't feel fair that I'd get that much more than everyone else. And even though I wasn't close to them, I didn't want to drive a bigger wedge into my relationship with them. I hoped that one day I'd be able to be the fun auntie their kids came to hang out with when they needed a break from their *connard* parents. If I fought the will I knew any chance of a relationship with their kids would be impossible. I'd decided that that wasn't worth the $73,000 of what my share would have been.

But listening to them, and how petty they were, made me want to take every dime I could. Plus, it was becoming more and more clear that I was so far from their minds as an auntie to their kids, that my dream would never come to pass anyway.

I'd paid Dylan to represent me on the house sale but he'd

said he'd still fight the will *pro bono* if my situation fit his criteria and I decided to pursue it. In that moment, I was thinking I'd be a fool not to.

A heavy bang on my door pulled me from my thoughts.

"Where are Mom's rings, Sophie? Where did you put them?"

Sarah shoved my door open and stood in the doorway holding Mom's jewelry box in her hands. Within seconds, three people had crowded my small room. They were looking at the bracelets and necklaces in the box, most of it obviously department store quality.

"Nowhere. I didn't touch them," I said.

"Come off it, Soph, where are they? Have you already sold them?"

"Oh my god! I didn't touch anything. I'm not going to steal from my own family." As soon as I said that I regretted it. These people were less my family than Murray and all the guys at the firehall. All except Nick, of course.

"Okay then, do you know where Papa put them? Did he have a safety deposit box?"

"No idea," I said, using all my energy not to use every curse word I'd ever heard to emphasize the point.

"Well they didn't walk out on their own, now did they? And Papa couldn't have walked them out of here without you knowing, so that means that you either have them or know where they are," John said, looking at the others with an expression that suggested he thought his powers of deduction were comparable to Sherlock Holmes.

The others nodded and smiled, saying, "Good point," and "He has you there, Sophie."

I took a deep breath and glared at each of them in turn, now one hundred percent convinced I'd fight the will.

"If any of you had bothered to spend any time with Papa in the last two years you'd know how utterly ridiculous that is. You think I was sitting beside him twenty-four hours a day? You think just because he was in a wheelchair he didn't have a social life outside of time with me? He did all kinds of things without me. Went places with friends. Had friends over. He wasn't incompetent, he was still Papa.

"And I didn't take Mom's rings, *chalis d'hostie de tabernak.* I bet he sold them just so none of you could get hold of them."

The fight was on. I'd never spoken back to any of them like that before. Papa always told me that nothing good ever came from investing energy into hate, that love was always the more sensible way to live life. I cast my eyes up and quietly mouthed, "Sorry."

John pointed at my jewelry box, "Maybe she's hiding them in plain sight."

Sarah put Mom's box down and picked mine up, pulling the top open. A ballerina stood and spun in a pirouette to tinny music. Inside were small charms and mementos. She pulled open the drawer and found a 24 karat gold cross. She pulled it out and said, "This was Mom's. You stole this so why should we believe you didn't take her wedding ring, too?"

The guys agreed that they'd remembered Mom wearing that cross. And they were right. It *had* been Mom's. She wore it everyday. I don't know if she even took it off to sleep or bathe. But she had taken it off once.

"Mom gave that to me when I left for boarding school. She put it around my neck when I was saying goodbye to her and Papa at the airport."

"Bullshit. Why would she have given it to *you*?" John said, emphasizing the 'you' in a way I was sure he meant to hurt me.

My nostrils flared. I wanted them out of my room. Out of my home. "I don't know, John, probably to save my soul since I was illegitimate."

There was a collective gasp and they all looked at each

other as if now that the secret had been spoken, it made it real. But it was already real. The DNA test proved it. I was their niece, raised as their sister. Almost sister. Sort of sister. Never really their sister.

"I may not be your sister, but I was still Papa's daughter. And a better child than any of you lot, too."

Sarah was the first to speak, "Well, at least now you understand why you don't get a share of the estate."

"No," I said, "I still don't understand that part. I was raised as your sister and as far as anyone outside this family knows, I was Mom and Papa's little girl. And you all were happy to have me act as Papa's child for the last two years I took care of him. And you know what? After today you've convinced me that I'm willing to fight to prove it.

"Here," I said grabbing the crucifix from my jewelry box and throwing it back at Sarah, "you take this. My soul is just fine. The one thing I'm trying to figure out is which one of you is actually my parent. My best guess is Dick."

By the way Sarah's eyes snapped open and John hung his head and sighed, I knew I was right.

"And by the way, Pat, it's thanks to you and Peter making your family trees public that I was able to figure out my relationship to you all."

"Dick is going to kill you," Sarah said.

"Whatever. So what? She was going to find out anyway. Dick's lawyer said as much. It's part of the argument, the fact that she's *his* kid, not Papa's."

I kicked them out of the house and sat down in the living room to write an email to Dylan, to tell him what I thought I knew about who I was, since it might help with my case.

Hi Dylan,

I got the results of the DNA test back this week and it looks like

I'm dealing with the worst-case scenario—the one situation that needs a good lawyer.

I had to stop typing as my vision contracted so I could barely focus. I'd spent twenty years trying to convince myself that what felt like a memory had just been a dream. But with the DNA report confirming that I was related, but not as a sibling, to two of my supposed brothers and sisters who'd also done the test, I had to accept that I was not Mom and Papa's *Oops*, I was someone else's accident. And, I had to accept that I'd been lied to by every single person in my family for my whole life.

As I tried to control my breath, I looked up the stairs and could see myself at four-years-old on Christmas Eve, laying in bed. It was after Midnight Mass so I was supposed to be asleep, but I was wide awake, waiting for Santa. I could hear my family—Mom, Papa, all eight brothers and sisters and a few married-in aunts and uncles downstairs talking and having fun. It was all happy background noise but I wanted them to go to bed so Santa could come.

I pictured myself getting out of my bed and starting down the stairs. That's when I heard my oldest brother, Dick, yelling at Papa.

"I'm taking Sophie with me tomorrow. And you can't stop me."

The whole house went silent. I didn't move. I was afraid they'd hear me breathing.

"Richard, don't be ridiculous. You're in no position to care for a little girl," Papa said.

"André," my mom said, "Neither am I. We're old. Too old. And she's not our problem."

That's the only time I ever heard Papa yell. He was so angry he was swearing, taking the Lord's name in vain.

"Sophie is *not* a problem. She's our daughter. Richard,

you gave up that right when you and Marie left her on our doorstep. You do not get to come back and take her now."

"André," now Mom was angry, too, "It's for the best. I already packed her things. Richard is taking her tomorrow and that's that."

I remember laying in bed crying, not understanding. I don't remember any of the time I lived with Dick and Marie. It might have only been a day for all I knew. That's why I always thought the memory had been a dream, since I had nothing to back it up. Except the way Papa treated Dick.

Mom talked to Dick and Marie on the phone sometimes, but they never came to visit and Papa always refused to talk to them. And when I'd ask him why, he'd just wave his hand and say, "I'm busy with you. I have no time for them."

I looked at the half-written email on my laptop, dreading having to say what I remembered, out loud, knowing I'd have to.

When can I book a time to talk to you? My house would be easiest if you happen to be heading up this way anytime soon.
   Kind regards,
   Sophie

I hit 'send' and felt both lighter and heavier at the same time.

25

NICK

I had barely seen Sophie in the two weeks since she unceremoniously kicked my ass to the curb. I wish I could say I was surprised since it really felt like we had something good, but if life had taught me anything, it was that it's best not to get too comfortable with an idea or a belief. The only thing a person can really trust are facts. And feelings are not facts.

The facts I had working for me were that I'd not yet rented out my condo in the city so I had a nice place to live and sleep, that I could do all of the paperwork part of my job as chief from the city, and that Sophie had made herself scarce. I figured she, too, was doing all of her deputy chief work from home.

Whatever. She'd been a distraction from my main goal: to earn my street creds so that the next time there was a hiring round for a city chief, I'd be a viable candidate. In the last two weeks I'd been singularly focused on that goal. I had a perfect canvas to work with in the Lily Valley Department since they had enough members to adequately serve the community's needs and most of those members were woefully undertrained. All I had to do was move this motley crew closer to the National Fire Protection Association standards in the next five months.

Of the thirty members, the last six weeks of practices and calls showed me that half were reasonably up-to-speed on the basics and that some even had advanced skills. The other half… they varied between seriously rough around the edges and as useless—and dangerous—as water on a grease fire.

Since we only had gear and space for thirty members, my first significant act as chief was to clear some dead wood—volunteers who arrived late to practice, stayed after to take advantage of the cheap beer, and who showed up for fewer than one in five of the calls—to make space for fresh new volunteers. Those men, and one woman, were of no use to the department. In my opinion, they were destructive and bad for morale.

Since all the former chiefs had been volunteers and had a history with the department, they were soft on these guys. I had nothing motivating me to accept their excuses. And so on my sixth Thursday training practice, I laid down the law.

"Pass these around," I said dropping a stack of papers on the table.

What I'd printed out was the member list with the number of practices and call-outs each member had attended in the past twelve months, listed alphabetically by last name.

"Find your name on this list. If you've attended forty or more practices and twenty or more calls in the last year, head to the truck bay. Your job tonight is to do a full equipment check on all three vehicles. Joe, you're in charge of Engine One. Take three members to help you. Martin, you've got the Quint and two members. And Sophie, I want you to take apart and check Rescue One with three members. Clear?"

"Yes, sir," came a chorus of the department's eleven most dedicated volunteers.

"Kasieta, French, Frebel, Kohn, Jones, and O'Reilly! On your feet."

"Why?" asked Kasieta with clearly no intention of standing.

"Because I just told you to. Do you need any more reason than that?" I barked.

"Actually, yeah, I do."

"All right, I'll give you a reason. I'll give you six actually since it looks like you're the only of this lot who bothered to show up tonight. Here are six garbage bags," I said tossing them on the table in front of him. "Take the member list and go to the truck bay with these bags and fill each one with all the gear for the six members who have attended fewer than twenty practices or fewer than ten calls all year. Can you figure it out or do I need to say the names again?"

Kasieta's look made it clear that I needed to be more explicit.

"Circle these names: French, Frebel, Jones, Kohn, O'Reilly and your own. Then put theirs and your gear in the garbage bags. Then take those bags up to the storage space. Drop your hall keys on my desk and you can go home. Thanks for your service." *And lack thereof.*

There was an audible gasp, not just from Kasieta but several members around the table.

Kasieta stared at the list and then at me. "You can't fire me. I'm a volunteer."

"Actually, I can and I just did."

"But Chief, shouldn't you give them a warning or a second chance or something," Mason Aspin, the youngest member asked.

All eyes were on me. I had their rapt attention. "Mason, how long ago did you join?"

"As soon as I turned sixteen. Like, six months ago or so," he said

"Right. And do you remember what you agreed to when

you joined?" I asked, not even a hint of anger in my voice since I wasn't the smallest bit angry.

"That I'd attend at least eighty percent of practices and fifty percent of calls."

"Exactly!" I said. "Now you work hard and let's see… you've hit quite a bit better than the basic minimum attendance for your six months. So, do you think it's fair that there are members who barely show up and can't be counted on to either help train you or support you on calls?"

"This is bullshit," Kasieta said. "I didn't sign that fucking piece of paper when I joined so you can't hold me to a so-called 'contract,'" he said the word making air quotes, "that I didn't agree to."

"Ah, well you may not have signed that contract specifically, but you did agree to the terms in it. All of you did, in case you've forgotten." I pulled a stapled stack of papers from a folder in front of me and held it in the air.

"These are the Lily Valley Volunteer Fire and Rescue bylaws. Each year in advance of the annual general meeting, they're distributed to each of you by email and hard copies are offered for those of you who would prefer to review them that way. And," I flipped the pages until I came to the last one which was a list of members and their signatures, "this is where you signed your name stating that you've read, understood and agree to abide by the bylaws or risk losing membership in this organization."

I tossed the stack to Kasieta who let the papers hit the table without looking at them.

He finally stood. "Fuck you, I quit."

"Leave your keys, please," I said with a smile.

"Sorry. Lost 'em."

"Understood. We appreciate your service."

Kasieta didn't leave the meeting room through the main door, he turned and entered the truck bay where he made it crystal clear that I was a piece of shit not worthy of being wiped from his ass. Since he was no longer under my command, the disrespect rolled off me like water on my turn-out gear.

"I'm sorry if you think that was harsh treatment, but those six members, as you can all see by their attendance records, have not been contributing. Your—*our*—community is about to undergo a huge growth spurt but this department will never have more than thirty members and the ones we have must be reliable and bringing value to the table.

"I was hired to make sure that in two years this town would be properly protected and all volunteers would meet the national standards that all firefighters, career and volunteer, must meet. Now, if you're not comfortable with this, I will not hold it against you. You can leave now or come to me to discuss your concerns in private.

"Over the next two years you'll be given more opportunities to develop your skills and those skills will be tested. If you fail a module, you'll get additional training and try again. To be clear, nobody will be fired as along as you're showing up and making an effort."

"Chief," Mason interrupted, "We're just volunteers. We're not here to become career firefighters. So why do we need to train to career levels. It seems like… a lot of work, frankly, for something we're not paid to do."

I smiled, appreciating the question, which I'd fully expected.

"How many of you were on the first crew to attack that forest fire last summer?"

Three guys raised their hands.

"How long were you working to control it before the smoke jumpers and water plane arrived?"

They looked at each other and agreed three or four hours.

"Hard work, right?"

Nods.

"Dangerous, too."

"Oh, fuck yeah, Orzel lost his footing and had to be long-lined out since he fell down a steep slope."

"Yeah. He was lucky. The fire didn't give a rat's ass that you guys were all *just* volunteers. The trees that were falling around you? They didn't lean away when they fell to not hurt you since you were *just* volunteers. You need to be trained to national fire safety standards since fire does not discriminate. And, before a hand goes up and informs me that you've not had an actual structure fire here in town in almost a decade, all that tells me is that you are long overdue for one.

"So, if you choose to stay, you'll be getting free training that is costing taxpayers a shit tonne of money. Money they're mostly happy to pay since it means they also get better premiums on their home insurance. Insurance companies expect fire department staff—career *and* volunteers—to be able to do the job they're supposedly trained to do.

"That is what you'll be getting if you choose to stay. And, if you decide to stop showing up for practice or calls and your stats fall below what the bylaws require, you will not be given a second chance. You'll simply find your gear packed up and soon enough, another member's name over your cubby space."

I let that information settle as I looked at each member, making silent bets with myself about who would rise to the occasion and who would rise from their chair, pack up and leave.

Childerston spoke, "Chief, I'm in. What do you want me to do tonight?"

Ha! Two points!

"Anyone else feeling sure that you want to remain in this new structure?"

Several hands raised.

"All right, you guys can self-organize. By the end of

practice I'd like an inventory of the sizes of turn-out gear, gloves, boots and helmets from the six former members. I also want a separate list of any gear that current members are using that either doesn't fit properly or should be replaced. I know a few of you have helmets that look like they did time in the second world war. If there's a helmet that's new to the inventory and it fits, grab it. And last, I need both the truck bay and the meeting room external door locks changed. The new cylinders are on my desk."

"Do you want us to distribute keys, Chief?"

"Nope, you'll each get your key from me when you sign your new contract of understanding."

Six guys rose and moved through to the truck bay where the gear and tools were. That left two guys still sitting in their chairs.

"You two want to take this to my office for some privacy or do you want talk here?" I asked.

"Oh, I have no problem with anyone hearing what I have to say," growled Roberts.

"I'm listening," I said, laying my chin in my hand and smiling.

"I've been a member of this department for almost twenty years and we've done just fine without the likes of guys like you coming in to mess with what's not broke. You're playing with fire, Chief, you know that? You think you can lock out volunteers to keep us from showing up and the district won't hear about it? Goddamn right they will. You'll have Decker riding so far up your ass to get Frebel, Kohn and the other guys back you'll be choking on your own dick."

I stopped myself from asking how my dick was going to end up inside my ass with Decker and by the way James looked at Roberts, he too was trying to picture this.

"So do I take it that you'll be leaving your keys when you leave tonight?"

"Not a chance. I'm staying on whether you like it or not and whether I hit your arbitrary targets or not. I am going to make your life so fucking miserable you'll wish you'd stayed in your fancy city department."

I continued smiling not because I was amused at the pain in the ass this guy was going to be but because I figured the more entertained I looked, the more it would piss him off. Roberts was one of the members who'd been given a courtesy interview for the chief job and Murray warned me that he'd be my biggest challenge. I also knew from Decker that there was no love lost between him and Roberts so he could bluster all he wanted. It was just white noise as far as I was concerned.

Sophie came into the meeting room looking concerned.

"Chief, can I see you in your office?"

I stood and spoke to the two still in the meeting space, "If you guys are staying, I need you to go up to the rec room and clean the kitchen. The stove looks like a yak shat on it and the fridge smells like the yak died in there."

Sophie and I were inside my office before they rose and by the sound of it, neither of them took the stairs to the rec room. I smiled inwardly and then outwardly at Sophie.

"Hey Soph, what's up?"

She stood with her hands on her hips, her pupils were so big her eyes looked black.

"I was going to ask you the same thing. Kasieta says you fired him and a bunch of others."

I nodded.

"But... those are some of our most experienced firefighters. They might not show up to many practices but when they do they're really great at showing newbies the ropes. And, Frebel and Kohn are the only two who have actual building fire experience."

"I'm not going to argue with you, but from what I've seen in the last six weeks and on the cluster fuck of a car accident last week, the department will be stronger without them."

"But—"

"You know that two other members applied for the chief position, right? I can't tell you who they were but I can tell you that the other guys were given a courtesy interview but never for a second were they serious contenders. You were, Sophie. They were not. The fact that these guys I just fired have a long history is actually a detriment to this department. We need change and we need it fast. We need solid leadership. We need members who respect the chain of command and the authority of the officers. The guys who've had their cubbies cleaned out were never going to be that.

"Now we have space for six new members who are willing to help grow us into the department we need to be, to be able to serve and protect this community."

Sophie was still standing, scowling at me. She had the same energy, that seemed to me to be half rage, half resignation, that she had the day she sent me packing. I knew the emotion well and I also knew that fear was at the core. It made me want to grab her and hold her and tell her everything would work out, in part to convince her but also to convince myself.

"You just fired five guys who weren't even here to defend themselves or, I don't know, argue their cases. That's a seriously dick move."

"Those five who weren't here? I texted each of them last week after practice and let them know it was critical that they show up tonight. They could have texted me back to let me know they couldn't make it. They had their chance. And frankly, I'm glad they're gone. It's going to make your job a whole lot easier."

"Oh yeah? Why's that?" Sophie dropped into her chair and spun so her knees were touching mine.

Instinctively, I laid my hands on her legs, the way I

would place them on a dog's back to calm him. She didn't jerk away which I took as a good sign.

"Hey," I said to get her to make eye contact, "how well did Frebel, Kohn or French follow orders when you were IC?"

She shrugged shoulders, "Well, they had more experience than me, so…"

"Sophie, if I assigned Mason as the Incident Commander on a call, and he suggested a course of action that you thought wasn't the best course, what would you do?"

She sat back in her chair, relaxing a little. "I guess that depends. If nobody was going to get hurt, I'd not say anything since he might see something that I didn't. But if I thought someone might get hurt following his orders, I'd go and talk to him and let him know what I saw in the situation and hope that he'd see a different approach. I guess. It's never happened, though. The chief would never put someone with so little experience in charge."

"Really? So, why did Murray give you the IC role so often even though you're one of the newest members?"

She looked at me like it was a trick question, so I answered, "Because you show up to every practice, every call-out, do more than is expected. Hell, you even took extra training on your own time… come on, Sophie. It's not rocket science. You're smart, you work hard and you were rewarded. These guys are being rewarded, too, for their level of commitment. It's just that their reward is to not have to carry a pager with them 24/7, to have Thursday nights free to go drinking or whatever they want without guilt."

Sophie had dropped her gaze and was staring at my hands, laying on top of her thighs. Her jaw was tense. I lifted my hands and she followed them, making eye contact with me again.

"Their gear wasn't being used to the best benefit of this

community and you know it. We need that gear for volunteers like Sophie Beaulieu."

By the way she was looking at me I figured she got it. Hoped she was onside because I knew I couldn't rebuild what I'd just blown up without her support.

26

SOPHIE

I didn't know how to feel about Nick's little pep talk. I was angry that he'd so cavalierly canned some of our longest-serving members, I was sad that the chatter among those who remained was not kind toward Nick, and I was flattered that of all the people he could have chosen to be his deputy, he chose me and didn't fire me when I kicked him out of my house.

But that also confused me since wasn't I the one person who was supposed to be bad for his career? How could he think that *and* still let me have a position that had the most power to undermine his authority and send him back to the city? I was just about to ask him when there was a knock on the door.

"Come," Nick said, motioning for me to open the door since I was sitting closest. Mason stood there, looking apologetic.

"Sorry to interrupt, Chief, but I thought you might want to know that a bunch of guys you didn't fire are putting their turn-out gear into garbage bags. You know, in case you want to come out and convince them to stay?"

My heart sank. There was no way we'd have enough

people to respond with two trucks with the loss of this many members. I watched Nick consider his response. He didn't get upset or change his energy at all. I bet Mason had won the short end of the straw in being sent to tell Nick since we were all used to Murray's reaction to bad news—he'd shoot the messenger. With a poison-tipped arrow.

"Thanks for the intel, Mason. You can let them leave. I'll come out in a few minutes and have a look at the damage. You and the guys who were assigned to sorting out gear, can you handle the new inventory or do you need me to assign someone else to help you?"

"No, Sir. We can handle it."

Nick smiled at him, "Good man!"

Mason beamed. I suspect he didn't get called a man very often.

Nick turned his attention back to me. "So, Deputy Beaulieu, are you ready to help me recruit some fresh new blood to this department? Looks like we've got at least ten positions to fill."

"Okay? I'm not sure how to go about that, though. I mean, since I moved home and joined, there's never been a recruitment. People just join when they feel like it," I said. "Do you have a plan?"

"Half-baked at best," he said. And then he told me to figure it out. And he also told me that I had to start doing my deputy work from the firehall. I guess he'd noticed I'd been avoiding him. Whatever. I thought he'd appreciate not having my bad influence around.

Fortunately, since that fight, he wasn't making my blood boil in all the inappropriate places anymore. I mean, a sexy body can only take a man so far if he doesn't also have a sexy personality. And there is nothing sexy about a man who misleads and lies and uses a woman to get what he needs, like a bed in a town with no vacancy.

I hated myself for being such a sucker and thinking Mr.

Arrogant Calendar Man would ever have actually been interested in me. I hated myself even more for caring enough to go searching for photos of him on Instagram. Well, not him *specifically*. At least, at first it was the opposite.

Since Nick had awakened my sexual energy and then left me without an outlet to expend it, I'd found myself having to rely on myself for that relief. But that *connard*'s face was what I saw in my fantasy and I needed to replace his with another face and his calendar firefighter body with another hot bod.

So I searched #sexyfireman on Instagram and *ostie de callise* don't you know I saw over ten photos of Nick-fucking-West, each with a different woman hung over him like a freaking shawl. And maybe it wasn't kind of me to have thought it, but I did: *she looks like a good lay.* God, somehow I was channeling my mother.

It looked like the photos had been taken on three different dates, five from the time before I met him but five of them in the last three weeks. And in those, he was virtually naked with each of the women who were all very happy to have their hands on every inch of his body. And he sure looked like he was having the time of his life. I broke into a stress sweat staring from photo to photo, trying to understand who this man really was. Was he actually a firefighter or was he a male model. Or a stripper? Could he be all three?

And oh my god, I'd had sex with him. Instead of feeling worthy of his attention, I felt even more used since it was abundantly clear that whatever chemistry there was between us, Nick West was an element that caused anything he touched to explode.

Those photos were all the proof I needed that I was never his type and that my utility to him had nothing to do with friendship or a budding relationship and everything to do with him excelling at his job. And that giving me what I needed—physical human contact—was done in service of giving him what he needed. Bet he never saw it coming that I'd catch on so fast, even though he'd all but predicted it when he told me, "You're smarter than you are pretty."

Of course, in my desire to believe a man like Nick would ever want me, I'd twisted that to mean he thought that I was both pretty and smart, but now I realized what he'd meant was that what I lacked in looks I made up for in brains. I took a breath and brought my focus back to the challenge at hand.

My tone was unintentionally sharp. "So, are you going to share your half-baked plan or do I have read your mind to know what it is?"

And to Nick's credit, he was as calm with me as he'd been with Mason.

"Neither. I trust your plan will be smarter than anything I can come up with."

Argh! I hated him.

"Timeline for these new recruits?" I asked grinding my teeth.

"Next week," he said, as if that was a totally reasonable request.

I glared at him.

"What? You have a problem with that? Do you think it'll take you more than ten hours to find ten guys willing to join? You want more money, is that it?"

"No! That's not it. It's… I'm just pissed that you call me your right hand and I have the title of deputy but you didn't give me a heads-up that you'd be firing a bunch of guys tonight. In fact, you even made me leave the room when you did it so I heard second hand. Doesn't really leave the impression that I have your trust, you know?"

I broke eye contact first and I hated myself for it.

"You know, you're right. It was an asshole move. I should have filled you in—"

"You should have had a discussion with me," I interrupted.

"Yes, I should have talked to you first to get your input. I know it's a lame excuse, but it's been weird between us since, you know, and I have this strong sense you want to spend as little time with me as possible. I guess I let that override the right thing. I should have talked to you.

"But I am talking to you now. And I really do want you to lead the recruitment. I trust your judgment implicitly. You know this community, the people, who'll be a fit—"

"Actually, I don't. Aside from the guys in the fire department, I barely interact with anyone. I haven't made any friends here, really. I was too busy taking care of Papa and well, apparently putting all my free time into one day becoming your supposed right hand." I might have sounded more angry than I needed to.

"And," I added, "if you want ten new recruits by next Thursday, I'm going to need to use two weeks of my time in the next week and then I'm going to take a week off." I stared at him and did not allow myself to break eye contact this time. "Deal or what?"

He reached his hand out to me. *Don't touch him, don't touch him, don't touch him.* I reached toward him and let my hand fall inside his. My stomach flip flopped. *Merde.*

The following Thursday, I showed up with ten new recruits. All of them had agreed to making a three-month commitment, which was all we ever asked of a new member. All of them understood that they'd be expected to show up every Thursday from now until the first week of September. And since every new recruit had to agree to First Responder training, they also knew that they'd be giving up three full weekends and about one hundred hours of their own time for studying.

I told them that we responded, in an average week, to one vehicle accident, one fire alarm, usually false, and one medical call that almost always required an ambulance so we were there to stabilize and, if the patient was large, sometimes help move them onto a gurney. Three calls a week on average and they were good with that.

Toss on top the fact that for the first couple of months we'd have small campfires to put out, maybe fires in the highway median from morons who thought nothing of throwing a cigarette butt out their car window, and a motorcycle crash virtually every Monday night at around 7pm since upwards of a hundred guys on crotch rockets road raced from the city to the Squamish Starbucks to try to win a kitty that each racer put five bucks into. Because all men under thirty years old are morons.

In any event, all ten recruits said they'd do their best to make as many of those calls as they could. And I believed them.

I'd asked them all to arrive an hour early so I could get them turn-out gear, which I knew would be hit-and-miss at best. I'd let Nick know we were going to need new pants, jackets and boots for most of the new folks. At over two thousand dollars per volunteer I worried we might not have that in the budget. He said it was all good and told me to use what I could and then let him know what was needed after the recruits had been fitted. I hoped he had a line on a deal because seven of the new members left the fitting with only partial coverage—in one case, just a pair of gloves.

At 6:45, the regular guys started to show up. My new recruits and I were already seated around the meeting table. Nick had been in his office with the door closed and I didn't see a reason to bother him. He'd meet them soon enough. The guys sat down, nodded at me, some asked "how's it going," others chatted with each other about the Formula One race that had taken place in Montreal last weekend. Nobody asked who the strangers at the table were. Not unusual. When we had guest speakers from the utility company or ambulance services, they ignored them too, until they were introduced.

At two minutes to seven, the room was packed and Nick opened his office door. He looked at the full table and smiled at me. Then he took a closer look, taking a full second to stop and smile at every person at the table. But his smile looked less like delight and more like confusion. His head was tilted a bit towards his right shoulder, and I could see the questions forming in his head, which he finally shook, not like a wet dog, more subtle, like to clear a bad thought.

"Glad to see everyone here tonight," he said. "I can't help but notice a whole bunch of faces I don't recognize. Sophie," he directed his furrowed brow at me, "what can you tell us about all of these new faces?"

I stood up and walked to the seat beside him at the front of the room, but remained standing.

"In case any of you suffered a stroke last week, you know that we lost one third of our volunteers. Chief asked me to recruit ten new members who were up to the challenge of being Lily Valley Fire and Rescue firefighters. These ten ladies have enthusiastically accepted the challenge. I'll let them introduce themselves."

27

NICK

What the actual fuck?

I did *not* see that coming. Sophie asked each new member to stand and tell everyone their name, say a sentence or two about their background and share why they were interested in being firefighters. One thing was clear, Sophie no longer held the title of 'smallest firefighter I'd ever seen.' But she'd earned a new one, one I shouldn't have been surprised about, 'biggest balls on a woman.'

Part of me wanted to strangle her and the other part wanted to hug the shit out of her while we laughed our asses off, preferably naked, but I knew that wouldn't be happening again.

I had to hand it to her, she clearly recruited for talent and keen interest. Every one of these women had a valuable skill to contribute—one was a traffic flagger, two were nurses, one was a mechanic, one had been a climbing guide and knew ropes better than I ever would. Their reasons for joining were almost all the same: they wanted to be ready in case of an emergency with loved ones and were happy to contribute to the community to get access to that training. Damn. Sophie had done well.

Roberts didn't let us down and was the first to offer a personalized welcome.

"All right, ladies! That's a good joke. Now be good girls and head up to the kitchen." He turned and looked directly at me, "The fridge smells like a yak shat in it. It needs to be cleaned out. Run along while the firemen do their job and you do whatever the fuck it is that you do in the Ladies Auxiliary."

I let him finish since I thought it only fair that the new recruits got to know who they'd be dealing with. I was about to tell him to stand down when young Mason stood up, proud as punch and fuming mad.

"Roberts, you're an asshole," he pointed at one of the the new members, "That's my mom and she's gonna be a way better firefighter than you are."

Roberts was non-plussed, "Well I hope your mommy has invisible muscles because when you get stuck in a burning building she's going to need them to pull your ass out, kid."

Sophie looked at me with raised eyebrows which I interpreted to mean she wanted to address this. I gave her a nod.

"You raise a really valuable point, Roberts—"

"Right? I know. Chief," he said making eye contact with me and pointing at Sophie, "you're insane to—"

Sophie cut him off and continued. "As Roberts was saying, it's pretty unlikely that most of our new recruits, or myself or Lynne for that matter, could *ever* carry a two hundred pound member out of a building. Hell, I'd be hard pressed to drag any of your asses more than a few yards. And the reality is, it doesn't matter—"

"What are you saying, Beaulieu, you'd let us burn?" Roberts barked.

"If you were at the meeting back in January or February when Chief Rollit explained the new standards for volunteer departments, Roberts, you'd know that we are not allowed to do interior attacks anymore. When the day comes that we have a structure fire, we'll all be standing on the outside, shooting water in."

"Just burned yourself, Roberts!" Mason said with snark made even more pointed by the fact that he was still a high school kid and his voice cracked when he said it.

A number of guys chuckled and repeated, "buuurned."

Roberts looked around the table, his face red. Of course, Sophie was right. Members needed less strength than they did stamina and judging by the apparent fitness levels of these new recruits, stamina wouldn't be a problem for most of them.

"This place has gone to shit. I'm out of here." Roberts pushed his chair back so hard it fell over and when he peeled out of the parking lot he left no mistake that he thought he had a big cock.

"Brilliant!" Sophie said, "I had one more person I wanted to bring on board. She's on stand-by."

"Anyone else have a problem with giving our new members a warm welcome? If you do, you know where the door is. Great job, Deputy Beaulieu. Welcome new members. It's going to take me a little while to get to know your names, so bear with me. I apologize if I get them wrong a few times.

"Old members, you've been assigned into three teams for training tonight. Check the board to see who your Captain is."

The officers stood and the rest of the guys followed. I was left with our new members and Sophie.

"So, we need to order gear," she said.

"I gathered as much," I said with a smile. "What size jacket and pants do you wear, Soph?"

"Small," she said.

"And have we got enough variety in sizes upstairs for you to figure out what sizes I'll need to order for everyone?"

Sophie pushed a sheet of paper over to me, "Already done, Chief."

I don't know if it was the way she said 'Chief' or the v-neck t-shirt that gave me a brief glimpse of her bra when she leaned over, or the fact that she was so damned cocky and smart, but I was starting to feel not very professional and if I didn't step into my office soon, eleven women would see my thoughts through my sweats when I stood up.

"I'm going to print some copies of a basic knowledge test, just to get a sense what you already know. Be back in five," I stood and quickly turned my back to the room, went to my office and closed the door.

Of course, ten seconds later there was one knock as the door opened and Sophie walked in to find me with my mouth open and one hand covering my semi. If she noticed, she was polite enough not to say anything. She closed the door behind her.

"You're not mad?" she said.

"Were you expecting I'd be mad?"

She shrugged her shoulders.

"Did you recruit these members to make me mad?" I asked.

"No! I recruited them because I think they can do what's needed to move our department forward."

"Then why would I be mad? Since you're here, bottom drawer in the filing cabinet. A folder called 'Knowledge Assessment.' There should be twelve copies plus an answer key."

Sophie squatted in front of the cabinet, her ass facing me. Jesus H Christ, what was she doing wearing running shorts to practice? I was going to have to implement a dress code just for her. I pushed my chair as far under the desk as I could before she stood with the folder in her hand.

"Give them thirty minutes then have them swap assessments to mark each other's papers. Clear?"

"Got it. You okay? You seem... agitated. You're sure you're not mad?"

"Close the door when you leave. I've got paperwork to do."

As soon as she left I locked the door and found a paper towel. That was the only paperwork I'd be able to do for the next several minutes.

28

SOPHIE

I t was moving day. Not that that meant much at this point since the house had been emptied of all furniture except what was in my bedroom. Being the generous souls they were, my siblings didn't instruct the movers to take my food. Generous or it had been so long since they'd watched *The Grinch Who Stole Christmas* that they forgot to take the last crumb that was so small it wasn't even fit for a mouse.

I'd arranged with Murray to borrow his pick-up truck and got help from a few of the guys in the department to load my bedroom furniture and take it to the thrift store in town. It was old but in good enough shape to find new homes. The things I wanted to keep I packed in moving boxes and took down to the firehall. Nick had said I could store them on the shelving that used to hold all the boxes of outdated gear.

Murray insisted that I stay at his place and make the guest room my own. I'd offered to pay rent but he refused, saying my company would be payment enough. We agreed that I'd cook dinner for us every night in exchange for the room.

Per my eviction notice, I gave my house keys to a real

estate agent at noon. She was pounding a For Sale sign into the front yard before she had the keys in her hand. I made note of her name and swore that if I ever needed an agent, she would not be the one I called.

~

Living with Murray was nice. He was respectful of my space and I was of his. We both knew it was a temporary arrangement, so I didn't make any effort to make my bedroom feel like home. It was just the space I slept in and where I spent time trying to figure out what my next steps would be. At Denise's advice, I'd invested most of the money Papa left me in a low-risk, interest-bearing savings account. The money was locked in for twelve months which was fine with me since I had nowhere smart to spend it. On bad days I felt like my best life choice would be to take the whole $240,000 and just travel the world until money ran out and then live wherever that happened to be.

Murray convinced me to give myself at least three months to let the dust and my emotions settle. Plus, he'd rightly pointed out, if my case against my siblings had to go in front of a judge, I might have to appear and coming home for that would be a nuisance if I was off gallivanting in some far corner of the world.

Dinnertime was my favorite time of day since chatting with Murray was a lot like chatting with Papa. They'd known each other for forty years but had never become friends since they ran in very different circles. Papa's circle being that of the church, and Murray's that of groups he said he didn't like to talk about anymore.

"Never doubt that people can change, Sophie. And that a person can both be willing to risk his life to save another and risk his freedom to take a life."

It was cryptic but clear that he didn't want to elaborate.

And I'd heard the rumors that he'd been part of a gang that had a reputation for engaging in the normal things that gangs did. I'd only gotten to know him since coming home and through the fire department so all I knew of Murray was that he had a heart of gold and would risk his life to protect mine or any of the other members, if push came to shove.

We'd only had one argument in the weeks I'd been living with him. He'd invited Nick over for dinner without telling me. It was hard enough to see him at the firehall but knowing I could keep him contained to my life as a volunteer made keeping my feelings for him separate from my real life a little easier. I couldn't understand why he'd agreed to come when he knew I'd be here. I thought it was incredibly insensitive of him, given I was such a bad influence on his future.

I plated two dinners and then excused myself and went upstairs.

Five minutes later Murray bellowed, "Our food is getting cold. Get your ass back down here."

I bellowed back, "I'm not coming down. You eat."

"Not eating without you."

"Then you'll be hungry tonight."

"Move your ass, Beaulieu," he yelled, no humor in his tone.

I obeyed, plated my meal and sat with them but didn't engage more than with single words when one of them addressed me directly. They seemed to make a game of it, talking about me like I wasn't there and asking me if they'd gotten some story they'd just made up about me, right. It wasn't as funny as they seemed to think it was. *Connards.*

After I'd cleaned up and Nick had left, Murray called me to the living room and tore a strip off me. He said if I was ever that rude to one of his guests again, I'd have to find a new place to live. I said if he ever invited Nick to dinner again, I'd leave willingly.

In the end, it didn't come to that. I was able to move out on good terms with Murray.

~

Linda, the post mistress, called to tell me that my parent's house had been sold.

"That's nice," I said, feeling quite un-nice about the news. "Do you know anything about the family that bought it?"

"I do, actually. I've been working with the buyer for the last week, helping him figure out zoning rules with the district."

My heart sunk, "They're tearing it down?"

"Oh no. Quite the opposite," she said. "He's going to turn it into a rental property. He needed to make sure he could do that without actually living in the house himself since Airbnb's aren't allowed. He's planning to renovate the upstairs and the attic so there are five bedrooms on the second floor, each with its own sink and toilet. The full bathroom will be re-plumbed so it has three shower stalls. Weird, huh?"

"Seriously. Well, thanks for the news," I said, not feeling at all thankful for the news.

"That's not why I called. The buyer was looking for a property manager. Someone to live in the house and make sure the tenants weren't behaving like animals. That's what the district requires: one permanent resident to act on behalf of the property owner."

My blood was boiling. This was my business plan.

"Your mom and dad's room will be renovated with its own full bathroom. They'll even pay you to live there," Linda's tone made it clear she thought this was a plum deal that I should be excited about.

I thanked her and asked her to put the details in my mailbox since I couldn't talk right now. I was too busy keeping myself from screaming, which I did as soon as I hung up.

Murray was up the stairs and in my room in under five seconds.

"Sophie! What happened? Are you hurt?"

"Someone bought my parents' house and are turning it into a rental, just like I'd planned to do."

"It got approval then? Good," he said.

"You knew about this? How could you?"

"How could I what? Know about it? I hear things. Lots of people knew. Dylan Rhodes, Nick's brother, is representing the owner and he's been talking to lots of people, making sure the community was onside before he put an offer on the house."

"He stole my business plan!"

"I don't think so, Soph. The plan isn't to rent it to international students. It's to rent it to temporary construction workers."

"What do you mean?"

"With all the building going on in town, construction companies are desperate for more guys than we have living here. And with no rental units, they're screwed. So the District has been changing bylaws faster than they raise taxes to encourage homeowners to put suites in their places. Your folks' house is perfect. It's more like a dorm but it'll get five guys here fast."

I sat with that for a minute. My anger settling.

"I'm going for a walk. Come on Max," I said stepping by Murray. Once I was in the woods and away from civilization, I called Dylan.

"What the fuck, Dylan?" I said without a hello.

"Hey, Sophie. You heard about the sale, I guess."

"Yeah, I heard. Were you planning on telling me?"

"No, it's not my news to share."

"What do you mean, not your news? You bought it, didn't you?"

"Not me. I don't have that kind of money."

"So who bought it, then?"

"It's a numbered company."

"Sure," I said, not believing a word of it. "Dylan, did Nick buy my house? Seems kind of suspicious that a) you're involved in the sale and b) they're using my business plan which only you, the bank manager and Murray knew about."

"I am one hundred percent sure Nick did not buy the house. The reason I know about the sale is that the buyer was referred to me, I assume by someone in Lily Valley. Like I said, I was paid by a numbered company. And, as for your business plan, come on Sophie. Your bank manager approved that plan with virtually no research since it's so obvious. The town is desperate for housing and even more desperate to attract guys to build that housing."

"Do you know how much the buyer paid?" I asked, dreading the answer.

"It's a public record. They paid $810,000 cash, no inspection, with immediate occupancy. Sorry. That must bite."

I leaned against a tree feeling sad and mad and broken but mostly, very much alone.

"Hey Sophie, on the upside, this morning a judge put a stay on dispersing the assets of your mom and dad's estate. That means you stand a solid chance to get your share."

I didn't care at all about the money. I'd have much rather had even one sister or brother who loved me as much as Nick and Dylan loved each other. "I hope we win so you get your five minutes of fame," I said.

"I hope we win so entitled asshats think twice before screwing family."

"Thanks, Dylan. Sorry I yelled at you."

"It's all good, Sophie. I've been yelled at by much more fierce clients than you."

I hung up and directed all my emotions into powering my legs. Max and I ran deep into the forest and along one of my favorite trails. It ran parallel to a glacier-fed creek. Max liked to splash around in it and on hot days like today, I enjoyed laying on one of the flat rocks that sat above the water level. When I positioned myself just right, the sound of the water was so loud a fire truck could drive by with sirens blaring and I'd not have heard it. I could gaze up the river and imagine I was in the middle of nowhere. Just me, Max and the universe.

It was a twenty-minute run and by the time I reached my spot, I was soaking wet from sweat. The sun was high and hot and felt great on my skin, so I took off my top and sports bra and laid them beside me to dry off. In all the runs I'd done since moving home, only once had anyone ever come up this trail so I closed my eyes and let myself relax.

I lay there for long enough that my body dried, my heart rate slowed to normal, and my anger dissipated.

I thought about my family—the people who grew up in the same house I did—and grieved for the little girl who always knew she didn't belong. I grieved for the twelve-year-old who didn't want to leave. And I grieved for my twenty-four-year-old self, feeling like I'd never know what it felt like to be so loved that someone would give up their life to be with me.

I felt in my pocket for the dime I'd found on the trail. Once it was squeezed in my palm, I heard Papa's voice in my head.

"Don't be silly, Sophie. You know exactly how that feels. You gave up your life to take care of me and I'd have done the same for you. I tried. God knows, I did what I could. And you knew that I loved you to pieces."

Tears rolled down my cheeks. Max came out of the water

and shook right beside me, covering me in icy cold drops. Startled, I sat up and came face-to-face with Nick.

"What are you doing here?" I yelled.

"I was going to do exactly what you're doing but you're on my rock," he said smiling.

"It's my rock. Go find your own," I said crossing my arms in front of my naked breasts.

"It's big enough for two," he countered.

"My rock!"

"Sorry. Hard to understand you over the water. It sounded like you just said, "My cock!" Then he pointed at himself. "Do you mean this one? Because technically it is mine but I'm willing to share it with you if you'll share that rock with me."

"Oh my god!" I wiped my face dry, hoping the water Max covered me in camouflaged the tears. "How long have you been standing there?"

"Not long. If you'd stayed asleep another three minutes, I'd have had more cock to share with you. It was growing."

"You're impossible. You're so arrogant." I kept one arm across my chest and reached for my bra and tank top with the other then turned my back to Nick and put them on.

"Thank you," he said taking a step onto the rock with me.

"Hey, what are you doing?"

"You moved your shirt to make room for me. But now we have another small problem. No room for my shirt." He pulled his tee over his head, looked around, shrugged his shoulders, then threw it into the creek where it slowly moved down the current.

I couldn't help but laugh. "You're such a goof."

Nick got serious sounding, "You okay? You looked kind of sad. I was going to keep running but when I saw," he stopped talking and pointed to his cheek making a sad face, "the First Responder in me thought it best to stay in case you decided to jump in or something."

I gave him my best, 'as if' glare.

"Honestly? I stayed since the horny, once-lover in me wanted to stare at your almost naked body."

I punched him. "You are not allowed to get horny looking at me. You gave up that right months ago."

"The way I remember it, I had that right stolen from me."

"Yeah, well, unlike the other women you date, I have some self-respect." I stood and jumped from the river back to the shore, leaving him alone on my rock.

"My rock," I yelled over the sound of the current. Then I turned and ran home, feeling just as agitated as I had when I started. Damn him.

29

NICK

I left a note for Sophie on my desk,

If you don't hear from me before closing time, call Search and Rescue. Meeting with Decker in Pemberton. He sounds pissed. xo

As my pen scrawled the 'xo' I wasn't sure if I was adding that to piss her off or try to make her understand that I wished she'd give me another chance.

The drive to Decker's office was epic. A sunny day, not too much traffic and no cops. I might have gone just a few miles over the speed limit.

Like the last time I'd been up to meet with Decker, he met me in the parking lot and drove me to his favorite greasy spoon just out of town.

"Why not meet at your office?" I asked this time.

He scowled at me, answering my question with one of his own. "How's it going sharing an office with Beaulieu?"

I wasn't sure what his point was but it felt like a set-up and I wasn't going to take the bait. "Well, it's a small space, really too small for two people. But you know, we manage."

He grunted. "My ex works in the same office. Some days it feels like she thinks we're still married. Any excuse to meet outside is a blessing."

I nodded, "That's too bad."

I thought about how much I enjoyed sharing a workspace with Sophie and wondered if that would change if we were dating again. Probably, too much of a good thing and all that.

"Business. Nick, I don't know what to tell you other than you're walking on thin ice right now."

"Thin ice?" I asked entirely unclear on what he meant.

"The shake-up in the department. I can't even tell you how many complaints I've had—"

I raised my hand, pointing a finger up, to try to interject but Decker didn't let me.

"And before you tell me that you did what I asked and got rid of the dead weight, that's not where the problem is. Yeah, every one of those guys you fired has called or sent me a note, but you were totally in your right to let them go. They can cry all they want, I don't give a rat's ass."

Decker stared at me as if waiting for me to say something. I waited for him to add more.

"Jesus, West, what were you thinking, replacing eleven guys with eleven women? Are you out of your fucking mind?"

My stomach lurched. This was not at all what I expected. All I could say while my mind spun, trying to figure out how to address this, was, "No, I'm feeling pretty stable."

"When I told you I wanted you to bring the department

into this century, break up the old boys club mentality, that was not an invitation to burn the whole fucking house down and rebuild it. Christ. I'm in an elected position, Nick, and your little drama queen act is going to make it hard for me keep my job."

"Right," I said, "Sorry about that?"

"Sorry? You're sorry? Sorry for making a dumb-ass decision? Sorry for making me look like I made the wrong call when I hired you? Sorry that you're now going to have to have to fire at least eight of those women and find eight more suitable recruits? What are you sorry for Nick? I'd love to know."

I couldn't tell him that what I really meant was that I was sorry I didn't care about whether he kept his job or not. I sure as shit wasn't sorry that Sophie had thought outside the box and shaken things up. Those new recruits were the best thing for the department. And it was an idea I'd have never thought of since no matter how forward thinking I'd thought I was, Sophie made it clear that even those of us with good intentions were still thinking with our dicks, or like dicks.

"I'm sorry you disagree with my leadership approach. Can you pass along the names of the people who've complained so I can follow-up with them directly, and put their minds at ease that they're still going to receive the best fire and rescue service of any volunteer department this side of the Rockies?"

Decker stared at me looking gobsmacked.

"No need since you're going to let eight of those women know that they didn't make it past the probationary period."

"Actually, all eleven recruits are doing exceptionally well and I'd be shocked if a single one of them wasn't ready to respond to emergency calls before their three-month probation is up."

"That's not my problem. Find a reason. Make it happen

or else someone else is going to find they don't make it past their probationary period."

"To be clear here, Mr. Decker, is there a threat in that statement?"

He shook his head and smiled. "Not at all, West. It's a promise."

30

SOPHIE

Nick hadn't been to the office in three days. I didn't get his note until the day after his meeting with the big boss so I called to make sure he hadn't driven into a ditch on his way home.

"Soph," he answered.

"Hey, what's up? Did you catch some kind of bureaucrat flu when you met with Decker?"

"Something like that," he said. His voice was flat.

"Everything okay?

"Had better days. Sorry I didn't call."

I waited for more and I could hear him breathing but nothing else came.

"I was kind of getting worried," I admitted, hoping I didn't sound as worried as I'd actually been.

"I'll be there for practice tonight. Can you do me a favor and send an email to the whole gang. Just let them know that I need everyone on time and to plan to stay for the full two hours. No practice—we're doing some strategic planning and I want all voices and opinions at the table."

"Sounds… ominous."

"You'll let them know?"

"Of course," silence hung between us. "Do you want to come early and have dinner with me and Murray?"

Silence on Nick's end.

"Nick? You still there?"

"I better not. See you at 6:45 at the hall. Gotta go."

"Drive safe," I said but the call disconnected before I finished.

I spent the entire day dreading our meeting, seeing Nick and hearing what was going on. It felt like he was about to walk away from the department. From Lily Valley. From any chance that I'd get to see him. I didn't have the stomach to have dinner with Murray and have to make small talk or answer why I looked 'so goddamned sad,' since he'd notice.

I made a lasagna and as soon as it was out of the oven, headed down to the firehall at 5:30, in case Nick came early. And failing that, I'd decided to log in to the department email to see if there were any hints about what was going on. I didn't normally check the chief's email but Nick had given me access and told me that there was nothing there I couldn't see as the deputy. So I only felt a little bit sneaky.

What I saw made my blood run cold: heated messages between Nick and Decker over the last two days. Heated and seriously confusing. It was clear that Decker was apoplectic about the new recruits and that he wanted virtually all of them fired by yesterday. What wasn't clear was what Nick was going to do about it. What also didn't make sense was that it didn't appear that Decker understood that I was the one who'd recruited them.

Why would Nick take all that heat that should have been directed at me? That didn't make any sense at all. He was clearly putting his job in jeopardy when he could have just pointed the finger at me and had the whole mess cleared up.

I spent an hour reading and rereading the emails. I'd broken into a nervous sweat and felt shaky and anxious. Was he going to fire the new recruits? Was he going to make me resign at the meeting tonight? Or maybe make me find ten more suitable recruits, men, and *then* fire me? I wanted to throw up.

The door alarm beeped three times. I leaned around the chief's desk to have a look at who'd come in. Him. The Chief. Nick was at the office door before I could move to my desk. I got up and sat in my chair so he could sit in his.

"Warmed it up for me. Thanks," he said with a weak smile. He looked at his monitor and nodded but didn't turn around when he spoke, "So you're up to speed. Good."

"Not really. I understand that Decker is enraged but I don't know what it all means to you or me or the department. That part I'm really not up to speed on," I said to his back.

He finally turned around, "That's why I want everyone here tonight. That's what we'll all decide together."

"So you're not firing them? Or," I sucked in a breath, "me?"

"I'm not firing anyone. And I'd never fire you, Sophie. That would be as stupid as cutting off my right hand."

"But I got you into this—"

"You got me into nothing. You did your job. I could have overridden you that night you brought the recruits in, but you did a fucking amazing job. No. I'm not firing you or them. What I'm going to do is let everyone know exactly what's happening and let them decide what they want to do."

"I think I should resign," I said.

"Them. They get to decide. Not you. You don't get an out, Beaulieu. You're stuck in this shit pile with me, hate to say."

I felt all of my worry evaporate right then and there.

Being the tough MoFo deputy that I am, I blinked so hard the tears that had started to pool did not have a chance to slide down my cheek. Nick shook his head but the corners of his mouth tipped up and he grabbed a paper towel from his desk drawer.

"Next time you place an equipment order can you add Kleenex to it, please? Seems to be needed around here."

I sucked in a breath and laughed. "Can I hug you? Would that be okay or too weird?"

He answered by standing up and opening his arms for me. I fell into them and let myself cry. I wasn't sure exactly why I was crying because although it didn't feel like a properly sad cry it also didn't feel like a happy one. Maybe relief, the way I sometimes cried after a stressful emergency call where we'd at least managed to keep a patient alive until they were put into an ambulance. That feeling that things were okay right now, in this moment, but who knew where they'd be in a minute from now.

"I'm glad you came early," Nick said as he rubbed my back.

I just nodded then buried my face into his chest, not caring that I was getting it all wet. He didn't seem to mind either since he didn't make any effort to push me away.

The door beeped letting us know we weren't alone. I pulled back and looked up at him. The only thing I wanted to do was kiss him but as soon as I gave him his freedom he stepped away from me, toward the office door and poked his head out.

"Martin, can you do me a favor and bring down some pitchers of water from the kitchen? And a bunch of paper cups, please?"

"Sure thing, Chief."

Nick turned back to me, "Go splash your face with water. If the other women see that you've been crying it'll probably set them off and I don't think I could handle thirteen of you all bawling in the meeting."

I took a step to the door but he grabbed my hand and pulled me back toward him.

"I need you to trust me tonight," he said, holding my hand longer than needed. Then he raised my hand to his mouth and kissed it.

I managed to make it into the women's bathroom in the truck bay before I totally fell apart. No amount of cold water was going to hide the fact that I'd just spent ten minutes ugly crying.

Nick needed me to trust him. I interpreted that to mean not to argue with him. He could have thrown me under the bus with Decker but he didn't. He also said he needed me like he needs his hands. For a minute that made me happy but as I stood, trying to get my emotional shit together, I realized that he only meant as a deputy since that was all I was to him. He wouldn't have meant it any other way and that almost set me off down fire hose lane again. I waited until five to seven and entered the training room with a big smile and a happy, "Hello, everyone!"

Nick motioned for me to join him at the head of the table where he'd written a bunch of stuff on the white board. I quickly scanned it before sitting down.

Go with the flow, Sophie.

Nick had a pad of paper in front of him. He picked up a pen and wrote, 'BREATHE' on it.

I looked at him and pointed to myself with questioning eyes.

He shook his head and pointed at himself with big eyes, like he was pretending not to faint.

He stood up at seven on the nose and cleared his throat.

31

NICK

"Tonight we're going to do something a little different than normal. There are a few stacks of paper and pens everywhere on the table. Grab one pen and a few pieces of paper each, please."

I turned and winked at Sophie while people got paper and pens. "You, too, Deputy."

I stood and looked down at my note that said 'Breathe,' and took a deep breath. I spread my legs a little wider than normal and clenched my hands behind my back, a Superman power-pose Dylan had showed me he used when he was facing a judge who intimidated him. I'd laughed at the idea, but it felt good.

"I want you to write down a list of what you see when you look around this room. I'm going to time you for thirty seconds and you just write until I say stop. Clear?" Everyone nodded. "Good. Start."

Twenty-four of the thirty members, including Sophie and I, looked around, wrote a word or two, looked up, wrote again… until the time was up.

"Good. Now put your name on the paper and hand it forward to Sophie, please. Next exercise. Grab another piece of paper. In thirty seconds write down the most important qualities you think a volunteer firefighter needs. And go."

Once they were done everyone wrote their name on their paper and passed it forward.

"And last exercise. This time, I want you to start by writing the following at the top of your page, *Chief West was smart to recruit me or keep me, whichever the case may be, as a firefighter because I…* and once you've written that, finish the sentence and then hand your work forward. Please and thank you. And make sure your name is on your paper."

As everyone wrote I watched Sophie who stared at her incomplete sentence until the time was up and then scrawled something quickly.

"So, I don't know if any of you have heard the rumor that the regional district mucky mucks want to fire me because they don't like the make-up of the new membership. Now, they can't actually fire me since I've not broken any bylaws or laws or anything. So if you were hoping to see me packing this week, sorry. I've got eleven more weeks in my probationary contract. But I'd like to stay, as I'd originally planned, for a couple of years.

"Apparently, we have some neighbors who don't think this fire department can do its job any more. Instead of going door-to-door trying to figure out whose knickers are all in knots to try to change their minds, I came up with a different idea. I was going to ask you all permission to spend some of the discretionary funds we've accumulated from the call-out and practice money on a full-page ad in the township newspaper. I called to find out how much that would cost and when I explained who I was and why I wanted to run an ad, the sales manager put me through to the editor-in-chief who decided that we had a good story here.

"In about fifteen minutes, a photographer and a reporter will be showing up to take pictures of you guys and ladies and to interview me. He or she may also want to talk to you and that's entirely your choice. In fact, if you'd rather not have your service acknowledged in the paper, that's fine, as well. I'm going to give these sheets of paper you've written to the reporter who's going to use them as photo cut lines and pull quotes. They're expecting to do a two-page spread.

"Any questions or concerns?" I looked around the room, gave everyone a chance. Nobody said a word.

"I'm going to change into my official chief clothes and I want you all in your turn-out gear looking sharp."

Chairs scraped and everyone but Sophie went through to the truck bay to put on their turn-out gear.

"Smart," she said.

"Wasn't my idea. Can't take credit."

"But you do take the blame for ideas that aren't yours..."

"Do you want to be photographed in your turn-out gear or in your deputy uniform? Choice is yours, whichever you're more comfortable in."

"Since my formal wear is at home, I guess I'll just put on my gear."

"You have time to go home. If you want to wear your official uniform I think it would be amazing to have you and I standing in solidarity with our members. But, only if you don't mind the extra attention. You won't be able to blend in as easily."

"I don't mind at all. I'd be happy to stand beside you. I mean, you're taking the fall for what I did. I feel terrible. I—"

"Sophie. If you'd been chief would you have made the same decision to recruit eleven women?"

She nodded.

"Okay, so there's nothing to feel bad about. It was and is the best thing for this department. I actually don't even believe that Decker's been inundated by letters of concern like he says. But I can guarantee you that he's going to get letters after this story runs. As pissed off as he is right now, he'll be ten times more pissed off next Monday when the paper drops. And that is one hundred percent on my shoulders. I'm walking into this house on fire with my axe swinging. Hell, I'm the one who set this house on fire and I cannot wait to fight it."

"But," she looked pained, "this could ruin your chance of fast-tracking your real chief position. Wouldn't it be easier to just tell Decker it was my idea, do what he says and then you can stay on here and earn your stripes so you can leave on your terms?"

I shook my head. "Would you respect me if I did that?"

She stared so deep into my eyes I felt like she was trying to crawl inside my brain. Her head moved ever so slightly left and right.

"And I wouldn't respect myself," I said. The way she looked at me I just wanted to grab her and tell her I'd throw myself under an actual bus to protect her. "Okay, Beaulieu, if you're going to stand by me as my trusted deputy, I need you to get home and back as fast as you can."

After she left I rifled through the sheets of paper to find the one she'd written. Bingo!

Nick was smart to promote me because as his right hand I can do things he wouldn't dream of.

I laughed out loud and pocketed the paper. If only she knew all of the things I'd dreamt about her right hand doing.

32

SOPHIE

As promised, Linda put the details about the property manager job at my old family house in my mailbox for me. It was a hand-written note with just the bare facts: free rent, pay of $1,000 a month to make sure the house was maintained, and more for every dinner I prepared for the five guys who lived there, which could add an extra $500 a month per guy, which they'd pay me directly. Easy money, I thought. Too easy.

There was a phone number and a name, Gabe, with instructions to text him my answer and any questions.

> This is Sophie from Lily Valley. Got your note from Linda at the post office. What's the catch?

His reply was quick,

GABE

> You'll be living in a house with five 20-something construction workers. All guys. Isn't that catch enough for you?

I mean, what's the downside? You're
offering up to \$3500 a month to move back
to my old home. There must be a catch.

GABE

Have you ever smelled construction boots
after a day of work? Five pairs of those.
Avalanche of a downside.

This guy was funny. He emailed me a contract that outlined all the things I'd have to enforce, like no smoking in the house, no overnight guests, quiet by eleven PM... the catch was that I was being hired to be these guys' mom. They were going to hate me. But for that kind of money, I didn't care. Murray had convinced me that the best use of the money Papa left for me would be to invest it in buying a smaller house in Lily Valley, one that wasn't built for a family of eight but had enough room for me and Max. I had the downpayment ready for when a suitable one came on the market but I still needed an income to pay the mortgage on a small house, and renting out rooms wasn't going to be the business plan. So accepting this job was a start to proving I had the stability to be a home owner.

The plan was to have two guys, a framer and a plumber, move in immediately and do all the renos to add the new ensuite on the third floor in the master bedroom, which would be my room. And once that was done, to turn the original full bath on the second floor into a multi-shower room then to plumb a toilet and sink into the five bedrooms.

Gabe gave them two weeks to get that work done. The third guy in was a tiler. He had the other two assist him and together they were supposed to get the bathrooms completed one week later. It was an insane schedule but they all seemed motivated and worked long days.

During those weeks I still slept at Murray's place since it was too dangerous for Max to be walking around with the nails and lumber and rough tile edges all over the place. But I was at the house to cook dinner every night for the guys. During the day I'd been charged with furnishing all the rooms, which was a lot more fun than I'd expected.

Gabe gave me a company credit card with a total spend limit of twenty-five thousand dollars. My incentive to be thrifty was that I'd get to keep twenty percent of the amount under the limit that I didn't use.

As easy as it would have been to shop in a build-your-own furniture store, I couldn't justify spending money in a store that hired black market loggers to cut down forests to make their cheap furniture.

It was actually Nick who gave me the idea I ended up going with, which was to buy gently used furniture and beds from Whistler hotels since several were renovating during the low season. He even offered to help me since he had connections from all his years as a ski bunny... or whatever a male version of that would be. Though to be fair, he didn't frame it like that. What he said was that he spent much of his misspent youth at Whistler hotels and became friends with people who eventually became managers, so he had access to the stuff they'd be selling before it was all made public.

He also managed to get a free dinner thrown in at a restaurant I'd only ever dreamed about going to, the Araxi Oyster Bar.

I rented the biggest U-Haul available, a 26-foot truck which was supposed to be big enough to move a four-bedroom house. I hoped that we'd be able to get six bedrooms worth of furniture in since we weren't moving personal belongings. To his credit, Nick didn't suggest I was delusional nor did he offer to drive the hour to the resort town. In fact, he was so relaxed with my driving that he fell asleep on the way there. Granted, he'd had to leave his house in the city before five AM to make it to Lily Valley by six so we'd have time to choose and load all the furniture before ten, when the warehouse space would be open to the public.

I didn't understand why he would do that for me and when I asked he just said, "All I did was make a couple calls and set my alarm an hour early. Seriously, it was nothing."

My heart broke a little since in my delusional mind, he'd done something that was evidence that he cared for me even a tiny bit more than as just an easy to get along with co-worker.

Picking the beds was easy: six queen frames, headboards, mattresses and box springs, all exactly the same. Nick's pal, Dustin, threw twelve sets of sheets and six comforters into the back of the truck at no charge.

Then we needed six bedside tables and six dressers which were easy enough to pick since they all looked the same to me. I chose five entirely different bedside lamps just because it was fun. While the guys were dragging all of that furniture to the truck, I looked at dozens of couches and chairs to find enough living room seating for eight people.

With Nick and Dustin packing the truck, they got everything in with just enough space for a dozen pieces of art which I splurged on at the very last minute. I let Nick choose the prints to put in the rentable rooms, but I chose the ones I was going to hang in the living room.

"What about your room?" He asked me as we stood looking at all the pieces we'd chosen.

I just shook my head. "I already have something to hang in my room. Sort of. Well I did, I mean…"

He squinted his eyes and sighed. "There are some really nice forest shots that I think would be perfect in your room."

"If I want to see a forest all I have to do is open my curtains."

"Beach scene?"

"I'm good, thanks," is what I said but I felt my mood

shift. The joy of having fully furnished an entire, six-bedroom house for under ten thousand dollars poofed-up in smoke when I thought about the picture that I really wanted to hang in my room—a photo of my own magic Genie, arrogant sexy firefighter.

But we still had the rest of the day to hang out while we waited for our dinner reservation, so I gave myself a mental slap and smiled my happiest smile,

"So, can I take you out for breakfast?" I asked.

It was only 10:30 and I figured since he'd just lifted several hundred pounds of furniture he might be peckish.

"Absolutely. I know a great little place in the village. Want to leave the truck and walk over? It'll take us twenty minutes."

Hanging out with Nick, talking about everything and nothing, I started to feel happy, truly happy for the first time in eleven weeks. Not that I was counting, except that I couldn't forget the day I got my eviction notice, which sadly coincided with the day I actually evicted Nick. Meh.

We'd been working really well together doing fire department duties, keeping it professional but also fun. I never felt like I had a bad idea even when he disagreed with me. He was a fantastic mentor, a patient trainer with the new recruits and had developed a strong rapport with more community members than I'd ever connected with. He fit well in Lily Valley but he still wasn't living there, choosing instead to commute from the city.

"Have you tried to find a room to rent in Lily Valley?" I asked over breakfast. "The commute must be a pain."

He shook his head, "I don't mind the drive. I actually like it. I do a lot of thinking in that hour. And honestly, Soph, there's not a hope in hell that I'll be staying a day longer than my six-month contract. Decker's made it crystal clear that he won't be extending it. So I'm doing the best job I can in the time I have. In three months you won't have to deal with my sorry ass anymore. I put my money on you being appointed as the new chief."

He smiled. I didn't.

"So, you're not going to fight to stay on? You've got the support of everyone in the department and virtually the whole town. You could fight this. Why won't you fight it? Wouldn't Dylan give you a deal on legal advice?"

Nick put down his fork and clasped his hands together, resting them on the table. I wished I could read his mind. I could tell he was thinking lots but he wasn't saying anything.

"Well? Why won't you fight to stay, Nick? Stay until you get offered a real chief job like you originally planned?"

"For the record, being the chief in Lily Valley is a real chief job. It was arrogant of me to think otherwise before I got here. And in case you hadn't noticed, I'm not a fighter, Sophie. I don't enjoy being in conflict situations. Working with Decker as my boss, if he was forced to keep me on, would be hell. It *is* hell."

"But," I wanted to ask if working with me could make up for having to work with Decker but stopped myself since I didn't want to ruin a good day by hearing him speak the truth out loud. Better to live in a fantasy, even for a day, that Nick and I could be more than just co-workers. That we could be friends. Or more.

"But?" Nick said when I didn't finish my thought out loud.

I looked down at his plate and reached across with my fork. "In my family, putting down your cutlery meant you were done and whatever was left on your plate was up for grabs. I'll have that bacon, thank you." I stabbed it and started to pull it toward my mouth.

"And in my family, if anyone dared touch the food on anyone else's plate they forfeited their dessert to that person.

Too bad for you cause I know a place right here in Whistler to get the best *pain au chocolat* this side of Paris."

After a tussle for the bacon that I let him win, I looked down at the floor and saw a dime. I walked a few tables over and picked it up.

"Did either of you drop this?" I asked the couple at the closest table.

They looked at me like I was crazy, and said, "No."

Nick also looked at me like it was a weird thing to do so I explained.

"When I was in the hospital with Papa, in his last hour or so, a nurse came in to sit with me. We were chatting about the transition of life after someone you love dies. She told me that she's heard lots of stories about the ways that people continue to communicate with their loved ones after they've died."

"You mean like turning lights on and off, moving things?" Nick asked. He looked serious and sympathetic. There was no 'you've got to be kidding' in his tone or his eyes so I kept telling the story.

"I guess that could be a way but the way she was explaining was more subtle. She said that people talked about finding dimes, specifically, and when they did, having a feeling of the person they loved being there."

My eyes glassed over while I talked. They usually did when I was thinking about Papa. Nick handed me a clean napkin and held my hand for a second when he passed it to me.

"That's interesting. Like the dime is for a phone call."

I laughed. "Exactly."

"And you've been finding dimes since your dad died?"

I nodded.

"That's cool. And when you find one, do you, I don't know, do you hear your dad's voice or see a vision of him or…"

"No, but I think about him. And in the moment that I find the dime, I choose to believe that he has something to say to me. So I try to imagine what it would be that he'd be saying."

Nick let me wipe my eyes and blow my nose. I was embarrassed, but not because Nick could see how emotional I was. I didn't want other people in the restaurant to see me cry.

"Sorry," I said giving him a smile. "It's goofy. And it's silly that I still cry about it."

"Sophie, there's nothing goofy or silly or to apologize for. I think it's a great way to keep your dad in your life. So, are you going to tell me what you just imagined him saying to you? I mean, you're sitting here with me so I assume he has something to say about that."

I was mortified. How could I tell him what I imagined Papa had said? I couldn't. But I couldn't lie to him either. I stared at the dime in the palm of my hand, rubbing it with my thumb, desperately trying to conjure Papa's words, his advice, something, anything to not have to tell Nick how I was feeling.

"And?" he asked.

"He really likes you," I whispered loud enough for Nick to hear only if he was really paying attention.

Nick took my hand with the dime in it and held it open in his palm, placing his thumb on the coin.

"I wish I'd had the chance to meet the man who raised this young woman," he said. "Well, done, Sir."

And then he waved to the waitress to bring more napkins.

33

NICK

I couldn't remember having had such a good day off. Despite having to get up before the sun, spend two hours in a vehicle, and lift the contents of an entire household before breakfast, this was a better than good day.

After breakfast, as Sophie and I walked back toward the van, it took everything I had not to grab her hand. I can't even count how many women I'd done this walk with over the last decade, from a restaurant back to a hotel. Easily a hundred—sometimes at night, sometimes the morning after—and I couldn't remember a single time when the woman I'd been walking with was actually having a conversation with me. They were all gawking in shop windows and asking me where certain designer shops were. The real winners would ask me to buy them a gift to remember me by. And sometimes I'd give in and get her a scarf or a pair of gloves with the Whistler logo on it, especially if I'd stayed in her hotel room. Seemed like a fair trade, a thirty dollar memento for a bed in a three hundred dollar a night room.

Before we reached the van, Sophie saw the trail that runs outside of the shopping part of the village, along the creek.

"Feel like some nature?" She asked.

We walked slowly, meandering, enjoying the fresh air for a mile or so when we reached a direction sign, pointing toward the path to the Scandinav Spa.

"I've always wanted to go there. I'd like to come back one day and do that. Have you been?"

"I have," I said. "You know it's silent? Like, you can't talk at all when you're there. People get pretty perturbed at whisperers."

"Yeah, I think I heard that. Was it nice?"

Was it nice? How could I tell her that it was heaven since each of the times I'd been had been with a woman who I'd had nothing to talk to about but enjoyed seeing wet and virtually naked?

"It was okay. I mean, the saunas and hot tubs are great. The food is even pretty good. But it's a crappy place to go on a date, you know? Have you been on the Peak to Peak gondola? Now that's a great place for a date."

She stopped dead in her tracks and stared at me with a pinched mouth. "This is not a date, Mr. Arrogant Calendar Man. Thank you for helping me with the furniture but this, what we're doing now, is just two," she paused, clearly looking for two right word, "friends hanging out and waiting for a free meal."

I smiled inside but forced my face to contort into a look of concern and apology.

"I know. I'm sorry. That came out all wrong. What I meant was… so do you want to go to the spa to kill the next six hours?"

"Yes, actually, I do," she said with her hands on her hips. "But I need to find a bathing suit. Do you think they sell them there?"

"I know they do but they have only one style, it costs almost a hundred bucks and you'd never wear it again."

"Why's that?" she asked with suspicious eyes.

"Imagine what a Catholic nun would think is appropriate

swimwear and now double the fabric. On the upside, the suit they sell is black," I gave her a second to think and then suggested we go to SwimCo where for less money she could buy a more suitable for Sophie suit. I didn't say that in my definition, 'more suitable' meant less suit.

I placed my hands on her shoulders and turned her back toward the village and the bathing suit store.

When I dragged my ass out of bed at four-thirty this morning, I had no idea that I'd be spending an hour bathing suit shopping with Sophie so we could hang out in said suit for the afternoon. I would never have believed my luck was that good.

"You have to model for me," I said as she pulled bikinis from the rack.

"Not a chance," she said not bothering to look up at me.

"But I'm going to see you in it in an hour anyway," I tried to reason.

"You will see me in one suit for very brief flashes when I'm taking off my robe—they have robes at this spa, right?"

I nodded. "Make you a deal, then. Mr. Arrogant Calendar Model will try on any bathing suits you want him to and let you decide which one he buys."

She laughed. "Why are you talking in the third person? You sound like a goof."

"That's not the message you were supposed to take away. You can choose as many bathing suits as you want me to try on and I'll model every one of them for you and let you pick the one that I wear today, *if* you let me see you in your choices. I won't even demand to choose the one you buy. Come on! Have some fun with me."

I could tell she was considering it by the way she was smiling and looking at my chest. I flexed my pecs for her.

"Any suit?"

Oh, shit. She was looking at a rack of Speedos. I was a 'surfer trunks to my knees' kind of guy.

She waggled her eyebrows.

"Any suit," I finally said and Sophie squeaked in delight and ran right over to the offending rack.

"What size are you?" She pulled a man's bikini bottom off its hanger and held it up in position in front of my crotch, but from a distance of at least five feet. "This looks perfect," she said, tossing it to me. "Try it on!"

I looked at the tag. "This is a Small. I'll never get this on."

"Okay. Never mind. I'm going to take these into my change room. I'll see you in about twenty minutes."

"No wait, Sophie," I reached out and took her by the arm. "Fine. I'll try it on."

I wish I'd had my phone out to take a picture of her smile. I hadn't seen her this happy since the day before she kicked me out. I felt a pang of sadness. Why couldn't she see how good we were together? She had fun when she was with me. I had fun when I was with her. Sure, we pushed each other's buttons but in the best possible way. I couldn't understand what I'd done that made her decide she couldn't live with me and why she refused to talk to me about it.

I shook my head of the thought before I started down a track I didn't want to go down. One that would reek of relationship insecurity. No matter how good she might think I looked in this far-too-small suit, it wouldn't be able to override the scent of despair.

34

SOPHIE

Nick and I spent almost two hours modeling bathing suits for each other. I don't think I've ever had that much fun shopping in my life. It took a lot longer than it needed to since we agreed to go suit for suit, I'd model one then he'd model one, back and forth. And we only stopped after he ran out of suit styles to try on otherwise I think he'd have been happy to just keep dropping new bikinis at my door.

"Okay," I said, "you have to leave the store while I buy your bathing suit. I know which one it'll be."

"Wait. No, you can't do that, you need to let me see what it is. And, you're not buying my suit, that's ridiculous." Nick looked horrified and it made me laugh. I'd laughed so many times my glutes felt like I'd run a half-marathon.

"It's not ridiculous at all. Your idea helped save me thousands of dollars today and I'll be getting a twenty percent cut of all that saved money. That's literally three thousand dollars. And you're taking care of dinner. So the least I can do is buy you the bathing suit you might never wear again."

"Well, if you're changing the rules then I get to as well," he argued.

"How?"

"You let me choose and buy your bathing suit."

"But mine costs twice as much as yours. That's not fair. And anyway, no. The suit you said you liked best was that piece of string that would have me arrested for indecency if I wore it outside a shower stall."

"Whoah, Nellie! Why would you think that I'd want anyone else to see you in the suit I liked the best? Not a chance that I'd buy that one for you. Are you kidding? I'm counting on a ride back to Lily Valley with you after dinner —hell, I'm counting on having dinner with you. But if you wore that sexier-than-sex string bikini, there is a one hundred percent chance that some other guy would scoop you up and you'd leave me stranded," I said loud enough that the cashier started to laugh. "Do you really not have any idea how men think?"

"I guess not," I said, feeling like he was making fun of me. "Okay, then. Deal. But I'm buying both passes to the spa then."

He nodded and then shoo'd me out of the store so he could buy my bikini. I sat on a bench and people-watched for the few minutes it took. We were having such a good time, I couldn't wrap my head around what it was that made me so bad for him and his future. But, if this was all he was willing to give me, I'd take it.

"You're up, Buttercup. Please remember that too tight might be funny for a few minutes but urinary tract infections are not. I beg you to let my junk breathe a little.

"Relax, stud. I'm more likely to buy you a 1920s style one-piece for the very same reason you wouldn't get me the string bikini. I might want to have a drink with dinner tonight which would require you driving home. And I can tell by the way women here look at you fully clothed that if you paraded around in a Speedo, I'd be driving home alone. So whatever I buy for you will be hot enough to get you the ogling your ego loves, but not so much you leave *me* stranded. Now out you go. My turn at the till."

I'd decided to buy Nick the suit that looked more like shorts than a bathing suit, flattered the hell out of his ass, showed twice as much thigh as board shorts, and left enough room in the crotch for the imagination. The only thing I hadn't figured out was which color and pattern to choose: a 1950s green gingham or fire engine red. I took both to the cashier to ask her opinion.

I also grabbed the bikini that I loved most for myself. Not that I'd go back on my promise and wear it today, but I loved it and decided that it would be okay to have two new bathing suits.

"Which one of these do you think I should get for the guy I was in here with?"

She looked at the two men's suits and at mine.

"I know I shouldn't ruin the surprise, but that suit you have for yourself is the exact one he bought for you."

My heart did a little jump.

"Would you like to choose another one instead? How about that string bikini? It really did look amazing on you. And you should have seen the muscles in your boyfriend's neck pop when you walked out wearing it. It got his blood pumping!"

"Oh, he's not my boyfriend. We... just work together," I said, feeling like I was apologizing which was weird.

She raised her eyebrows as if she didn't believe me. Or maybe was now going to give me her number to pass on to him. Great.

"Fine. I'll take the damn string bikini, too. And the red trunks for him." I'd decided on the red ones since the bikini he got me would have clashed with the gingham print.

At the spa I paid for both our entrance tickets, robe rentals and flip flops. At the bottom of the stairs, where I had to turn left to the ladies change room and he had to turn right for the men's, we swapped bags.

"See you in five," we said giving each other a thumbs-up.

I was already standing by the first hot tub I'd decided I wanted to sink into when Nick came out. He was walking funny and had an unusual expression on his face.

"Oh no. Did I buy the wrong size?"

He nodded. Looking like he was in pain.

"Nick, I am so sorry. I don't know how. I'm sure I grabbed the large."

He shook his head, biting his top lip. His eyes were squinting. "Look," he said, untying his robe.

My squeal was loud enough to hear at the top of the mountain and then our shared laughter was anything but silent. I fell to the ground, barely able to breathe. Nick had let his robe fall off him entirely and stood with his arms out to his sides, as if holding back a crowd. He said in a loud and authoritative voice, "Stand back. She needs medical attention. I am a first responder."

From the gasps I heard it was clear that several people took in the full view of what was his naked ass under my string bikini which I'd forgotten to take from his bag.

Nick bent over me and sweet Jesus, when I looked past his face and saw that his 'bags' were only barely contained, I thought I'd die. On the upside, I was laughing so hard I'd stopped breathing which meant I was finally silent.

I have to give the staff credit for refunding our money when they threw us out. Honestly, though, I'd be happy to pay $150 to have that exact same experience again. I would never unsee what I'd just seen. And that was the only downside of the joke—that I'd never get to see it again.

35

NICK

When we got back from the best day and best meal ever in Whistler, it was almost midnight so I crashed on the couch in the firehall.

And, because I'm a sucker for punishment who refuses to take 'no' for an answer, I insisted that Sophie let me help her unload the furniture and set up the bedrooms on Sunday morning, even though she insisted she didn't need the help. Turns out, she was right and the three guys she'd lined up to unload the truck and put together the beds were perfectly suited to the job. Eager too. A bit too eager.

These guys were all under twenty-five and as fit as I was. And, even though I'm not an expert, it was pretty obvious that they weren't ugly. I didn't love the idea of them—and two more like them—sharing this house with Sophie. I knew what could happen if they got drunk and handsy. If Sophie didn't like it I knew she'd put up a good fight. What I worried more about was that she might actually like one of these guys. I hated that somehow I wasn't good enough to share the house with her but these strangers were.

I helped Sophie move the dining room table in, which was in pieces, and asked if I could help her put it together.

"Thanks but I'm pretty handy with a screw driver," she said.

"Okay then. So what can I do?"

"Like I said, I think we're good. You've been amazingly helpful already. And yesterday was the most fun I've had in…ever. So thanks for that."

She smiled and turned to the table legs on the floor, picking one up and putting it in position. She reached into her hoodie and pulled out a screw. The way she held the screw driver in her palm gave me a visceral memory.

"Do you have a lock on your bedroom door?" I realized that my voice was breathy, like I'd just been for a run.

She made a face that made it clear she did not.

"You need to have a lock. I mean on the inside of your door so that when you're sleeping, one of these guys doesn't accidentally wander in, thinking it's his room."

She laughed, "That won't happen. I'm on the third floor. They're all downstairs."

"Sophie, when I say 'accidentally,' I mean 'accidentally on purpose.' Put a few beers in these guys and…" I couldn't finish the sentence.

She looked herself up and down and shook her head. "Highly, highly, *highly* doubtful," she said, oblivious to how attractive her lack of worrying about the fact that she'd made no effort to try to be attractive made her.

"Will you humor me? Let me put a lock on your door. Just in case. You don't have to use it but I'll feel better knowing it's there in case one of these construction monkeys comes home wasted."

She shook her head like I was being an idiot.

"No. Thanks for worrying, but really not necessary. I've got this." She turned back to screwing in her table leg. "If you still want to help you could put together a bed."

"Yeah. Sounds good," I said turning to leave. "Do you

think the bedding needs to be washed or would you put it on the beds as is?"

"I'd say it's clean. You can put it on. Thanks! You're the best."

Upstairs I found each of the guys in what I assume was the room they'd chosen as their own, putting their beds together and moving dressers into place.

I stopped in the first room and stood against the door frame, "Hey," I said, tilting my chin up in a subtle act of dominance.

"Hey," the guy said, barely looking up.

"What's your name again?"

"Aiden."

"Right. You have a girlfriend, Aiden?"

He looked up and gave me a quizzical look.

"Uh, no but I'm not gay, dude, if that's what you're getting at," he said.

And Sophie thinks I'm arrogant. This guy was too much. I walked into his room, right up into his face. Both so I could speak quietly to him but also to show him how much bigger I was.

"Sophie is off-limits. Got it? She's going through shit right now and doesn't need one of her tenants hitting on her. Clear?"

"What the fuck, dude? She's not my type."

"Hmm," I said. Unfortunately that's what I would have thought too, before I'd spent a few hours getting to know her. She's exactly the type a smart man wants. "Well, if she suddenly becomes your type, she's still off limits. Am I being clear, Aiden?"

Aiden stood up and faced me square on. He wasn't afraid of confrontation. I expanded my chest. He expanded his. We held eye contact.

"Yeah, dude. She's yours. I got it. Not a problem," then he rolled his eyes and went back to work.

"When you're done with your room, do one more. Make the beds, too. Sophie's not your mom and that's not her job."

"Whatever," he said.

I had similar encounters with the other two and felt a little better when I went to Sophie's room and started to put together her bed for her. I had two legs on before she came up.

"Hey! What are you doing? You didn't have to do that," she said, clearly happy that I was.

"Those guys didn't want my help and since you didn't need me on the table… this was what was left to do. Where do you think you're going to put it? This is a nice room. Big. Lots of options. How about…" I stood up and walked behind her, put my hands on her shoulders and turned her to face her door, "against the door so those guys downstairs can't get in?"

She laughed but when she turned to face me her eyes didn't look happy. "Nick, nobody is going to be breaking down my door to get in. Seriously. I lived in a co-ed residence for three years and I was still a vir—" she stopped talking and blushed. "Well, you know. So you should also know that I'll be just fine. So stop worrying, okay, Dad?"

It took every fiber of my being to not grab her in a hug and tell her how wrong she was. Tell her how much I missed her and how I wouldn't stop worrying since if I was sleeping in one of those rooms downstairs I'd be up here and into her bed the first chance I got. I knelt on the floor and started to connect another corner of the bed frame.

I decided I'd talk to Murray and have him tell her to put a lock on her door. She'd listen to him even if she didn't want to. Even if she didn't use it I'd be happy to know it was there. Sophie hummed a bouncy 80s song to herself as she connected the fourth corner. It was a song I'd hated but she made it sound happy, not sappy and I found myself quietly humming along.

She looked up and smiled at me but her eyes still didn't match the curve of her lips or the happiness in the song. She was breaking my heart.

"What's up? You look sad."

Her expression totally changed, like she'd just done one of those sad clown/happy clown face swipes.

"Nope. That's just my resting thinking face."

"So… what were you thinking about?" I wanted her to say, 'you.' I wanted her to say, 'us.' I wanted her to say that she'd made a terrible mistake when she asked me to move out.

"My mom and dad. Just wondering how they'd feel about their family home being used as a fancy flop house for temporary workers with me as their house mom."

"And what do you think they'd say?"

"I think Mom would be appalled. She'd probably find a way to blame me for losing the house in the first place." Sophie shrugged her shoulders and rolled her eyes. "Papa, however, would say something cliché but supportive like, 'Way to turn lemons into lemonade, kiddo.'"

"Do you think your dad would be proud of you if he could see you now?"

She bit her bottom lip and her eyes got glassy. "I know he would be. I didn't know that when he was alive, but I do now." She took a deep breath. "Did Dylan tell you anything about my financial situation or the lawsuit?"

"Not a word. I told you, he totally keeps business and family separate. Not a gossipy bone in his body."

"Not one single bone?"

"Even as a kid he was always the best secret keeper of anyone I've ever met."

"Do you think he thinks I'm a fuck-up?"

"What?! No. Why would you think that? That's ridiculous."

She looked at her feet, "Just something I overheard him say about me. Never mind."

What the fuck did she overhear him say about her? I was going to kill Dylan.

Sophie inhaled deeply. I was probably scowling hard when she looked up since she stopped her smile mid-way. "You probably need to get back to the city. I really, really appreciate all your help this weekend. I feel bad that you used your days off and had to come back here when you could have been, you know, living your city life."

"Nothing to get back to. And our work here is not done. Let's finish getting your room set-up."

She looked at her phone. "I actually have to get the truck returned otherwise they'll charge me for another half-day, so I'll finish this up later."

"Okay. I'll take my car and give you a lift back home after, then."

She literally looked like she was going to cry. "Why are you being so nice?"

What the hell could I say to that?

"Because you're my friend and I like spending time with you." And that was the second lie that I'd told Sophie. At least by her definition, since it was only a half-truth. The other half of the truth was killing me not to tell her, but I knew if I did she'd push me even farther away: I was falling in love for the first time in my life.

36

SOPHIE

The last two construction workers moved in the day after we got the bedrooms furnished. Gabe hadn't been joking when he asked if I'd ever smelled construction boots. And five pairs of them? The first rule I had to enforce was a 'no boots in the house' policy. I bought a bench to put on the landing outside the front door so the guys could sit down to take off and leave their toxic materials outside. And, I bought a giant plastic bin with a cover for the guys to throw them into. It wasn't pretty and Aiden, in particular, was mightily offended that I'd refused to allow the stench of death into the house. But they adjusted.

Cooking for these guys was also not quite what I expected. When I'd agreed to provide seven dinners a week for $500 a month I'd had no idea how much construction workers ate and what they'd demand as meals. I was spending almost two thousand dollars a month on meat and carbs. Fortunately, they didn't seem to care if they ate the same meals over and over, and since I was working weekends now, training new first responders at the fire department, they were left to heat frozen lasagna on

Saturday night and reheat leftovers from the week on Sunday.

I'd started spending more time at the fire department, even when I didn't need to be there, because, even though Nick was driving me crazy, it felt more like home than my old family house did filled with hotel furniture and strange men.

Since our weekend in Whistler, Nick had started sleeping at the hall again, in his loft bedroom above the truck bay. Not every night, but many, if not most. He said it was since we'd been having so many evening calls and were still short on trained volunteers to attend. And it was true that having Nick on-call was as good as having three of our regular members.

I'd invited him for dinner with the guys and me a few times once I realized he wasn't going back to the city. I wasn't surprised that he always said yes since the food in the fridge at the firehall was nothing that he was making healthy meals with, which meant he either wasn't eating dinner or was eating at one of the crappy restaurants in the next town over.

Sharing the table with the five guys meant that Nick and I didn't actually talk about anything meaningful or interesting. The only contribution he made to dinners was showing the guys who were paying rent that he was the alpha male at the table. It would have been flattering if there'd been any legitimate reason for him to act like he had some stake in my life.

In fact, since our day in Whistler, the day those construction workers and I started living together, things had gotten strange between us. Like we'd stepped over a line that shouldn't have been crossed by having had so much fun together.

Oh my god, he was driving me crazy, like I was his property to protect. He was worse than Papa had ever been.

Maybe this was how older brothers treated their little sisters in a normal family. And if that was the case, thank god my brothers took no interest in my life since just three weeks of this was enough to make me want to pack my bags and leave town. Or worse, let one of the guys into my room just to prove to Nick that I was my own person who could do whatever I wanted with my body in my bed. It's not like who I slept with was going to have a negative impact on his career, which wasn't going to be in Lily Valley for much longer anyway.

When he wasn't hovering and giving me advice about how to live in my house, I'd think about our day in Whistler and wish I could conjure and bottle that version of Nick.

I loved the Nick who made me laugh and how *that* Nick made me feel. For a minute there I thought I loved him, but this over-protective side was about as unlovable as a rabid doberman.

The way he was acting made me think of how my mom would hoard nice chocolates when I was a kid. She'd get a box of hedgehogs, which I loved, and let me have one for a special occasion. I don't know where she'd get them, but it was always a big box, the biggest one, big enough for each of us to have at least two.

But she'd allow one per person and then put them away. Hidden. By the time she'd take them out for the next occasion that was worthy of a nice treat, the chocolate would have gotten white and the filling would be stale. They wouldn't be delicious anymore.

I felt like Nick had made me into that box of chocolate and wanted to hide me away so nobody could enjoy me until he was ready to bring me out. Like after he'd gotten his promotion to a real chief position? It was so obvious that he liked me, but he was making zero attempt to either show me in a nice way or to let me show him how much I wanted to be more than just his deputy.

When we were both at the office, sometimes I'd accidentally on purpose take advantage of the too small space and sit sideways in my chair so that my leg would touch his. And what would he do? He'd move to give me more room. Or he'd find a reason to get up and leave the office. I'd quickly figured out that if I wanted a cup of coffee but didn't feel like going upstairs to make one, all I had to do was bump his leg three times and he'd offer to get me one.

He was a lame genie who granted stupid wishes. He was a stupid, jock-like *connard* who didn't speak body language. Sadly, body language was the only way I felt comfortable trying to tell him that I thought we could have something good together if he'd just give it a chance. But he'd been clear that his only reason for being in Lily Valley was to get the experience he needed to leave our one horse town. And I'd been equally clear that this was my home and I'd do almost anything to stay here—including cook for and clean-up after a house full of man-children.

So I flirted, in part since I loved touching him, in part to torture myself with his rejection and in part to torture *him* for being such a Class A jerk, treating me like a little girl who needed his protection from the big bad boys of the world.

Until meeting Nick, I'd never understood the relationship status, 'It's complicated.' Now I felt like the poster child for that tagline.

Some days, he smelled so good that I found myself almost hyperventilating because I was breathing so deeply to take in as much of him as I could. I don't know if it was all that extra oxygen that increased my blood flow, but on those days I'd get so horny I'd have to leave the office. Fortunately, the women's bathroom had the worst ventilation fan ever. It sounded like a broken refrigerator and was loud enough to cover the hum of my pocket-sized bullet vibrator. When I was in that state, all I needed was thirty seconds before my body gave in to what my mind fantasized, Nick between my legs bringing me to breathless, though never silent, waves of pleasure. Oddly, never guilty.

I could get back to the office so quickly, Nick wouldn't have ever expected I'd done anything other than pee and wash my hands to health code standards. And on the days he'd offer to make coffee, sometimes I'd be really brave—or maybe stupid—and use my bullet in the office. He always had a fire department hoodie hung over the back of his chair and I'd bury my face in it, breathing in his scent, while bringing myself to the edge, then easing off, over and over until the pleasure was verging on pain.

Usually I timed it perfectly so I was done a minute or so before I heard his footfalls on the stairs from the kitchen and rec room. But twice I was still climaxing when I heard the door at the top of the stairs open. In those moments I decided that if he saw me, he saw me, because there was no way I was going to stop that orgasm mid-shudder.

Today was one of those days. When he walked into the office, his hoody was still on my lap, the vibrator still in my pants but turned off. My head was back and I was breathing hard.

He placed my coffee down on my desk and we made eye contact.

"No porn in the office," he said with a dark tone.

"I wasn't," I said as normally as I could which, I realized was not my normal voice at all.

"Relax, I was joking," he said much more playfully. "Some people talk to counsellors to relieve the stress of the job. Others find different ways to cope. Each to his or her own."

He sat down and started typing. I watched him from behind, the tilt of his head, a roll of his shoulders, his back expanding and retracting as he breathed. After a minute he turned and faced me.

"You're staring. What's wrong?"

"Nothing. You're the best boss I ever had. Just wanted you to know that. I'm really glad you got the chief job."

"Oh yeah? How many bosses have you had?"

"Can I count university teachers? Technically they were like bosses since I was on scholarship so I was being paid to be in university."

"No, you can't count teachers," he said squinting, "Don't be ridiculous."

"Okay," I had to really think, "Well, there was Mrs. Cook. You're a way better boss than she was."

"What did you do for Mrs. Cook?" he asked, turning his chair and looking very interested.

"Well, I made sure her bratty seven-year-old son didn't burn down the house. And even though I was successful in that job, Mrs. Cook thought I should have also kept her devil spawn from cutting a hole in the drapes." I shrugged my shoulders. "We were playing hide and seek. How was I supposed to know he'd hidden scissors behind the curtains before I got there?"

"So, Mrs. Cook was your boss when you were… how old?"

"Eleven," I said proudly. "You are the best boss I've had since I was eleven years old. That is something to be seriously proud of, Chief West."

"And, the hottest, I suspect," he said keeping a straight face.

"And the most arrogant," I added.

"That goes with being the hottest."

I tried to give him a gentle punch on his thigh, but he grabbed my wrist before I made contact.

"Careful, or I'll write you up for aggression towards a superior officer."

"If you're going to write me up then I'd make it worth

the paperwork," I said, visions of tying the chief to my bed posts, dancing in my head.

"That's a wicked smile, Deputy. Do I want to know what you're thinking?"

"Probably not," I said, "It involves advanced rope skills."

"Does it also involve your bedroom?" he asked.

"That, Sir, is none of your business."

He squinted at me and suddenly our fun repartee was over and Nick was back to being the worst older brother ever.

"Sophie, I swear to god, you have to keep the line between you and those construction workers clear. Don't be flirting with them the way you flirt with me. They won't understand that this is just a game to you. And as soon as one of them thinks you're serious, you will be seriously fucked. Like fucked, fucked, whether you want it or not."

I hated him in that moment. I wasn't a flirt with the guys in the house. I'd told him that a hundred times. And it's not like I was playing a game with Nick. He was the one who was holding me at arm's length.

"I've done my work," I said abruptly and stood to leave. Of course, I'd forgotten about the little bullet vibrator that was in my underwear which wasn't tight enough to hold the weight of the double-A battery from succumbing to gravity. It fell out the bottom of my jogging shorts and hit the ground with a loud clunk, breaking apart at the battery seam.

We both looked down and then at each other. I was too mad and embarrassed to even try to explain. I prayed he wouldn't know what it was but the fact that he didn't ask as I scooped it up and put it in my pocket, told me that he did.

37

NICK

I wanted to lock Sophie in a room but I couldn't decide if I wanted to be in there with her or not. Ever since that day in Whistler she'd been flirting with me just the way those downtown chicks do, accidentally-obviously-on-purpose touching my leg with hers, coming into the office smelling like fresh air and cinnamon, wearing jogging shorts and tank tops so that it was impossible not to undress the rest of her and imagine any one of the three dozen bikinis I watched her put on.

It was driving me crazy since I hated that behavior in the women who lived to Instagram their conquests, but I loved it when Sophie touched me. I loved the smell of her when she jogged to the office, and the fact that even with no effort to try to look pretty she was the most gorgeous woman I'd ever met. And I hated her for it since I didn't stand a chance against that house full of testosterone she was living with.

Hell, I knew what happened to men when she walked into a room in her 'I'm not leaving the house' clothes. There was no way they weren't thinking about how to get her into bed. Those three weeks I'd lived with her were the best damned three weeks of my life.

I knew she wasn't mine to protect, but I saw how hurt she was when I fucked things up between us. I still don't know what I did but then I never did in any of the houses I lived in. It was some fatal flaw I'd had to accept years ago, that I'm not 'the living with' kind.

But that didn't mean that I was 'the fucking with' kind either, and the way Sophie was teasing me was really getting on my nerves. Either she wanted me or she didn't. I was sick of this game where everything was on her terms.

I'd been busting my ass, doing the best job I could as chief of this department, sleeping in a cot for fuck sake, sharing my room with fire trucks for the last month so that I'd be here for all the evening calls.

But the eyes she'd just given me when she said, "oh, sorry," after tripping and planting her hand on my thigh to keep herself from falling over? Those playful, tempting, come-fuck-me-eyes? Those eyes were breaking my balls. I couldn't stay in the room with her.

"I'm making coffee. Can I bring you one?"

Thank god the coffee maker took fifteen minutes to run its cycle. It was enough time to jerk off and get my head back on straight. I'd sit right there on the couch in the rec room, cock in hand, lean back and remember how she felt, what she smelled like, how she tasted. I knew there was a risk she might come up and catch me, but I almost wanted her to.

I wanted her to see me. See what she was doing to me. In one of my fantasies I grab her and throw her over the pool table, taking her from behind, hard and fast. In another, I don't touch her. I order her, as her chief, to sit down, take off her shirt and watch me bring myself to a mind blowing climax while I stare at her tits.

In my favorite fantasy, my go to when I was more sad about having lost her than mad at how she kicked me out, she'd come into the room and willingly undress for me. She'd lay on the couch beside the one I was sitting on and spread her legs to show me how wet and engorged she was for me. Then she'd touch herself while I stroked myself. And as she arched her back in a clitoral orgasm she'd order me to make love to her, slowly. We'd kiss first and as soon as my fantasy cock touched her fantasy pussy… that was it. Game over.

Today I had it bad for her. I'd be leaving in a less than a week. Decker had agreed that rather than fire me, since I would have taken his ass to court to keep that off my record, he'd allow me to resign at the end of the probationary period. I'd written him a letter stating that I was grateful for having had the opportunity to have worked with the district and the Lily Valley Fire and Rescue and that in the interest of continuing to build community assets, I believed it would be in the best interest of the district to promote Sophie to chief and allow her to assign a deputy of her choice. I said that there were several highly qualified members to take on the role.

He graciously accepted my resignation and our paper trail covered his sexist ass and wouldn't reflect as a black mark on my record. Two happy bureaucrats, except that I couldn't have been less happy.

Once I had the coffee maker filled with grounds and water, I pushed my sadness aside and walked to the couch and lay down on my back with my left arm behind my head and closed my eyes. Nothing to see here, just a guy taking a quick mid-morning nap.

That is, until fantasy Sophie joined me. It was her smile I saw first, then I heard her laugh. I could see her in my mind's eye, collapsed on the ground at the spa wearing the bikini I'd chosen for her, laughing so hard she couldn't breathe. She was joy, energetically, spiritually, emotionally, inside and out. Even when she pissed me off she still had this way about her that sucked me right in. Even when her eyes betrayed a sadness, she had this way of communicating that deep down she was a joyful person and that this moment would pass and she'd be happy soon.

I don't know what it was about Sophie, but she made me feel like I could be joyful, too. And as I pictured her smile and felt her energy and remembered how she moved and tasted under my tongue, my cock grew hard. I didn't bother resisting the urge. I drove my hand down the front of my sweats pulled my cock free.

With my eyes closed I imagined her hand swirling my pre-cum around my head. I imagined her taking me in her mouth as I wrapped my hand around the shaft and slowly stroked, holding myself at that place where just a bit too much pressure or the wrong thought would send me over the edge without apology.

I hung there until I heard the coffeemaker make a particular sound. It was my game to prove to myself that even though I couldn't control the fact that I was masturbating thinking about Sophie that I did have some control. I came as the coffee maker sputtered the last of the water from the tank to the pot.

I felt both full and empty. I lay on the couch for a few minutes, thinking about the fact that I had less than a week to tell Sophie how I really felt.

38

SOPHIE

Nick would be leaving in a few days and everyone knew it. They also knew I'd be given the probationary position of chief and would be looking for a new deputy. Two guys wanted and were perfectly capable of doing the job but the thought of sharing the tiny office with anyone other than Nick gave me anxiety. I'd been debating the best way to make things work—appoint the guy who was willing to work from home? Or give him set hours he could use the office, times when I would plan not to use it?

I called Murray to ask his advice and he invited me to discuss ideas over vodka at his place. I walked over and found Dylan's car in Murray's driveway. I wondered what business Murray had that would need a lawyer. He was widowed and never had kids so it wouldn't have been Last Will and Testament stuff. Lucky guy.

I knocked on the door, waited a beat and then opened it and yelled, "Hello!"

"Hey, Kiddo. Come on in. We're in the kitchen."

Dylan and Murray sat at the table, a stack of papers sat in front of Murray.

"I can come back if you're busy."

"Nope," Dylan said, "Just two more signatures and we'll be done."

"You seem to have become the lawyer of choice in this town. At least one good thing came out of Nick's time here—a bunch of us meeting the up-and-coming lawyer of the year. We'll all be able to say we knew you when…" I smiled but didn't feel in the least bit happy.

Murray stood and Dylan followed suit. They walked together to the front door speaking too quietly for me to hear anything except the way Dylan said goodbye, "Pleasure doing business with you, Murray. Sorry about the circumstances, though." And then Murray's grunt.

"So, here we are again. Must be desperate times if you're coming to me for advice," Murray said, motioning for me to get up and follow him to his living room. He poured himself a three-finger vodka and offered me some. I shook my head.

"So, I'm thinking of quitting. Well, of not accepting the chief position. Maybe moving back to Nova Scotia to finish my practicum so I can finally get my nursing degree and maybe do another couple of years and become a Nurse Practioner."

Murray took a long draw from his glass, "Big loss for us."

"Yeah, well, I'm not having fun being the house mom for baby men. And I'll have to give up being the first responder trainer if I become chief since it would kill me to do both and there's probably a conflict of interest somewhere in there anyway."

"Sounds like you've got it all thought out. You've got the money to finish your degree. I say go for it," Murray said without any hesitation.

"Really? I kind of expected a bit of discussion about the upsides and downsides of packing up and moving away," I said disappointed that he'd so quickly agreed with me.

"What downsides? You've got nothing to keep you here.

You came back for your dad and he's gone. You lost the family house so that's not your responsibility. You don't have a boyfriend… seems like leaving is a no-brainer."

"Well," I felt flustered, "maybe it's a no-brainer to you, but it's not to me. I mean, maybe I don't have anyone to keep me here but, maybe I do. I mean, why would you assume I don't have a boyfriend? That's kind of rude."

"Don't tell me you're fucking one of those nail benders living in your house?" Murray made a face like he'd just imagined one of them naked and did not appreciate what he saw.

"No! Of course not," I said, as appalled at the thought as Murray clearly was.

"So who's the lucky man who's captured Sophie Beaulieu's heart?"

I looked at my feet and shook my head.

"You're embarrassed by him? Interesting—"

"I am *not* embarrassed," I said giving him a death scowl, "I'm just not sure my feelings will ever be reciprocated."

"Oh, Christ," Murray said, dropping his head into his hands. "Why do otherwise smart women get all stupid when it comes to love?"

"I'm not being stupid. And anyway, I wasn't asking you for relationship advice, I wanted career advice."

"It's your lucky day then cause I'm giving you two-for-one. Career advice? You're not going to be happy being the chief of this department. You've already done all the fun work, shaking shit up and putting all the systems in place to get things running smoothly. All you'd be doing moving forward is maintaining crap. You're a builder not a maintainer. And what the fuck are you doing still living with all those guys? You don't need the money or the headache. Find a damned place of your own and stop being their mother.

"As for going back to Nova Scotia to finish your nursing

degree?" Murray raised his arms, palms facing skyward. "Did all of the local universities close? UBC, SFU not good enough for you? The only reason you'd even consider going back to the east coast is to run away. And that pisses me off since I pegged you as a fighter not a quitter."

"Maybe there's nothing left here worth fighting for. Ever think of that, smart ass?" I said, furious with him.

"Christ, Sophie, everyone but Nick can see that you're in love with his dumb ass. And everyone but you can see that he feels exactly the same way—"

"He's not in love with me. He might like me but that's only because…" I stopped, not sure if I should tell him.

"You've fucked. Of course, you have."

"Oh my god, Murray. What do you mean, 'of course you have?'" I thought for a second while he just shook his head and mumbled to his glass of vodka. "You mean because he's a player," I said, getting it.

"Sophie Marie Beaulieu, I've known you your whole life. And until this moment I've always thought that you were one of the smartest, most shit-together people I'd ever met. But you're being as dumb as that dumbass you're so head over tits in love with. You want my advice?"

"I'm not sure anymore."

"Don't accept the chief job. Tell the guy who owns the house that you're quitting and find your own place. Here, in Lily Valley. You love it here, so why would you ever consider leaving? So you can get a degree and spend your life taking care of people you don't even know somewhere else?" Spit flew from his mouth and his face was red. "Hell, if you love taking care of other people so damn much, move back in with me. Within the next few months I'll be needing a full-time nurse and ass-wiper."

"What do you mean? Why are you going to need—"

"Never mind. I'm just being as stupid as you are. Grow some balls, Beaulieu and tell Nick how you feel."

I couldn't hold back my smile or my snarky comment, "You know I have a vagina and it's very sensitive—"

"Yeah, yeah, just the way Nick likes it."

"Murray! That's not what I was going to say."

"But it's the truth. And if he's not going to grow a pair, you're going to need to."

39

NICK

I was having another restless night. I'd had a dream about being a dad. My dream wife didn't have a face—no one in my dreams ever had faces—but I knew it was Sophie by her energy and how happy I was. We were in a cabin in the woods and Max was laying in the dirt chewing a stick. Dream Sophie and I were watching him from the front porch. She was standing behind me and had her hands plunged into the pockets of my sweat pants. My cock was in her hands and I was hard as hell.

Then an alarm sounded and when I looked up our boy was gone. I woke with a start. No Sophie. No little boy. But the goddamned alarm was still with me. So was my hard-on.

"Lily Valley Fire and Rescue this is Dispatch. We have a report of a fire alarm at 2299 Eagleview Drive. Respond Routine. No sign of smoke or fire. Lily Valley Fire and Rescue, respond routine to a report of a fire alarm, no smoke or fire at 2299 Eagleview Drive."

I swung my legs out of bed and looked down at my raging boner. This was a call that didn't need me. One that as few as four guys could handle. I pulled on a t-shirt, stuffed myself into my jeans and headed down to the truck bay. I opened the bay doors then started Engine One and Utility One just as the first three cars pulled into the parking lot.

Sophie had obviously jumped into Tamara's car when she passed her place. The others were old crew. I called Sophie over to me.

"You can stand down on this one."

She looked at the guys gearing up. "But they need an IC," she argued.

"Someone else will show up," I said.

And someone else did. Four more guys, in fact.

"Joe, you're IC. Take Engine One. Matt, you're Captain on Utility One. The rest of you, find a seat and roll. No lights, no sirens. Keep to the speed limit."

Lots of "Got it's!" and "Copy that's!" and they were out the door. I pushed the button to close the bay doors.

"You want me to go home or stand by?" she asked.

What I want is for you to come upstairs and resume what you were doing in my dream.

"Come upstairs with me?"

She looked at me suspiciously but followed.

"Feeling like being beaten at a game of pool?" she asked, covering her mouth as she yawned.

I feel like being beaten, all right, but not at pool.

"I feel like we haven't made time to talk in the last couple of weeks. And I've missed that. And since you have to wait until Tamara gets back, I thought we could hang out for twenty minutes."

She gave me a weird look. "I could just walk home. I'd be back in bed in under fifteen minutes."

"I'd really like you to stay." God, I bet I sounded pathetic and needy. My cock was not helping me keep my cool, either, since Sophie was in nothing but jogging shorts and a tank top. No bra and, I was guessing, no underwear.

Stop thinking about that! I commanded myself.

"What's going on, Nick? You look uncomfortable. Is there something you need to tell me?"

I nodded and opened the door to the rec room.

She shook her head, but smiled. The faintest smile.

"Will you lie on the couch with me? It would really help," I said, holding my hands up in prayer position.

"You are a weirdo, Chief West," she laughed.

Yes! Sophie laid down on a couch and patted the space in front of her.

"Do you mind if I big spoon you? I'm worried if I lean back I'll suffocate you into the cushions."

She scooted out and made room for me behind her. I wrapped my arms around her ribs and felt my world collapse. There was no one else I wanted to hold this way.

She put her hands on mine and rubbed up my forearm. It felt electric. The charge went straight to my Levis and she noticed.

"Seriously, Nick?"

"Sorry? Not sorry. You just feel so good. And even though my cock might suggest in a sexual way, I also mean it in a, I don't know, just home kind of way. I was having a dream when the alarm went off. About you."

"Were you?" she said, squeezing my forearm. "And were we snuggled up on a couch like this? Is that what made you want to bring me up here while everyone else is out being good citizens?"

"No, in my dream we were standing. You were behind me."

"And what was I doing behind you?"

"It's kind of hard to explain. You know, the way dreams make everything kind of weird. I'm not sure if it's even possible. Can I show you?"

I could feel her starting to shake. She was holding her breath, I figured trying not to laugh. She silently nodded her head so I swung my legs around and dropped my feet to the floor with her still in my bear hug, then I stood up and placed her on her feet and walked in front of her.

"Okay, I'm not sure this is going to work since in my dream I was wearing sweats, not jeans."

She giggled. "Mm, hmm."

"Give me your hands."

Sophie pushed a hand to either side of my body and I took them in mine.

"So, imagine I have sweatpants on and you've got your hands in my pockets. Put your hands where you think they'd go."

She slowly and lightly placed her hands on the front of my thighs, avoiding my inner thighs and general crotch area. She pressed her breasts into my back and used me to balance herself as she stood up on her toes to whisper in my ear, "I can't find the right position with the jeans on. They're... confusing me."

"I should take them off, then."

"If you want to know if what you dreamt was possible, yeah, you better take off your jeans."

She didn't have to tell me twice. With my jeans at my ankles her hands found their mark without any trouble. She swirled my precum around my head with her right thumb and pulsed my shaft with her left.

"Wait! We need some our special SophNic lube," she said. She dropped my cock and took four steps to the kitchen area and came back with a tub of coconut oil. Against every jurisdiction's food safety codes she drove four fingers into the solid oil and came out with a large lump of it which she rubbed between her hands.

"Face me. Take my top off," she ordered.

I pulled off her tank top. Her nipples were hard. My cock throbbed.

"Lean against the pool table. Hands behind your back," she ordered. I did as commanded while she lubed up my shaft. My eyes rolled back as she stroked and pulled. Then she grabbed the base of my cock and dropped to her knees, taking me in her mouth.

"Fuuuck," I exhaled. I opened my eyes and watched as Sophie, my Sophie, not some faceless dream-Sophie or nameless cheap date, took me inside her. She worked me slowly, deliberately. Her tongue traced the vein down the underside of my cock, then she took one testicle into her mouth and gently sucked while she stroked me. I moaned and pushed my hips forward to go deeper inside her mouth.

She moaned and the vibration on my cock made it harden even more. She reacted by moaning again, longer, playing with the tone as her tongue ran around the head of my cock in quick circles. If I'd let her suck for even five more seconds I was going to lose it. Too soon. I wasn't ready for this connection to end. I bent forward and put my hands under her armpits, pulling her back to standing.

"Your turn," I said.

"Did you do me in your dream?" she asked wiping her mouth before tilting her head up to kiss me.

"Every fucking night, Sophie, since the day I met you."

40

SOPHIE

I'd missed him so much. The way he felt in my arms and wrapped around me. The way he tasted and the way he devoured me, like I was the most delicious thing he'd ever eaten.

I let myself melt into the moment, even though I knew it was temporary, brought on by a horny dream. But I'd take it. Living with five buff bodies was making it even harder for me to stop thinking about Nick. If I'd been living with Murray it would have been a cakewalk since I wouldn't have all that testosterone energy filling my kitchen at breakfast time.

And damn those boys flirted. Aiden made it crystal clear that if I abused my landlady power and entered his bedroom without notice, he'd let me in. But I didn't want him or any of them. I wanted Nick. They were just there to taunt me and remind me that I wasn't going to get what I wanted. Not in the way I wanted it, at least.

I got my house, but as an employee. I got cash flow, but at the cost of losing Papa. I was even about to get the chief position, but it meant losing Nick.

Stop thinking, Sophie! Give in to the moment.

I grabbed Nick's hair and brought myself back to the moment. I felt his flat tongue against my sex, warm and hungry. He pushed my labia open with a now firmer probe and found my clit. Sweet Jesus. He moved in circles until my hips were arched so high he had to pull me back toward him.

"Stop squirming," he stopped to say.

"Stop talking," I breathed.

I missed him so much. The way he made me feel. The way he made me laugh. How comfortable I was just being myself with him.

Neither of us had a condom—what was I thinking coming to the hall at two AM without personal protective equipment?—so everything we did was oral. And touch. It was slow and erotic and I could have spent hours laying on that vegan leather couch like the teenage girl I never was, exploring a boy's body in the rec room.

I heard Engine One's back-up beeps then the first truck bay door opening.

"Oh, no. Make them all go away," I said.

"Your wish is my command," Nick said, pulling on his jeans and t-shirt, backwards and inside out but who would notice at 2:30 in the morning?

I grabbed my shorts and tank top and took them into the loft area, just in case anyone decided to come up to the kitchen for a drink. I sat on Nick's bed and listened to the chatter as the guys got out of their gear.

"Hey, where's Sophie? I can't leave without her," Tamara said.

"She walked home. Don't worry about her."

The crews left and Nick locked up the hall again before coming back upstairs. I wanted to say so many things to him since we both knew that in a few days he'd be getting a visit from Decker with the official request to hand over his keys. I'd be left to re-key the hall again. Not that I worried that

Nick would come to wreck things. In fact, my worry was just the opposite, that he'd have no reason to ever come back to Lily Valley.

He came back up to his room and found me laying on his cot, which was barely big enough for him to sleep on, let alone both of us.

"How do you manage to sleep on this? It's not even as long as you are."

"You get used to it."

"You're really leaving, aren't you?"

"Seems so."

I sucked in a breath to settle the nerves in my belly and asked the question I'd been wanting to ask for weeks, "Since I already fucked up your career chances of fast-tracking a life to a city chief, you want to spend your last few days sleeping at my place?"

I laughed out loud at Nick's face. His eyes went wide and he looked like I'd just given him the keys to a new Ferrari. "You know my answer."

"I don't have to ask you twice?"

"Please tell me you saved the icing covered condoms we didn't manage to use or ruin," he said making prayer hands.

"One or two. Maybe five."

Max met us at the door. We came in as quietly as humanly possible. Nick was still taking off his jacket and petting Max when I reached the landing on the second floor.

Aiden's door opened, "I heard the other cars go by ten minutes ago. I was getting worried since you didn't take your car. Thought, I don't know, something happened."

"That's nice, Aiden. All good. I got a lift down with Tamara and a lift back with Nick."

"You amped? Want to hang out? I don't work tomorrow."

Nick did not come up the stairs quietly. I'm sure he woke the other four guys when he roared, "Yeah, no. Sophie and I are 'hanging out' if by that you mean about to have sex. So, put on your music—"

I put my hand over his mouth before he could finish. I was mortified. Kind of angry. What sort of possessive bullshit was that coming from the guy who'd be leaving in five days, probably forever? Was it sweet that he wanted to mark me as his territory? I didn't know. Nobody had ever treated me this way before. Hell, even my fiancé was never, ever, one single time, jealous of how any other man spoke to me or looked at me. Compared to Nick it was like he didn't care.

But Nick was so far at the other end of that spectrum and we weren't even dating… I wondered how he treated actual girlfriends. And then I remembered he said he'd never had an actual girlfriend. Maybe this was why. Maybe he scared them away with his psycho over-possessiveness.

My hand was still on his mouth since he'd grabbed the squishy bit of my palm in his teeth and wasn't letting go. It didn't hurt but it was weird. I used my other hand to point up the stairs to my room. He bent over and scooped me into his arms, carrying me up the stairs and carefully sitting me on my bed, releasing my hand at the same time.

"I'm sorry. I couldn't stop biting your hand since I knew I'd keep talking and it was clear you didn't want me to."

"That was… just a bit over the top."

"And can I just say, 'I told you so,' now? He so wants to shag you. He had a boner ready to go."

"Oh my god, Nick, you're projecting. He really didn't."

"Oh, he really did."

We had a small stare down and I started to worry that the moment had been ruined. That Nick was finally here again but it would end badly, like the last time. I started to feel nauseous. Nick saw it right away.

"Take a breath. I'm not mad. Are you mad?"

I shook my head.

He held my shoulders lightly and looked me right in the eye. Even if he hadn't spoken, I'd have known he was telling the truth. But he made sure it was clear, "Okay so the moment was kind of ruined, but that's okay. That moment was a moment ago and I know my body. If you give me another moment with you, I'll be so back to ready you'll forget every moment between the firehall and this one."

"I don't understand half of what you just said but if you get naked, I'm sure it won't matter anyway."

We dropped our clothes on the floor and lay down facing each other.

"This is a touch more comfortable than your old single bed," Nick said.

"And safer. If one of us falls out of this bed I'd take that as a bad omen."

"Interesting," he said, "because I'd think it meant that we were so focused on the pleasure of being together that we forgot about everything around us, including where this magic bed ended and where the real world started."

"So… the bed is like a Genie's bottle? Do I get to make a wish when we're both inside?"

"Wish away, Princess." Nick pushed his hips closer to me so his hard-on pressed into my belly just enough to know it was there, like it was saying hello. I took him in my hand.

"I wish you weren't leaving in five days."

As we stared into each other's eyes, I felt his erection soften. I pulsed my hand around it, to bring it back to full attention, but it continued to retreat. Nick took my hand off of him and kissed the back of it, shaking his head.

"Sorry," we both said.

"My fault," we answered at the same time.

I kissed him gently on the mouth then rolled over so my back was pressed against him. He wrapped his arm over me and pulled me in tight.

"I'm going to miss you. I wish I'd never recruited all those women. I ruined everything."

Nick didn't say anything. What could he say? From his point of view, I'd ruined his career goal. That made me sad but what made me sadder was that I'd ruined any chance of ever taking our friendship to a deeper level since, 'out of sight out of mind' and all that. He'd go back to his city life which he clearly enjoyed, and I'd stay here, me and Max against the world.

"You did what was best for the community. I respect you for that, Soph. It does suck that I was collateral damage, but the upside is I don't hate my old job and I still have it."

We lay quietly for minutes. I matched my breathing to his, slow and deep, to keep me from melting down. In my head, I asked him a million questions. In my mind, I replayed tonight differently, with us laughing, planning our next dumb project together, making love. It felt like that was off the table now. The energy between us was no longer hot and hungry.

"Will you stay in touch?"

"If you want me to," he said.

I twisted around to face him, to look into his eyes hoping to decipher what he was thinking. He gave me a small smile.

"I'd like to," he added.

I nodded but said nothing. I hoped he could decipher what I was thinking as we held eye contact. *I can't just be friends with you because I'm in love with you.*

We didn't have sex that night. I woke up a little when he left sometime before dawn. I thought he was just getting up to pee and so I fell back to sleep. But at six, when my internal alarm went off, I was alone. I wished that I'd find him in the kitchen making coffee. No luck. I didn't want to see the guys this morning, have to take their comments about last night, so I went back to bed.

I didn't want to go to work. Didn't want to see Nick.

He'd left without saying goodbye. Seemed like a pretty clear message that he was happy to fuck me but didn't want to wake up with me. As I fell asleep in his arms I'd had this dumb idea that things could be the way they'd been before I kicked him out and he'd lost his job because of me.

Of course, that was stupid. I was stupid. I was just another willing body and the only one that was available in our small town. That's all. If I wasn't so sad about the whole situation I'd have laughed at how naïve I'd been.

I texted Nick,

Not feeling well. Taking a sick day.

NICK

Copy that

41

NICK

Even though she didn't normally come to the office until after lunch on Mondays, Sophie was at her desk when I came downstairs to shower at eight AM. I wasn't dressed, since I hadn't been expecting company, and she looked embarrassed to see me with just a towel wrapped around my hips. I was glad I'd dealt with my morning woody upstairs, hadn't waited for the shower since simply seeing her would have triggered an unwelcome, premature ejaculation. *As if premature ejaculations were ever welcome*, I thought.

"First, good morning," I said. "Second, why are you here so early? And third, why are you wearing your formal deputy uniform?"

"Um, good morning," she said, staring at my chest which made me laugh inside. To her credit, Sophie was not one of those hypocrites who would check me out then, when I returned the favor, say "Eyes up here, Asshole."

"I came in early to be prepared for when Decker gets here to, you know…" She paused and looked up at me with sad eyes.

"Take my keys. You can say it."

"I don't want to say it. And I'm dressed this way so he knows that I'm acting in my official capacity as the deputy chief. I don't want him thinking that I'm just... I don't know... not credible, that's all." She sounded flustered and was cute as hell.

"So you have a plan?"

She nodded and stood, bouncing on her toes.

"Why haven't you told me?"

"I just thought of it at about four AM. So I came down and started getting ready."

"You've been here since four?" I was horrified. What if she'd heard me moan when I came? Did I say her name? I know I thought it, over and over and over, but for all I knew I said it out loud over and over and over, too.

"What's wrong? You look confused or something."

I scratched at my ear, "I need to shower. I'll be back in ten minutes and I'd love to hear this idea of yours." I threw her a smile and headed to the shower, kicking myself every step of the way since I wanted to ask her to join me, to be with me one last time.

Her idea was one that I did consider, sort of seriously, but it would have left me too vulnerable if Sophie and I ever found ourselves accidentally, maybe on purpose, crossing that professional line of colleagues who worked really fucking well together and fucked really well together, too.

She knew Decker was going to have her sign a contract to be the probationary chief for six months, as soon as I'd signed away my right to the title. She offered to hire me as her deputy, a position that reported solely to the chief so I'd not have to have any contact with Decker. She also offered me the chief's salary. In her perfect world, everything would stay exactly the same except for the number of service stripes we'd have on our dress shirts, something we'd worn exactly once in the last six months. People would still call me Chief and her Deputy inside the hall. Members would still defer to my authority. Officially and publicly, she'd be the chief, but internally it would be a name only.

I couldn't tell her that my real concern was that not crossing the line with her from work colleague to a not-complicated relationship status, was killing me. That if I lived here, I'd never be able to give up the hope that Sophie and I could become a family in the truest sense of the word. And I knew if I told her that, she'd likely convince me that we should try. And then it would end and I'd have developed even deeper relationships here but I'd be the one to have to leave since Lily Valley would always be her home first. So I told Sophie an out and out lie—the first and only time.

"My whole point in becoming the chief and staying in this one-horse town was to earn the credibility to become a career department chief sooner than later. Being your deputy won't fast-track my career. In fact, if anything, I'll be better off back as a rank and file firefighter, working my ass off and my way up the ladder the normal way.

"I appreciate the offer, really I do, but it's a short-term solution to a longer term challenge."

I felt like I was punching myself in the gut as I said it. And by the look on her face, I'd say she also felt like I'd punched her in the gut.

She dropped her head and didn't make eye contact with me, "Of course. I'm sorry. I... I way overstepped. I was thinking about everyone's needs but yours."

The sad truth was that Sophie's plan could never meet my needs since what I needed more than anything, more than the stability of a pay check, more than a promotion, was to escape the feeling that I carried from Day One in Lily Valley to my last day there: that I was reliving my youth, the years when I didn't have a place to call home, people who'd notice I wasn't at the dinner table, call me to find out where I was and when I'd be back, and tell me to hurry home soon.

At least in the city, I had a bed in a home that was my own. And all the brothers a guy could ever hope for.

Decker texted and let me know he'd been delayed, that he'd be an hour late. I vented my frustration at Sophie.

"I'm not on the payroll anymore so really, why stay? I can leave the keys with you. Stupid policy."

She nodded agreement but looked so sad I was sure she was about to cry. I felt like a shit but I wanted her to cry so I could take her in my arms and tell her that I wanted to stay. That I wanted to be wherever it was that she was.

She took a deep breath, exhaled hard and said with force, "Give me your keys. I'll tell Decker you had an appointment and couldn't hang around."

Soft Sophie was gone and Strong Sophie was in the room. I wanted to stay and spend every last minute I could with her, but her tone was one of dismissal. *You can leave. I've got this. We're fine without you.*

I placed three keys on the table. Adjusted them so their tops were all at the same height, then decided they'd look better with their tips lined up. I could feel Sophie watching me.

"I guess this is it," I said after fiddling with the placement of the keys for at least a full minute.

"I guess so," she said, staring at the table, not looking at me.

"Car's packed so…"

"I'll walk out with you."

I opened the car door. Sophie stood a few paces away from me. As I bent to get inside, she said, "Wait!"

She threw herself into my open arms and hugged me hard.

I kissed the top of her head and silently mouthed, *I love you* into her hair.

She let me go and looked up, blinking away tears. "I love," she paused and as I was about to say, 'I love you, too,' she finished, "working with you. If you ever need a deputy again, I'm your man."

I got into my car and drove away faster than I'd planned, so she wouldn't see Mr. Arrogant Calendar Man cry.

42

SOPHIE

When Decker finally showed up to take Nick's keys, he offered me a six-month probationary period as the chief. No surprise since that's what we'd discussed. What did come as a surprise, as much to me as to Decker, was that I refused the offer and didn't sign the contract. I suggested a counter-offer: I'd sit in the chief's chair until Decker could find a suitable replacement.

It took Decker two full weeks to post the position and he put a four-week application deadline on the job. Interviews would be done during the last week of November and first week of December. He promised me that I'd be free by the end of the year so that's how I kept myself going, knowing that I wouldn't have to keep showing up to the empty office forever.

And since the new chief would want to assign his or her own deputy, we left the position empty. I realized, having not filled the position, that there were not ten hours of deputy work to do every week. Heck, I was hard pressed to find thirty hours of Chief work to do and I was being paid to do forty. It became clear that Nick had been putting lots of work on my desk that he could have been doing himself.

At first I was seriously pissed off since he was being paid to work full-time and after that first month, after I kicked him out, I wasn't being paid anything as his right hand and yet he still kept me committed to ten hours a week. And it's not like I was sitting around playing with myself... much.

But after spending four weeks alone in the hall, I understood why Nick wanted someone around for some of the time—it was lonely being the chief of an on-call, volunteer department.

Today, however, was not going to be a lonely day since I had a date in the city. A date I had not been looking forward to one bit.

I stood at the front of the courtroom with Dylan feeling like I was going to vomit. I had no idea how many of my so-called siblings would show up but even one was going to be two too many.

Dylan assured me that it was unlikely I'd have to speak. He said he'd do all the talking. I was there to witness, basically, and so the judge could see that I was a decent human being, not a harpy bitch out to ruin eight people's lives.

My oldest brother and his lawyer came in but I didn't see anyone else with them. My oldest brother who was really not my brother at all. He knew what I was to him and I had to assume that Sarah, John and or Patrick had told him I'd finally learned the family secret. Well, the Sophie secret since I'd been the only one who didn't know.

When Dylan found out that the brother leading the efforts to erase me from the will was actually my biological father, he made a little 'whoop' sound and then quickly apologized. I guess the whole thing was kind of Shakespearean and that, he said, would make for a really great story. It would also give the judge the opportunity to exercise some creative problem-solving, which, if she was a 'family first' kind of person, would give me a healthy settlement and Dylan a healthy media bump for a few days.

He was cautiously optimistic. I was cautiously trying to hold my lunch.

"All rise," the court clerk said. "Court is now in session. Judge Lisa Khan presiding."

As much as I tried to focus on all that was being said and argued, I struggled to keep my mind from wandering to how hateful Dick, my brother/father was, trying to understand why and how he hated me so much and why my mom, the one who raised me, was so mad about being stuck with me. I wanted to ask Dick about my bio-mom, but Dylan made it clear that I was not to talk to him until after the court decision had been made.

The whole thing took less than an hour. It seemed to me like the judge had already made up her mind by the time she entered chambers since her questions were almost all directed at Dick's lawyer and they seemed pretty nasty to me.

In the end, she found in favor of me and not only did she award me my full eleven percent of the inheritance as an equal sibling, she also awarded me Dick's share, arguing that he'd, in effect, avoided paying nineteen years of child support that he should have been paying.

When Dick argued that that wasn't fair, despite being shushed by his lawyer, the judge said if he said one more word she'd have Revenue Services calculate the exact amount he'd avoided paying based on his income for those nineteen years and make sure he paid it in full before I had one more birthday. And, she awarded Dylan's legal fees which made me happy since he'd refused to let me pay him, even though I had the funds to.

Dylan was reserved and gracious when he thanked the judge. All I could muster was a smile a nod and a quiet whisper of "thank you." Somehow, even though I'd just been awarded almost two hundred thousand dollars, I didn't feel like I'd won anything. In fact, I felt like I'd just lost any chance at having a relationship with anyone I'd grown up believing was a sister or brother. Worse, I knew I'd never have a chance to be an auntie to any of their kids.

I wondered, for the millionth time in the last weeks, how different my life would have been if I'd been raised by my biological parents. Somehow I knew it wouldn't have been better. Despite the hurt of not having had that unconditional love most kids get from their mother, I knew in the deepest part of my being that I got that from Papa.

"Time for a traditional celebratory lunch," Dylan said, "on you, at a restaurant chosen by me."

I laughed but agreed. A celebratory lunch, it turned out, wasn't lunch at all. It was Manhattans at the Five Sails Restaurant in the five-star Pan Pacific Hotel. After two drinks, I was feeling relaxed enough to ask the question that had haunted me since I overheard his conversation with Nick and Josh.

"Do you remember that day I texted you to tell you that I wanted to pursue this case? You were out at that shit-hole bar with Nick and Josh. Do you remember?"

"Of course I do. Why?"

"I walked in and overheard you talking to Nick.

Dylan said nothing.

"You were giving him advice."

"Okay…"

"About me."

"Advice about you? I can't say I remember that exactly. But you do, I'm guessing," he said, sounding calm as a cucumber.

"I do. Your words have played on repeat in my brain for the last six months—"

"And they were?"

"You said, in this loud, particularly deep voice, looking

right at Nick, "She's no good for you. If you pursue her, you can kiss your career goals goodbye."

There! I finally said it. I felt a combination of relief and grief all mixed up in a swirling bundle of four ounces of rye. I really doubted I'd make it to bedtime without throwing up.

Dylan was rubbing his forehead and looking at me with a very serious stare.

"Is this how I sounded?" he lowered his chin and puffed up his chest. He looked at me down the bridge of his nose, scowling, and then spoke in a much deeper voice than was normal for him, "She's no good for you. If you pursue her, you can kiss your career goals goodbye."

I nodded. "That's *exactly* what you told Nick. And I just want to know why. Why do you think I'm so bad for Nick?" I fought to keep the tears at bay.

Dylan shook his head and then closed his eyes and smiled. A look of understanding on his face.

"You know, about two months ago, Nick came at me like a Canada goose in heat, he was so pissed that I'd said something negative about you. He said you overheard me talking. I had zero idea what he was talking about since I've never said a bad word about you. He wouldn't believe me. I've never lied to my brother in my life and he believed your word over mine." Dylan shook his head and rolled his eyes.

"Well, it was a really shitty thing to say about me. You didn't even know me—"

"Sophie. I wasn't talking about you. And I wasn't giving advice to Nick. I was telling him what our dad had said to *me* about a woman he saw me with in a morning-after situation. That voice, that look, that's the way I mimic Dad."

I let that sit. I'd kicked Nick out because I'd jumped to a wrong conclusion. I destroyed what could have been a really great relationship because I was an idiot. On the one hand I felt better since it meant that Nick hadn't thought that I was bad for him. But after what I'd done, I'd actually created a self-fulfilling prophecy and proven that I was bad for him.

"I messed up. Understatement of the year."

"Yeah, you pulled some classic, over-reacting female drama," Dylan said.

I wanted to be mad but he was so right.

"And you know, my stupid brother, despite that, is still in love with you."

I shook my head, "No he's not. Have you ever searched #sexyfireman on Instagram?"

Dylan's look of disgust would have made me laugh had I not been so sad.

"Well, it's a thing. And there are at least a dozen pictures of Nick with these hot women posing with him. I know he has a life in the city and that I'm not the kind of woman he's attracted to. I know that I can't ever be in a relationship with him, but I do love him and even just getting to work with him, spend office hours with him, maybe go to the spa again and not get kicked out… have Nick as a friend. I'd be happy enough with that."

"That's too bad because if I know anything, I know that Nick will not be happy just being your friend. I haven't seen those pictures on Insta of my brother—seriously, hashtag sexy whatever? As if his ego needs that. Anyway, I can tell you with one hundred percent certainty that he did not go home with one of those women. Sure, maybe he let them take a picture ,but he and I left together, just the two of us, every single time we went out."

This didn't make any sense to me. "I don't buy it. I tried to get him to stay in Lily Valley. I even offered him the chief salary if he'd stay and keep working with me. But he said—"

"He said what was safe, not what he actually wanted to say. And, I've just said too much. Talk to Nick."

"But I *do* talk to him," I argued.

"No, you talk to Chief West. And he talks to you as

Deputy Beaulieu. You two need to talk to each other as Nick and Sophie."

I shook my head, "It won't make a difference. It's too late."

"Did I not just prove to you how smart I am and how good my instincts are? Trust me, Sophie."

I had to smile. "My god, you brothers are all arrogant in your own special ways, aren't you?"

He shrugged, "Come for dinner with my dad one night and I guarantee you'll understand why."

43

NICK

I'd been back at my old job for a month and man it actually felt great to be back doing city firefighter duties and not pushing papers across my desk. The parts of the job I loved the most about being a firefighter, I'd gotten to do the least when I was chief, like on-the-ground stuff. The best part of the six months in Lily Valley was Thursday night practice when I got to lead the training of the new recruits with Sophie. Well, that and the ten hours a week we worked together in the office.

But, as nice as it was to be back with my old crew, the six months I'd been away had changed the feeling of family I'd once had with the guys. None of them had aspirations of becoming a chief. They'd razzed me for wanting the gig and didn't ease off when I came back with my hose between my legs.

"The prodigal son returns," they'd cheered on my first shift.

I didn't know what the fuck a prodigal son was so I laughed it off until I could look it up. And sure, I left my firefighting brothers for a foreign land to pursue a dream they didn't approve of, but there was one part of that parable that wasn't true: I didn't feel at all sorry for what I'd done. In fact, I was feeling sorry that I hadn't been able to figure out a way to stay.

Dylan called to let me know, with Sophie's permission, that the mess with her family had been settled in her favor. He told me I should call and congratulate her but I knew that she wouldn't be celebrating. She'd told me that if she won, she was going to put the inheritance aside until she could think of a way to use it that would make her dad proud.

"Who cares what your dad thinks?" I'd said. This was before she shared her dime story with me. I never would have said that now that I knew that she was still getting his advice. Of course, she'd given me shit. The more she argued that her dad's approval was important to her, the more I challenged her, saying it should be entirely irrelevant to how she lived her life. Even as I said it, I knew I was being a dick.

"Yeah, well, maybe you don't care what your dad thinks, but my dad was always my biggest cheerleader and he gave me great advice. So even though I know he can't actually be proud of me anymore, I still want to act in a way that he would be."

What she said had been weighing like a brick on my chest. The only thing I wanted more than to be spending time with Sophie again, was to stop caring that I would never live up to my dad's expectations. That was then.

In the last few weeks I'd realized that I'd never be able to change my dad to make him the father I wished he'd been. But more importantly, I realized that the only thing I wanted to change was myself, to be the kind of man that could earn and keep Sophie's love.

I dialed Sophie's number.

"Hey, Soph," I said, not sure what else to say.

"I guess Dylan just told you he won? I won? I don't know who won, it sure doesn't feel like me, but I got my share of the inheritance," she said, sounding entirely unmoved.

"He did. Have you decided what you're going to do with the money that would make your dad proud?"

"I think he'd be proud if I moved back to Nova Scotia to finish my degree—"

"You can't do that!" I couldn't stop myself. As soon as I said it, I regretted it. "I mean, of course you can do anything you want. And I'm sure that would make your dad super proud."

"Yeah, it would. But it would also make me super sad," she said.

"I hope you don't mind, but I'm glad to hear that."

"Really?"

"Yeah, really. Hey, I'm just wrapping up a four-day shift so I have the next three off. You want to go for dinner with me, maybe catch a movie? Have a big night out in the city?"

She hmph'd.

"As tempting as that sounds I don't have the attire for a date night with a hashtag sexyfireman."

"What do you mean, you don't have the attire… with a hashtag… what was that? Of course you do. And anyway, since when did you care what you were wearing?"

"I don't. Not normally. But I wouldn't want to wreck your Instagram reputation."

Ah shit.

"I wish I could say that I have no idea what you're talking about, but sadly I do. I swear to you that I can't even tell you the names of the women I posed with for any of those pictures."

"And that's supposed to make me feel better?" Sophie's voice was strained.

"Yes? They're just pictures. Kind of like the pictures I

took for you, to replace your teeny bopper boy band poster—"

"That was different!" she interrupted.

"No, you're right. It was very different. For one, I was a fully willing participant to have those photos taken for you because it made me happy to believe that you might lay in bed fantasizing about spending time with me. And for two, those pictures on Instagram are not even about me or the dozens of other firemen you see with women hung around their necks. They're about the women who posted them, showing off… god knows what."

I let silence sit between us until Sophie spoke.

"You wanted me to fantasize about spending time with you? Seriously? Did you ever fantasize about spending more time with me? Aside from, you know, wet dreams?"

"Why do you think I stayed on in Lily Valley after Decker basically put my balls in a vice? He'd have been delighted to have me resign three months early, you know that, right?"

"Because you're trying to fast-track yourself into a city chief position. Everyone knows that."

My turn to let the silence sit since I didn't know what to say. She wasn't wrong but it wasn't the full story either. As good as it felt to have a proper place to shit, shower and sleep, I missed some things about living in the Lily Valley firehall. Well, one thing specifically: hearing Sophie come in. She was almost always humming some bad song from the eighties. I kept meaning to ask her why she had such weird music tastes but I never wanted to embarrass her. And as awful as the originals were, there was something about the way she'd make the songs her own that made them just a bit like walking on sunshine. God, I can't believe I thought that.

"You're right. I was. But I'm not sure that's what I still want. I'm trying to figure that out."

"Nick, I screwed up. Did Dylan tell you?"

"The only thing he told me was that you'd won the case. What did you screw up?"

"Everything."

"Wow. Now who sounds arrogant?" I said trying, hoping to lighten the mood.

"Ha ha," she said, without sounding amused. "I mean, I screwed up with you. I just found out that what Dylan had said, what I'd overheard, wasn't about me or you… so I kicked you out for nothing."

I let that sit, not sure what she meant, trying to make it make sense. If she kicked me out for nothing did it mean that I hadn't done anything to drive her away? I felt a spark ignite. It felt like hope.

"What do you mean you kicked me out for nothing?"

"I thought I was bad for your career, so I kicked you out of the house to save you from my bad influence. But in the end, I still got you fired, so… I kicked you out for nothing."

This still didn't make sense.

"I resigned," I corrected her.

"You had to resign because you took the heat for my decision, which you didn't have to do."

"Of course I did. We've been over this, Sophie.

I heard her inhale, slowly, deeply. I waited. Hoped.

"I'd love to have dinner with you—"

"Fantastic, I'll—"

"—but not this week. I need to figure something out first. Nothing is making sense right now. Rain check?"

"Maybe I can help you figure things out. I'm a good sounding board, aren't I?"

"The best. When you're being Chief West. But I don't know when you're just being Nick."

"Only one way to find out. Have dinner with me." I was starting to feel that pressure in my chest that warned me I was about to shut down, to walk away from facing the potential of being rejected. "Dinner. Yes or no?"

Silence.

"Yes or no. Easy answer, Sophie," I hoped I didn't sound as frustrated as I felt.

"Not right now Mr. hashtag sexyfireman."

I hung up without saying goodbye since the next thing out of my mouth was going to be, and was, a string of expletives.

44

SOPHIE

I was miserable. I hated being the chief and couldn't wait until Decker replaced me. I was sick of living with a bunch of adult children who needed to be cooked for. I missed Nick and tortured myself by looking for proof that he was happy back in his city life by stalking him on social media. Not his feeds—he didn't have any that he kept updated. But places he was tagged, either by name or worse, by photograph.

He'd called twice after that day he hung up on me, to see if I wanted to get together, but as much as I wanted to see him, to hang out and have fun with him again, I knew it wouldn't be enough. That it would actually make me feel more sad in the end. I'd been so wrong thinking I could just be friends with Mr. Arrogant Calendar Man Nick West.

I wished I'd had the courage to ask him if Dylan and Murray were right, that he felt the same way for me that I felt for him. But if I asked and he said No, I'd never be able to face him again since he'd know that I was in love with him and it would make him too uncomfortable.

I knew it was stupid since I was avoiding having the conversation I needed to have because I was afraid that the result would be us not having more conversations. Murray was right, I was being a stupid girl. But that was all I knew how to be.

In my free time, which I had far too much of, I half-heartedly applied for live-in caregiver jobs far away from Lily Valley. I had a dozen applications out in the wild, with private clients and with agencies that matched palliative patients with people to keep them fed and clean until their dying day. I felt no joy in this as my future but then, I felt no joy in any future these days.

Weird as it was, Murray and I started hanging out together more. When I was with him, at his place, I felt like I could be myself. I didn't have to be the confident boss or the responsible caretaker. I could just be me. And if I felt like being the lazy twenty-something who had no idea where her life was headed, Murray was great company since he had no more life or career aspirations. We just hung out and watched movies.

He'd drink until he fell asleep. I'd eat popcorn until my stomach ached and then I'd let myself out. Sometimes we talked, but mostly we sat, the way Papa and I had, just happy to know there was another human around to acknowledge that we were alive. Still breathing. Still here.

"You're depressed," he said one night in the middle of an old Steve Martin movie. "You're laughing and acting like things are hunky dory, but I can tell. You're depressed."

"Oh yeah? What's my tell? The fact that I'd rather hang out with a cranky old man than have a life? You should have been a psychiatrist, Murray."

"I'd have been a damn good psychiatrist. I know what the solution to your depression is."

"Let me guess: a bottle of vodka?"

He scowled at me. "I'm not depressed. I'm thirsty. And no, you can't have any. What you need is to get laid, fuck some happy back into you."

I rolled my eyes. "Won't work and not happening."

"You've got a house full of men who I'm sure would be happy to climb those stairs to your room."

"Oh my god! You and Nick. You're ridiculous."

"You should be watching movies with Nick, not with me. What's your problem, Beaulieu?"

"No problem, Chief. Everything's under control." It was my pat answer to his rhetorical questions.

"Bullshit. You've left the scene of a forest fire without digging up the roots to kill the heat that's going to build until it reignites into more flames."

"Your metaphors need some work," I said, shaking my head, "But I take your point. Yes, I have a crush on Nick. I'll get over it. And hanging out with you is the perfect cure since I see what my future would have been if things had worked out with him. Watching TV with a cranky old man who interrupts the movie when things get interesting."

"Spoiler alert: he grows some balls and she toughens up her sensitive vagina." He made a face like it pained him to say the word 'vagina,' "They talk it out and live happily ever after."

"Only in the movies, Murray. You know better than I do that that's the truth."

"For a smart young woman, you can be a dumbass." He finished his vodka and held his empty glass out to me. "Three fingers, no ice. Please and thank you."

45

NICK

I'd never checked out the photos that got taken of me when I was out boozing with my brothers or other fire fighters, but with both Sophie and Dylan mentioning them I had to have a look. And yeah, I could see why Sophie had been upset. It did look like I was a Class-Asshole player. I wanted to call and assure her I'd never done more than pose for a photo with any of the women. I wanted to point out that some of those photos had been taken before I'd even met her, but somehow I didn't feel like it would quite say what I needed it to. As for the ones from the stagette—Jesus Christ, I should have just bought the dog food myself. What was I thinking?

So with Dylan's help and the agreement of a dozen of my #sexyfireman pals to play, we hatched a plan to show Sophie that I didn't want to maintain some reputation of being a player. We arranged to have photos of ourselves taken with the clients of a bunch of charities we all believed in and we hired a professional photographer for a day to get great shots. Everyone came down to the firehall to make the best use of the time.

We got in touch with the SPCA who brought puppies,

cats, a bunny and a turtle to be cuddled by bare-chested, first responders.

The Food Bank arranged to have some of their volunteers come down and pose. Ally, our photographer, was brilliant and created what she called 'little tableaux' with our bare-chested bodies and different props, like soup cans and Wheaties.

The Senior Center drove their minivan over and we posed with eighty-year-old men who mirrored our shirtless poses while their lady friends ignored us and draped themselves on the older men. They were beautiful and hilarious shots.

For the whole day different organizations dropped in and we provided our bodies to help them with their fundraising efforts, the only condition being that they had to post their images to Instagram and include #sexyfireman with whatever their own tags were.

Within forty-eight hours, the number of posts using the #sexyfireman hashtag had more than doubled and the massive attention to the photos drew media interest from news sites around the world. The charities got most of the coverage which was exactly what should have happened, but a few news outlets wanted to talk to the brains behind the campaign—and that's where Dylan got his glory as our chosen spokesman. It was a win for him, and a win for the charities.

But the only win I cared about was that Sophie would understand that I'd be more than happy to take her out in the city, to be seen with her, to have our picture shared across all social media, if that's what she wanted. Which I knew she didn't but since she seemed so concerned that she'd make me look bad I wanted to put her mind at ease.

I waited four days before caving in and texting her:

> Have you seen the latest #sexyfireman shots?

SOPHIE

> The whole world has seen them.

I'm not sure what I expected her specific reaction to be but somehow this didn't feel like a positive response. Shit, shit, shit. What to say to that? I hoped she could read between the lines since I wasn't sure what the lines should say.

> Dinner?

SOPHIE

> Non-Sequitur

> On me!

SOPHIE

> I'm not one of your charities

Fucking hell. I called her. She let it go to voice mail.

> Sophie talk to me

SOPHIE

> Can't. Busy. Will call in an hour or so.

I checked the time: 10:22am. I decided to workout for the next hour to keep my mind off how badly that had gone.

It didn't work. At noon I texted her again:

> Free to chat now?

The message was unexpected.

SOPHIE

She's driving. Chill. She'll call you when she calls you.

I pictured her out with one of the guys who lived with her and I saw red.

"Chief," I said, knocking on his door. "Emergency at home. You good without me for rest of my shift?"

He looked at the schedule on his screen and then back at me, "Emergency? At home in your condo? Where you live alone?"

"No, up in Lily Valley," I said. "So, am I good to go?"

"I want those extra hours on your next shift."

"Deal. Thanks, Chief."

I drove home and packed an overnight bag. Even if I had to sleep on the couch at the firehall, I wasn't leaving Lily Valley until Sophie and I settled what this relationship was going to be, once and for all.

46

SOPHIE

"**M**urray! Why did you do that? What did you say?"

"I told him to relax. What's the big deal?"

The big deal was that Murray had trusted me with his most personal, private life. I hadn't told a soul about Murray's health since he swore he'd take me with him if I did. Of course, I knew he wasn't serious about killing me, but he was dead serious about keeping his cancer a secret.

But now that he'd replied to Nick's text it left me in an uncomfortable position of likely having to lie to him by avoiding either the obvious question, *Who were you driving with?*, or *What were you and Murray doing?*

Not that it was any of his business but if I didn't tell him who I was with, he'd probably assume it was someone I didn't want him to know about and that might lead him to think I was dating which was not what I wanted him to think. At all.

"It's a big deal because when Nick asks who replied I'll have to tell him it was you. And then he'll ask what we were doing and I'm going to have to lie. I don't want to lie to him."

Murray was silent. He sat with his hands in his lap,

clasping and unclasping his fingers. I'd already had a good cry at the doctor's office and it was pretty clear that he was bottling up his reaction to have once he was alone.

"Just tell him it's none of his goddamn business where we were."

I let that float around in my head. It's true that it was none of his business, just like it was none of my business who Nick was spending his nights with. Of course, that didn't mean I didn't want to know.

I'd seen all the photos he and the other firefighters had taken and was confused by the whole media thing and why he wanted to know if I'd seen the pictures. I'm sure he was proud of them, being Mr. Arrogant Calendar Man and all. He—and all the guys—looked amazing. The photos were funny and touching and got a ton of attention for the charities. But the comments made me want to cry. Correction: the comments made me bawl my heart out.

If his goal was to create his own personal Nick West screening app for potential dates, he got full points. Literally hundreds of women commented on his photos, offering to pose with him to promote their obviously made-up charities, to take him out for drinks to say thanks for his community service, to let him pat their kitties. Vomit.

He knew I was insecure about my own lack of either an Instagrammable life or photo-worthy appearance, so it made no sense for him to rub my nose in it by making sure I saw his and Dylan's media coup. And why invite me to dinner again? So I could see first-hand how many beautiful women would fawn over him when we were out?

I didn't think he actually thought that or intentionally wanted to hurt me but that was part of the problem, that Nick West would never understand how it felt to be inadequate compared to everyone else. He was the goal everyone set their impossible-to-achieve standards by.

Since he'd left, I had the space to realize that the only

reason we'd worked so well together when he was in my one-horse town was because I owned the horse he needed to ride.

"You missed the turn," Murray bellowed as I drove past the road that went into Lily Valley.

"Oh! Sorry. I was lost in thought, I guess."

"Well, we may as well go to town then. I feel like a milkshake. How about you? DQ. My treat."

I turned to look at Murray who kept his gaze straight ahead. The doctor had just told him that his best odds of living more than a month meant he'd have to stop drinking and start eating, in his words, "goddamn hippie food."

"The doctor said—"

"I don't give one good goddamn what that doc said. A milkshake is not going to kill me. The vodka I buy after we have milkshakes is not going to kill me either. I'll be dead before my next birthday whether I keep living my life the way I enjoy it or not. So I'm going to keep enjoying it."

I nodded. "Okay."

"Okay. And when you're talking to Nick, I want you to invite him for dinner. On a night when Dylan can come, too. And you have to be there so it can't be Thursday."

"All right. Will you be telling Nick and Dylan about… your health situation?"

Murray scoffed. "Health situation? Dylan already knows I'm dying. And yes, I'll be telling Nick."

Since Murray loved chatting up the cashiers at the liquor store, I knew I'd have a good ten-minute wait so I called Nick back.

"Hey," he answered.

"Hey, yourself," I said.

"Are you mad at me?"

"No," I said in a way that might not have sounded totally convincing. "I'm not mad at you. I'm confused, maybe? I'm,

I don't know," I shrugged my shoulders hoping he could imagine what I was doing.

"Confused about what?"

"I don't know. About everything. Can we talk about this in person, maybe?" I asked.

"I can be there in an hour."

I laughed. "Murray wants to talk to you, too. And to Dylan. He asked me to invite you both for dinner. I was thinking that after dinner, you and I can talk. Does that work?"

"What's Murray want to talk about?"

Emotion rose from my chest up into my throat and out my eyes. I gasped a breath. "Himself, I guess." It wasn't my news to share but I was pretty sure my voice said what my words didn't.

"You okay?"

"Had better days."

"I'm off work now. You want me to come up tonight? I'm serious. I can be there in an hour."

There was nothing that I wanted more than to lay in Nick's arms, just be held by him. The thought that that wasn't what he was offering, layered on Murray's imminent death, made me sob a "No, thanks."

"You're crying," he said.

"Just a little."

"Like it or not, I'm coming up with dinner. Just for us, not sharing with the man babies you're living with."

"Nick, you don't have to—"

"Pizza or Japanese or cheese, olives, salami and stuff? The only option I won't accept is 'nothing' because I'm coming up with food whether you want me there or not."

"The cheese, olives and stuff option, please. Does that choice come with wine? I really need wine tonight."

"Red and white. And rosé if you want."

A small laugh pushed up from my chest, from my heart.

"All of the above?"

"Your wish is my command," he said.

"I wish," I whispered.

"Has your genie let you down yet?" he asked.

I didn't know how to answer that. *Yes, because he can't read my mind?* That would be accurate. *No, because I've never asked for what I really want?* That would be accurate, too. So, I said, "Yes and no."

Nick sighed loud enough for me to hear. "Sophie Beaulieu, you challenge me. And you'll explain when I get there. But right now, I've got a grocery store and liquor store to hit. So, I'll see you around four."

"Nick?"

"Ye-es?" he said, sounding like he was scared of what was coming.

"You're the best. Thank you for being my friend."

"Anything for you, Soph."

If only he knew what I'd ask of him if he was being serious about 'anything.'

"Drive safe. Watch out for asshole Audi drivers."

"No need. I've got Dylan's car today so I'm the asshole everyone else has to watch out for."

I laughed. Despite how awful the day had been, Nick could still make me laugh.

47

NICK

Max met me at my car while Sophie stood in the doorway. Her lips turned up into a smile but her eyes were anything but happy.

"What's up with your mom, Max?" I said as I scratched his head. "We're going to make her laugh tonight, okay boy? You with me?"

Max licked my hand and I swear he nodded. I grabbed the smallest of the grocery bags and put the handles in his mouth.

"Take this to Sophie."

Max held his head up and carried the bag right to the front door, placing it in Sophie's hand. We didn't get a laugh, but her smile was a little bigger.

"Good boy," we said together.

"Do you need help carrying anything in?" she asked walking toward me.

"Sure." I handed her the first grocery bag, then the second, then the bag with the wine. Her hands were full and there were no more bags in the car. She looked at me quizzically.

"Don't move," I said, closing the car door. I grabbed my

backpack from the hatch and put it on then scooped her up in my arms. "There! That's everything."

She was laughing but she still had those damned sad eyes that broke my heart.

"When will the kids get home?" I asked as I placed her on her feet in the kitchen.

"Any minute now."

"I'm not sharing any of this—or any time with you—with them. So let's take everything we need into your bedroom, lock the door and pretend you're not here."

She didn't move. She didn't speak. She blinked and one tear escaped from each eye.

"What? You don't like that idea?"

"I love that idea." Sophie collected dishes, glasses, cutlery, and cloth napkins. She filled Max's food bowl then wrote a note and left it on the kitchen table,

You're on your own for dinner tonight guys. And clean up after yourselves.

Once we had everything we thought we'd need for a night in, I looked around the room to make sure there would be no reason for her to leave.

"Aha! You thought you could outsmart me by giving yourself a legitimate reason to run away," I said, turning off her pager. "No emergency calls tonight, Missy. You're already on-call with me. I am the only patient you'll be performing first responder duties with."

"Oh yeah? You look pretty healthy to me. What are your symptoms?"

She sat on her bed with her knees pulled up to her chest, protecting every vulnerable part of her body. I sat down on the edge and gently unwrapped her arms from around her legs, placing her hands on the mattress. I put my hand behind her left thigh and lifted it enough to raise her foot off the bed so I could straighten her leg. I did the same with her right leg. She didn't say a word.

And then I placed one palm on her chest, over her heart and my other in the same spot on my own chest.

"Mine is broken. I left a big chunk of it here and you're the only person who can help me put it back together."

I will remember the kiss that followed for the rest of my life. Sophie put her arms around my neck and pulled me toward her. When our lips met neither of us moved, we simply breathed. There was no urgency. It wasn't a sexual or hungry kiss. It was slow and gentle. I felt like Sophie was breathing life into me.

"I love you," I exhaled into her, needing her to breathe that truth into every cell in her body.

She pulled away, just enough to look at me, questioning in her eyes.

"You heard me. I love you. And I need you. I need you in my life. Not as my deputy. Not as a friend. I need you like I need air. Like I need water."

She moved her arms to my back and pulled me toward her, toward the bed. I lay down facing her.

She didn't speak. She stared into my eyes. The muscles in her face moved slightly, like she was debating what to say.

"What are you thinking?" I kissed the spot beside her mouth. She turned toward me, mouth open, and pressed hard against my lips. Her energy had changed. It felt electric now. Blood rushed from my big head to my small one. But I didn't want sex to be part of this conversation. I needed her to know that I wanted all of her, not just the parts of her that made my cock hard.

I took her hand and placed it over my hard-on. She gave a squeeze. I gasped. Then I brought her hand to my mouth and kissed her palm.

"You're the only one who has that effect on me, Soph. The only one. But I need you to know that that's just one small part of why I love you. Every emergency call I went on in the last month felt like work because you weren't there with me. I haven't laughed, like really laughed, since I left here. I've started listening to terrible eighties pop music just to feel like you're in the room with me. I miss every damn thing about you."

She still hadn't said a word.

"Say something. For the love of all things holy, please, say something, Soph."

"I love you, too," she whispered. "And I'm really scared."

"So am I. Scared shitless. But I realized that I'd rather have a year or a month or even a week of the happiness I feel when I'm with you than live in a place where I know I can't get hurt. That's not a life. Not a life I want anyway. I want a life with you for as long as you'll have me in it."

"Forever," she said planting a kiss on my mouth.

"That works for me."

48

SOPHIE

Even though I'd spilled the beans to Nick, Murray still wanted to have him and Dylan over for dinner. I made a Hungarian goulash using Murray's favorite recipe. He told me it was as good as his first, or maybe it was his third wife, made. Which was a compliment, he assured me.

But I'd refused to make dessert since, if he wanted to speed up his death by eating sugar, he'd have to make it himself. That, he told us all, was the kind of bullshit control his second, or was it his first, wife used to pull on him and why she wasn't his last wife.

"No matter," he said. "I expected no less and no more from you, Sophie. So Dylan was kind enough to buy donuts."

Dylan went to his car where he'd left the two boxes of Tim Horton's. I rolled my eyes at Dylan but when I made eye contact with Nick couldn't help but laugh.

"Put them in the living room," Murray barked. "Dylan do you let numb nuts drive your car?" he said, squinting between him and Nick.

"Yeah…" Dylan said, sounding concerned.

"So, which one of you is driving home tonight?"

They both shrugged. "Me, I suppose," Dylan said.

"Good. Nick, you're drinking with me. Dylan, you're doing girl drinks with Sophie."

"Works for me since I've got an eight AM," Dylan said.

"Really? You sure about that? You don't even know what girl drinks are. At least, my version of a girl drink," I said raising my eyebrows.

"By the way I've seen you throw back Manhattans, I'm guessing the only difference between what Murray is having and what you are is the number of maraschino cherries in the glass."

Murray laughed for the first time in three days.

"Sophie, pour yourself and the boys a couple fingers of vodka each, then give me the bottle."

"You want a glass or—"

"Bottle," Murray interrupted. "Take what you want now. The rest is mine."

Nobody laughed. We all knew he'd been drinking himself to sleep.

I poured the drinks, dropped a cube of ice into Nick's glass, added orange juice to mine and Dylan's, and handed Murray the bottle.

"Cheers to family, old and new," he said.

I teared up immediately which got an eye roll from Murray, a weak smile from Dylan, and Nick's arm wrapped around me. I leaned in close and lay my head against his chest.

"Dylan's got papers for you all to sign," Murray said, no explanation. He tilted his chin up toward Dylan who reached behind him and pulled a manila envelope from the table beside his chair.

As he opened it, Murray continued. "This is not a goddamn conversation starter. This is not a debate. You can read the details or not. It won't change anything. Just sign the goddamn papers so I can go upstairs and die peacefully."

I looked at Murray to see if he was joking. He appeared to be deadly serious.

"Well there are actually a couple of documents," Dylan said, holding the papers in his hand. "Murray, are you going to tell them or…" He looked at Murray.

"I sold my house to Dylan a few months ago. So when I'm gone, Sophie, you negotiate with him how much your rent is going to be. You get first right of refusal. That was the deal. But how much he charges you? That's his business."

Dylan's lips were pressed together and he gave me a small, quick smile. Nick inhaled so hard that his chest jerked and my head bounced. I looked up at him and saw anger in his eyes.

"Seriously, Bro?"

"Calm your tits, lover boy," Murray said, which drew Nick's death glare to him. "I needed to sell the house to get the cash to buy that flop house you used to call home," he said looking at me.

"You?" The rest of my words caught in my chest.

"Yes, me. And before you get your vagina all up in a huff, I didn't want you or anyone other than him," Murray pointed his thumb at Dylan, "to know until your lawsuit was settled with those pieces of shit. I didn't want your brother's lawyer to have anything he could point at that might suggest you'd been in cahoots."

"You're Gabe?" was all I could think to say.

He shook his head and pointed at Dylan again.

"You're Gabe?"

Dylan shrugged and nodded.

Murray was good enough to give me a minute to let this news settle. He took a long swig from his almost full forty-ouncer.

"Dylan, give Sophie the documents," he finally said.

"Sign those, Kiddo, and your house is yours again. All paid up. Do what you want with it. Keep it as a goddamn flop house, sell it, have a dozen kids and raise 'em there."

I looked down at the papers but couldn't see anything through my tears. I wiped them on the back of my hand but my eyes refilled.

"Breathe," Dylan said, giving me a real smile.

"Why?" I said, looking at Murray.

"Well, I can't take it with me. Not leaving it for the goddamn government to dispose of. Who else should I have left it to?"

"No, why did you even buy it? Why do that for me? I'm…" I didn't finish since I didn't know what I was. Words like "nothing to you," and "not worth it," came to into my head.

"Because you're goddamn family, Sophie. That's why. The daughter I never had."

I couldn't speak. I just kept repeating the word 'breathe' to myself as I pointed to the pen Dylan was holding.

"Actually, even though Murray wants you to sign this Bill of Sale for a dollar right now, I actually have to recommend that we have a chat about the tax implications. Yes, it's a mortgage-free house, but there will be expenses you need to be aware of."

"Oh, for Christ sake, Dylan, give her a pen."

I looked down at the paper and saw that Murray had already signed it and Dylan had witnessed his signing. I looked at Murray who smiled at me and rolled his hand in a hurry-up motion.

"Can I sign now and then you can sign the witness space for my signature after you've told me all the details?"

Dylan nodded. I signed. Murray said, "Good! Now the next papers."

Dylan handed a Ministry of Health government form to Nick. It had details filled in by hand, in Murray's writing.

Nick picked it up and I read it, too. It was a Medical Assistance in Dying Patient Request Record. Murray had initialed all the boxes that indicated he wanted a medically assisted death and that he understood all of the details. The only part he'd not filled in was his own signature which had to be witnessed by two people.

"I'm not signing this," I said standing up, intending to leave the room.

"Not asking you to," Murray said.

"Sophie, you can't sign since you'll be benefiting from Murray's death. Or, it could be argued that you are. So it's just cleaner that Nick and I sign it."

"You can't!" I said to Nick. "Did you know that's why you were coming for dinner. To sign this?"

Nick wiped a tear from his cheek and shook his head.

"Christ Almighty," Murray said, starting to sound drunk. "The paperwork's going to take ten days to process and I'll probably be dead by then from alcohol poisoning anyway. I'm not getting better and I'm sick of being in pain. So do a cranky old man a solid and sign the goddamn paper to let me move on."

"Murray, if you followed doctor's—"

"Sophie Marie Beaulieu, if you don't tell Nick that you won't bust his balls for signing that paper I swear to god I'll come back as one of your kids and I will live my next life exactly the same way I lived this one. You do *not* want to be my future mother, I can promise you that. So stop trying to be my mother now."

Nick looked at me with wide eyes. I bit my bottom lip and nodded. He initialed all the boxes that said he was eligible to be Murray's witness then signed the bottom and passed the paper over to Dylan who did the same. Murray grabbed the form, signed and handed it back to Dylan.

"Fax that in tomorrow. I'm going to bed. You people exhaust me."

Murray took his bottle and made his way up the stairs to his room with Nick spotting him all the way to the top.

"I'm going to head out. Do you want Nick to stay or head back to the city with me?" Dylan asked.

"Stay. If he wants to," I said watching Nick make sure Murray didn't require a 9-1-1 call for a fall.

Dylan shook his head, "Of course he wants to stay."

He'd spoken loud enough for Nick and Murray to hear. They both yelled down at the same time. Murray said, "he's staying," and Nick said, "I'm staying."

49

NICK

One year later

Murray died in his sleep three days after he had us sign his medically assisted death request. Dylan and Sophie talked about the implications of accepting her old family home from Murray and I witnessed the contract before he died.

I admit that I almost decked Dylan when I saw him the next day, I was so pissed off that he'd bought Murray's house without talking to me first since I'd always thought that if Sophie and I ever got together, a place like Murray's would be perfect.

And it was.

Today Sophie and I were celebrating our one-year anniversary of living together in it. Dylan literally traded me this house for my downtown condo. He reminded me that he'd actually floated the idea by me months earlier but since it was as one of our 'would you ever' games while we were out drinking, I gave it no thought after the game was done.

"Would you ever trade your condo for a house in Lily Valley?" he'd asked.

"If I was in a real relationship and living with Sophie, I would in a heartbeat. Would you ever…"

I actually don't remember what I'd asked him or anything else about the night other than the fact that a couple of hours later, after he'd invited two ladies to join us at the bar, that it was the last time I was my brother's wingman.

After Murray died, Sophie, Dylan and I spent a weekend working on a new business plan to use her house as a source of income that would support both her and me, so I could quit my job in the city and we could work together at the Lily Valley Fire Department—with neither of us as the chief.

She kicked out the construction workers—thank god— and I pitched the chiefs of the city departments on a program to train firefighters up to the National Fire Protection Association curriculum with on-the-ground experience as a farm team in Lily Valley. They loved it and found six guys willing to pay nine grand each for three months of full-time training with a guaranteed three-month probation in a career department, as long as they graduated our program.

The Lily Valley Fire Department got to keep the gear these guys needed me to buy for them to wear and use, which was a huge win for the volunteer team, too.

I worked with the farm team Monday to Friday, 8 to 4 and they were on-call, like all volunteers, 24/7. Sophie, of course, landed the contract to do the first responder training, which she delivered during normal, weekday training hours. I could have taken the time off but I volunteered to be her accident victim, heart attack victim, idiot who cut his own fingers off… because as far as work goes, nothing was more fun than working with Sophie.

It turned out that Sophie didn't actually need to have a

live-in caretaker in the rental house since we were in town and if there were complaints, we were two streets over to deal with it. The guys in the farm team program rented the five rooms with the shared showers for a thousand a month and the big room upstairs with the private bathroom went to the guy who was willing to pay fifteen hundred a month for it. And they all took care of their own food and meals.

We'd just started our fourth group of career-oriented firefighters and life was great. So great that we'd invited my dad and Isabelle, my step-mom, up for dinner. Sophie had met them a couple of times and they were gracious hosts who, according to Dylan, didn't have anything bad to say about her. Not that that should have surprised me, since there was nothing negative anyone could say about Sophie. But it did since Dad always found fault with my life choices.

"Who would like tea with dessert?" Sophie asked after dinner.

Everyone said 'Yes' and Dad stood up, saying he'd help.

"Where's the teapot?"

"We don't actually use one very often," Sophie said. "But I think there's one in the cupboard over the stove."

Dad had a look and found it. He took the cover off to rinse it out and as the hot water started to pour into the teapot he pulled it back.

"Well I'll be damned," he said pouring the water out, over the palm of his hand, catching something.

We all looked.

"There was a dime in your teapot."

I looked at Sophie, smiled and shrugged. I hadn't put it there. Finding dimes was not uncommon around here. Funny thing was that only Sophie ever found them, even when they were in places I know I'd walked by.

"That's Papa saying, 'Hello,'" Sophie said, standing to take the dime from my dad.

He closed it tight in his hand and shook his head.

"I don't think so. It's my father saying, 'Hello.' It's the most inexplicable thing, but after my father died I started to find dimes in the damnedest places. Like inside this teapot." He looked directly at Sophie, "Your father does that, too?"

"Yeah, he does. You're not just making fun of me, are you? Did Nick tell you about the dimes?" She gave me a stern look.

"No," Isabelle said, "he's been finding dimes in the strangest places ever since Leonard passed. Not every day or week or even month, mind you. But over the last twenty-some-odd years he's found dozens, if not a hundred, right, Honey? And never nickels or pennies or quarters. Only ever dimes."

"Papa seems to show up for me when I need his advice or when I need my ass kicked. Does your father show up at specific times?" Sophie asked my dad.

"Similar. But different." Dad stared at the dime in his palm and then he looked up at me and said, "Grandpa says he couldn't be more proud of you, Nick. And I agree."

I can't say with one hundred percent certainty, since part of our daily exercise was getting naked together, but Soph and I believe that that was the night we conceived the baby who would become the most loved child in the history of the world.

Sophie wasn't showing yet, but our twenty-week ultrasound showed us that our baby was a healthy, squirmy boy.

We played with the idea of calling the sprout Murray, but Sophie had a better idea.

"Let's name our first girl after him," she said, unable to hold back her glee. "I think he'd love having a sensitive vagina named after him."

"Name our daughter Murray? Funny. But not for her."

"His middle name, silly. Gabe, Gabriel. We can call her Gabrielle."

I placed my hand on her belly. "I know it's old-fashioned, but what do you think about Leonard, after my granddad?"

She put her hands on top mine, "What do you think, baby? Are you a Leonard? Maybe a Leo?"

"He kicked! Did you feel that? I felt it! Did you?"

Sophie's smile had so much love in it. "I did. But, what I haven't figured out yet is whether one kick means 'Yes' or 'No.'"

"Well then, let's figure that out." I moved my hand across her belly, rubbing in a small circle. "Okay, Magic Genie Baby, kick one time for 'Yes' and two times for 'No.' Do you understand?"

We waited and a few seconds later I felt one kick. I burst out laughing.

"Magic Genie Baby, do you love the name Leonard?" I paused and looked into Sophie's bright eyes as I asked again. "Actually, do you love the name Leonard *André* West?"

Sophie's eyes filled with tears and she pushed herself toward me then planted her mouth on mine.

"I love it," she said. "And he'll love it, too, because even when he's done something bad, something to invoke his full name, we'll say that name with so much love that he'll know that even though we're upset, we still love him to the moon and back."

"I love you to the moon and back, Sophie."

"Want to start practicing for number two? I hear if you want a girl you should have sex *a lot* since the X chromosome sperm live longer than the Y and that means that once I start to ovulate again—"

"Shut up woman and get naked."

. . .

Thanks for reading First In: Cheeky with the Fire Chief.

If you're not quite ready to say goodbye to Nick and Sophie, I have a treat for you—a bonus chapter that's only available to people like you, who've read to the end of this story!

Geni.us/first-in-bonus

Dylan's opposites attract story picks up in SECOND BREATH: Dazzled by my Blind Date.

I've just been given the chance to become the firm's youngest partner. All I have to do is go on a few dates with a grad student who's allegedly been breaking research rules.

The problem is, I figure out she's innocent. And I'm in a no-win situation with a choice to either protect her or keep my job.

Have you read all the brother's journeys to their happily ever afters?

- Nick & Sophie, his and hers firefighters, in FIRST IN.
- Dylan & Kama, enemies with chemistry, in SECOND BREATH.
- Josh & Paige, the love that never waned, in THIRD PARTY.
- Adam & Lizzy, fake marriage, true love, in RHODES TO LOVE.
- Morgan & Tamara, forced proximity, friends to lovers, in FRISKY WITH MY BESTIE.

GET A BONUS CHAPTER!

Thanks so much for reading First In: Cheeky with the Fire Chief.

If you're not quite ready to say goodbye to Nick and Sophie, I have a treat for you—a bonus chapter that's only available to people like you, who've read to the end of this story!

Geni.us/first-in-bonus

love&stuff,
 Danika
 DanikaBloom.com

ABOUT THE AUTHOR

Danika Bloom is a *USA Today* bestselling author who always wanted to be the mom in The Partridge Family or The Brady Bunch.

Since she only had one child, she lives out her mom-of-many fantasies in her rom-com series about bands of brothers ...

Actually, that's kind of creepy when you think about it ... Shirley Partridge (aka Shirley Jones) writing spicy stories about her hunky son Keith (aka David Cassidy, her real-life stepson) and his brothers ... ?

Hmm, she might want to rethink this bio.

Danika Bloom lives in a small village in BC, Canada and was a real-life volunteer firefighter in her community. She falls in love with all the heroes she writes and has a very patient husband.

Find all her books at DanikaBloom.com

www.ingramcontent.com/pod-product-compliance
Lightning Source LLC
Chambersburg PA
CBHW071409200726
48294CB00002B/328